GOTH
OTSUICHI

GOTH

OTSUICHI

SAN FRANCISCO

GOTH YORU NO SHOU
©Otsuichi 2002, 2005
Edited by KADOKAWA SHOTEN
First published in Japan in 2005 by KADOKAWA CORPORATION, Tokyo.
English translation © KADOKAWA CORPORATION
Translated by Andrew Cunningham

GOTH BOKU NO SHOU
©Otsuichi 2002, 2005
Edited by KADOKAWA SHOTEN
First published in Japan in 2005 by KADOKAWA CORPORATION, Tokyo.
English translation © KADOKAWA CORPORATION
Translated by Andrew Cunningham

GOTH BANGAIHEN MORINO WA KINENSHASHIN WO TORINIIKU NO MAKI
©Otsuichi 2008, 2013
Edited by KADOKAWA SHOTEN
First published in Japan in 2013 by KADOKAWA CORPORATION, Tokyo.
English translation rights arranged with KADOKAWA CORPORATION, Tokyo.
Translated by Jocelyne Allen
English translation © 2015 VIZ Media, LLC

Cover and interior design by Sam Elzway

HAIKASORU
Published by VIZ Media, LLC
P.O. Box 77010
San Francisco, CA 94107

www.haikasoru.com

Library of Congress Cataloging-in-Publication Data

Otsuichi, 1978–
  [Gosu. English]
  Goth / Otsuichi ; translated by Andrew Cunningham.
     pages cm
  Summary: "Morino is the strangest girl in school—how could she not be, given her
obsession with brutal murders? And there are plenty of murders to grow obsessed with
as the town in which she lives is a magnet for serial killers. She and her schoolmate
will go to any length to investigate the murders, even putting their own bodies on the
line. And they don't want to stop the killer, but simply to understand him." —Provided
by publisher.
  ISBN 978-1-4215-8026-5 (paperback)
  1. Teenagers—Fiction. 2. Serial murder investigation—Fiction. I. Cunningham,
Andrew, 1979– translator. II. Title.
  PL874.T78G6713 2013
  895.6'36—dc23
                    2015015143

Printed in the U.S.A.
First Haikasoru edition, August 2015
Sixth printing, February 2024

CONTENTS

I
GOTH

i

It had been about three weeks since I last saw Morino. It was summer vacation, but we had to attend school that day.

She arrived well before homeroom began and immediately threaded her way through the classroom bustle over to my desk.

We had never bothered with greetings. Morino stopped in front of me, pulled out a notebook from her pocket, and placed it on my desk. I had never seen it before.

It was small enough to rest on my palm, with a cover of brown synthetic leather—the kind of thing you see all the time in stationery stores.

"I found it," she said.

"It isn't mine."

"I know."

She seemed to be enjoying this.

I picked up the notebook, feeling the smooth fake leather against my skin. I flipped through it, skimming the contents; the first half of it was filled with tiny writing, the latter half was blank.

"Read from the beginning."

I did as she said, moving my eyes along letters written by an unknown hand. There were a lot of paragraphs; it was almost like an itemized list.

†

May 10
Met a girl named Kusuda Mitsue in front of the station.
She was sixteen.
I spoke to her and she got in my car shortly after.
I took her to T***** Mountain.
As she gazed out the window, she told me her mother was obsessed with the letters to the editor column in the newspaper.
I stopped the car at the top of T***** Mountain.
I took the bag containing knives, nails, etc. out of the trunk, and she laughed, asking what was inside.

†

It went on like that.

I had seen the name Kusuda Mitsue before... Three months before, a family had been hiking on T***** Mountain, a married couple and their son. The father had not had a day off in a long time, and he had lain down to rest when they reached the mountain. The boy had tried to get his father to play, but the man had not budged. So after lunch, the boy went to explore the woods alone.

The mother realized her son was missing. Then she heard a scream from the forest.

The couple went into the woods and found their son: he was standing still, looking at something just above his eyeline.

When the parents followed his gaze, they saw some reddish-black dirt on the trunk of the tree—something small and sinister was nailed to it at eye level. They gazed around them and found that all the trees nearby had something nailed to them...

Bits of Kusuda Mitsue. Someone had taken apart her body in the forest. Her eyes, tongue, ears, thumbs, organs—each was nailed to a tree.

One tree had, from top to bottom, the left big toe, the upper lip, the nose, and the stomach. Another had other bits of her arranged like Christmas tree decorations.

The murder was soon the talk of the nation.

The notebook Morino had found contained a detailed description of how Kusuda Mitsue had been killed, which bits of her were nailed to which tree, and what kind of nails had been used—but it contained no mention of the writer's emotions.

I had been following the case on TV, in the papers and magazines, and on the Internet, and so I knew a lot about it. But this notebook contained minute details that none of those reports had revealed.

"I believe this notebook belonged to the man who killed her."

Kusuda Mitsue was a high school girl from the next prefecture over. She had last been seen saying goodbye to friends in front of the station. And she was only the first victim in the gruesome murders that had caused a stir all across Japan. There had been another case, with strong similarities, and it was believed to be the work of a serial killer.

"He wrote about the second victim too."

†

June 21
I spoke to a woman waiting for the bus with some shopping bags on her arm. She said her name was Nakanishi Kasumi.
I suggested I give her a lift home.
On the way to H*** Mountain, she noticed that we were headed away from her home, and she began to make noise.
I stopped the car and hit her with a hammer until she was quiet.
I placed her in a small hut on H*** Mountain.

†

The nation had learned the name of vocational school student Nakanishi Kasumi a month earlier. The news and the papers had snatched it up instantly, and I had known there was a second victim before I even got home from school that day.

She had been found in a small hut on H*** Mountain. The building had been left abandoned for some time, its owner a mystery. It had been badly damaged by rain and was filled with mold and stains. It was about ten feet wide, and the walls and floor were planks.

An old man who had come up the mountain to collect food noticed that the door to the hut, which had always been closed, was now open. Surprised, he came closer—and noticed the stench.

He looked inside. It seems certain he could not tell what he saw at first. Nakanishi Kasumi was laid out in rows on the floor of the hut. Like the first victim, her body had been cut into pieces, and these had been placed carefully within a ten by ten grid on the floor, each bit about ten centimeters away from the next. She had been turned into a hundred small lumps.

The notebook described the process in detail.

There were no witnesses to either case, and the person who had killed them had not been arrested. The media were still talking about the two murders, calling them the gruesome work of a serial killer.

"I like watching news about this case."

"Why?"

"It's a strange case," Morino said flatly.

I had been watching for the same reason, so I understood what she was trying to say.

People had been killed—torn to pieces. People who had had that done to them and people who had done that actually existed.

Morino and I had a unique interest in this kind of awful event. We were always looking for stories that were so tragic that they made you want to hang yourself. We had never spoken about this strange inclination directly, but we both sensed it in the other without saying anything.

I imagine normal people would have been appalled. Our sense of these things was abnormal, so whenever we discussed torture implements or methods of execution, we always kept our voices low.

When I looked up from the notebook, Morino was staring out the window. I could tell she was imagining all Nakanishi Kasumi's parts laid out on the floor.

"Where'd you find this?" I asked, and she explained.

Yesterday evening, she had been sitting in a coffee shop she liked—a dark, quiet place with a shop master who never spoke.

As she drank the coffee he'd made, she flipped through the pages of *Cruel Tales of the World.* She heard the sound of rain, and when she glanced out the window, she saw it coming down really hard.

A few customers had been getting ready to leave, but Morino saw them sitting down again. They must have decided to wait out the evening showers. There were five customers there, not including her.

She stood up to go to the bathroom. As she walked, she felt something strange underfoot: she had stepped on a notebook lying there on the shop's floor, which was made of black wooded planks. She picked up the notebook and put it in her pocket, apparently never once considering trying to figure out to whom it belonged.

When she got back from the bathroom, the other customers were watching it rain. None of them had left.

She could tell just how hard it was raining from looking at the shop master, who had ducked outside for a minute and come back in soaking wet.

Morino forgot about the notebook and went back to her book.

When it stopped raining, the sun came out again. Several customers stood up and left, and the rays of the summer sun soon dried the roads.

It wasn't until Morino arrived home that she remembered the notebook and began to read it.

"I went to the bathroom twice. The first time, the notebook wasn't there. It began raining immediately afterward, trapping the customers there. When I stood up again, the notebook was lying there. The killer was in that shop, and the killer lives near here." She clasped her hands in front of her chest.

The two bodies had been found two or three hours away from where we lived, so it was not impossible for the killer to live there—but it didn't feel real.

This case would be talked about for years. It was still unsolved, but the sheer gruesomeness of it was enough to make that clear. Everyone in the country was talking about it—even children knew about it. It was too famous—making it hard for us to believe the killer was that close.

"There's a chance that this is only what the writer imagined, based on the news."

"Read more," Morino said, confident.

†

August 5
I gave a ride to a girl named Mizuguchi Nanami. I met her in a soba shop near S**** Mountain.
We went to the shrine in the woods on the south side of the mountain. She went into the woods with me.

†

In the woods, the notebook's owner had stabbed Mizuguchi Nanami in the stomach with a knife.

In the notebook, the killer broke down her body. In cramped handwriting, he described how he had gouged out her eyes and what color the inside of her womb was.

He had left Mizuguchi Nanami in the woods.

"Have you heard the name Mizuguchi Nanami?" Morino asked. I shook my head.

There had not yet been any reports of her corpse being discovered.

ii

I became aware of Morino when second year began and we found ourselves in the same class. At first, I thought she was like me, living her life without getting involved with anyone around her. Even during break periods or when she was walking through the halls, she always avoided other people, never joining the herd.

We were the only two people like that in our class. That is not to say that I gazed coldly at my classmates' excitement the way she did, though. I would answer if someone spoke to me, and I joked around enough to keep things friendly. I did the bare minimum to lead a normal life. But these were surface relationships, and all the smiles I produced were lies.

The first time we spoke, Morino saw right through that part of me.

"Will you teach me how to smile like that?" she'd said, standing directly in front of me after school, no expression on her face at all. She must have scorned me for it privately.

That was at the end of May. Since then, we had begun to speak occasionally.

Morino only ever wore black clothes—dark colors, from her long, straight black hair to the tips of her shoes. In contrast to that, her skin was paler than anyone else's I'd ever seen, her hands like ceramic. There was a small mole under her left eye, like the pattern on a clown's face, and it gave her a slightly magical aura.

Her expression changed significantly less than that of most people, but it did change. For example, when she was reading a book about a killer who had murdered fifty-two women and children in Russia, Morino was clearly enjoying herself. It was not the same as the suicidally gloomy look she wore when she was in a crowd of our classmates; no, her eyes were glittering.

The only time I didn't feign expressions was when talking to Morino. If I'd been speaking to anyone else, they would wonder why my face was so blank, why I never flashed a smile. But when

I was speaking to her, none of that mattered. I imagine she chose to speak to me for much the same reason.

Neither of us liked to attract attention. We lived quiet lives in the shadow of our livelier classmates.

And then came summer vacation—and the notebook.

†

The day after she showed me the notebook, we met at the station and boarded the train for S**** Mountain.

We'd never met outside of school, so it was the first time I'd ever seen Morino out of uniform. She was still wearing dark colors, nevertheless. So was I—and from her expression, she noticed.

The train was quiet and deserted. We didn't talk, keeping our noses in our books. She was reading a book about child abuse, and I was reading a book written by the family of a famous child criminal.

When we dismounted, we asked an old woman in a decrepit tobacco shop near the station how many soba shops there were near S**** Mountain. We learned that there was only one, and it was not far from where we were.

It was then that Morino said something very poignant. "Tobacco kills a lot of people, but cigarette vending machines are killing that woman by stealing her job."

She didn't particularly seem to be looking for a clever response, so I let it pass.

We walked along the side of the road toward the soba shop. The road led uphill, curving along the slope of the mountain.

The soba shop was at the base of S**** Mountain, in a row of bars and restaurants. It was not at all crowded, with few cars or people around. There were no cars at all in the soba shop's parking lot, but apparently they weren't closed; the sign said OPEN, so we went in.

"The killer met Mizuguchi Nanami here," Morino said, looking around the shop as if we were in a popular tourist spot. "Pardon me—that's still just a possibility. *May* have met her here. We are here to determine whether that's true."

I ignored her and read the notebook, which was written in with blue ballpoint pen. The story of the third woman's death was not the only other thing in the book; there were a number of other mountain names as well. They were on the first page, before the accounts of the murders.

There were marks in front of the mountain names: ◎, ○, △, and X. The mountains where the three bodies had been left were all marked with ◎, so this was probably a list of which mountains looked good for killing.

There was nothing that could identify who had written it. And neither of us ever considered giving it to the police. They would catch him eventually without our doing anything. If we gave them the notebook, they might arrest him faster, and there might be fewer victims—so it probably should have been our duty to turn it in. Sadly, though, neither of us had the kind of conscience that was bothered by keeping it to ourselves. We were cruel, reptilian high school kids.

"If a fourth victim were found, then it would be like we killed her."

"How awful."

That's all we said while we slurped up our soba. Morino didn't seem to think this was especially awful: her tone was disinterested, all her attention focused on the soba in front of her.

We asked the shop owner for directions to the shrine.

Morino kept her eyes on the notebook as we walked, stroking the cover with her fingers, touching it where the killer had touched it. Judging from that gesture, she had a fair amount of reverence for the killer.

I had a trace of that myself. I knew that was hardly appropriate. The killer was someone who deserved to be punished. He should not be looked at the way you would a revolutionary or an artist. At the same time, I knew that some unusual people worshipped famous murderers—and I knew that becoming like them was a bad thing.

We were captivated by the horror of what the notebook's owner had done, though. The killer had stepped over the line of ordinary life to destroy people physically, trampling their identity and dignity. Like inside a nightmare, we could not look away.

To get to the shrine from the soba shop, we went up the hill some more and then up a long staircase.

Both of us felt an entirely irrational anger at the idea of any form of exercise. We enjoyed neither slope nor stairs. And by the time we reached the shrine, we were both exhausted.

We sat down on the statues in the shrine and rested for a while. There were trees all around, their branches stretched out above us—and when we looked up, we could see the summer sun peeking through the leaves.

We sat next to each other, listening to the cicadas all around us.

Beads of sweat accumulated on Morino's forehead.

At last, she stood up, wiping the sweat away. She began looking for Mizuguchi Nanami's body.

"The killer and Mizuguchi Nanami walked this way together," she said, as we began walking side by side.

We entered the woods behind the shrine. We didn't know how far or in which direction they had walked, so we could only search at random.

For the better part of an hour, we looked—with nothing to show for it.

"Maybe that way," Morino said, moving away from me.

A few minutes later, I heard her call my name. I went in the direction of her voice and found her standing at the base of a cliff, her back to me, both hands dangling at her sides, her back stiff. I stood next to her and saw for myself what she had been gazing at: it was Mizuguchi Nanami.

Between the forest and the cliff, in the shadow of a very large tree, the girl sat naked in the dim summer light. Mizuguchi Nanami sat on the ground, her back leaning against the tree, her legs and arms flung out listlessly—nothing above her neck. Her head was inside her split-open belly.

Her eyes had been gouged out, and one was resting in each hand.

The empty eye sockets had been filled up again with mud, and rotting leaves had been stuffed into her mouth.

Something had been wound around the tree behind her... everything that had been inside Mizuguchi Nanami's abdomen.

There were dark patches of dried blood on the ground, and her clothes lay nearby.

We stood facing her in silence. Neither of us able to say anything, we simply stared silently at the corpse.

†

The next day, Morino sent a message to my cell phone from hers: "Return the notebook."

Her messages were always short and simple, nothing unnecessary. Likewise, Morino had no detestable clattery key holders or straps attached to her phone.

I had taken the notebook home with me. After we left Mizuguchi Nanami, I hadn't given it back to Morino.

On the train home Morino had stared into the distance, not yet recovered from the shock.

Before we left, she had picked up Mizuguchi Nanami's clothing off the ground, stuffing it into her pack. The clothes had been cut to pieces, but the girl's hat and bag—and everything inside—remained untouched.

Inside Mizuguchi Nanami's bag were her makeup, her wallet, and her handkerchief, all of which we looked over on the train coming home.

From the student ID in her wallet, we learned that Mizuguchi Nanami had been a high school student in the prefecture next to ours. In the bag, there was a small book designed to hold *purikura*; in those pictures and in the one on her ID, we could see what she had looked like while alive. Mizuguchi Nanami and an impressive number of friends smiled at us from the tiny purikura stickers.

I met Morino in the McDonald's near the station in the afternoon, after having received her message.

Morino was not wearing her customary dark clothes. At first I didn't even recognize her. The hat she was wearing was the same as the one we'd found lying next to Mizuguchi Nanami's body, though, so I was able to work out that she was dressed like the dead girl.

Her hair and makeup were the same as Mizuguchi Nanami's had been in the purikura. The girl's clothes had been cut to pieces, so Morino must have gone shopping for look-alikes.

As she took the notebook, she appeared to be enjoying herself immensely.

"Should we tell Mizuguchi Nanami's family that her body is in the woods?" I asked.

Morino thought about this for a moment, but then she shook her head. "The police will find her eventually." Morino spoke about Mizuguchi Nanami's death dressed exactly as the girl had been until a few minutes before she died.

What was Mizuguchi Nanami's family doing now? Were they worried because she was missing? Did she have a boyfriend? What had her grades been like?

Morino seemed a little different. As we talked, the way she spoke and gestured moved gradually away from her usual behavior. She worried about where her bangs were, and she mentioned how the couple at the booth across from ours looked very much in love—neither was the kind of thing that Morino had ever done before.

I had never met Mizuguchi Nanami—but now, watching Morino, I imagined that this was what Mizuguchi Nanami had been like.

Morino had her elbows on the table, and she looked happy. Next to her was the bag that had once belonged to Mizuguchi Nanami—on the clasp of the bag, a key holder with an anime character on it.

"You plan to dress like that for a while?"

"Yeah. Fun, isn't it?"

It let Morino pretend. But the way she smiled or looked in a mirror, examining her eyebrows, was not a copy of an ordinary high school girl—it felt as if Mizuguchi Nanami had slipped inside Morino.

As we left McDonald's, Morino very naturally took my hand, not even realizing she had done so until I pointed it out. Mizuguchi Nanami was dead, but I was sure it was her who had taken my hand.

We split up at the station.

When I got home, I turned on the TV. The news was talking about the serial killings, the first and second victims—the same information that had been covered countless times, nothing new at all. No mention of Mizuguchi Nanami.

There were images of the victims' friends and family looking sad. Pictures of the victims enlarged to fill the screen...

I remembered Morino and worried—but that kind of thing almost never happened. I dismissed my own concerns.

The victims in the photographs had hair and clothes like Mizuguchi Nanami's—which meant Morino was now the killer's type.

iii

Three days after we had met at McDonald's, my phone rang in the afternoon, indicating that I had received a message from someone...from Morino.

"Help."

That was it, just that one word.

I quickly tapped out a reply: "Something happen?"

I waited awhile, but she didn't respond, so I called her. I couldn't reach her phone—it was either off or broken.

In the evening I called Morino's house. She had given me the number once before—not because she thought I might ever need to call, but because the letters standing for the numbers coincidentally formed a deranged sentence, making the number easy to remember.

Her mother answered; she had a high voice and spoke very quickly.

I said I was a classmate and that I needed to talk with Morino about some class business.

She had not come home.

I had dismissed the idea that she would be attacked. Yet the contents of that notebook had been accurate, so it was probably also true that the killer had been in the same café as Morino. There was a chance that he had happened to see her in town dressed like Mizuguchi Nanami. The killer might have been surprised to see someone dressed just like the girl he had recently killed, and it might have tempted him... but the odds of his actually targeting her were very low. After all, any number of girls dressed that way.

The biggest reason to suspect that the killer might've captured Morino was the possibility that they lived near each other. They had been in the same coffee shop. Unless the killer had been far from home that day, his path might well cross Morino's regularly. The chances of his seeing her were high.

I thought about it that night. It seemed likely that Morino had been killed by then. Her body was probably scattered on some mountain.

I fell asleep imagining it.

†

The next day, I called her house again.

Morino still wasn't home. According to her mother, this was the first time she had ever stayed out all night without calling. Her mother was worried.

"So are you her boyfriend?" Morino's mother asked.

"No, not at all."

"You don't need to deny it so firmly. I know all about it."

Morino's mother had absolutely no doubt that her daughter had a boyfriend. Her daughter had never had any friends, and this was the first time anyone had called for her since she was in elementary school.

"Recently, she's been dressing in brighter colors, and I knew a boy was involved."

I began to worry about the cost of the call.

"Is there a small brown notebook in her room?"

The mother went and checked, putting the phone down. There was a short silence. Then her voice came on the line again. "There was something like that on her desk… I hope it's the one you meant."

It seemed Morino hadn't been carrying the notebook around. If she had, I'd been considering the possibility that the killer had seen her reading the notebook and had attacked her to keep her silent.

I told Morino's mother that I would come get the notebook, asking for the address.

After I hung up, I headed for Morino's house. I had known she lived not far from the station, but I had never been there before.

She lived on the third floor of an apartment complex behind the station.

I rang the bell and heard the voice from the phone call out as the door opened. Undoubtedly, it was Morino's mother.

"Come in, come in, come in."

Morino's mother was wearing an apron; she was a very domestic-looking, ordinary housewife—completely different from Morino. I wondered how a mother like this had produced a girl like Morino.

She invited me in, but I refused. What I was here for could be handled in the doorway.

I mentioned the notebook, and she had it ready. I took it, asking if she had read the contents.

She shook her head. "I can't be bothered to read such tiny handwriting."

She seemed much more interested in me than in the notebook.

"When second year started, that girl suddenly started going to school all the time. Now I know why!"

The year before, Morino had said school was boring and rarely went. I had not known that. Her interests were unusual, but more than that, she was awkward, unable to blend in. It was only natural she had ended up the way she was.

I asked her mother when she had last seen Morino.

"Yesterday, just past noon, I think. I saw her leaving the house."

"Did she say where she was going?"

Morino's mother shook her head. "Will you look for her?" she asked, as I turned to leave.

I nodded. "If she's still alive," I added. Her mother thought I was joking and laughed.

†

As I walked back to the station, I folded back the fake leather cover, opening the notebook to the page filled with mountain names—the list of mountains the killer had been considering as places to dispose of the bodies. It was clear that mountains marked with ◎ were mountains the killer considered ideal for that. There were only four of them, and so far all the bodies had been found on one of those four.

Of the four ◎ mountains, three of them already had bodies—which meant he would probably take Morino to the fourth mountain, N** Mountain.

I asked the man at the station ticket window which train I should take to get there, and then I bought a ticket.

I got off the train at the station nearest the mountain, but I had to take a bus from there. There were vineyards around the base of N** Mountain, and from the bus window I saw a number of signs advertising grape picking.

The killer would have come here in a car. Where would he have left the body? He must have carried out his ritual deep in the mountain, where nobody would hear her screams. I couldn't figure out where that might be.

The driver and I were the only people on the bus. I looked at the road map plastered on the side of the bus and talked to the driver, trying to figure out where the killer might have gone.

He said that people visiting N** Mountain from the direction Morino and I lived would almost always take the prefectural road, which crossed the east side of the mountain. There were few roads over it, and that was the only one that went in the direction we lived.

If the killer had driven Morino to N** Mountain, it seemed clear that he would have taken that road. According to the bus driver, it was the road the bus was on now.

I got off the bus at a stop near a fairly wide road that led all the way to the top of the mountain. If a car were headed down the mountain, then it would take this road.

I walked up the road. Although it was asphalt, there was no traffic.

There were several side roads branching off it into the woods on either side. I thought the killer and Morino might have taken any one of those.

The farther I walked, the steeper the road became. I could see the village through the trees, but in miniature.

I was close to the top soon enough. There was a small parking lot there and a building that appeared to be an observatory. Cars could go no farther. I hadn't been walking long, so I wasn't tired.

I was looking for Morino's body.

I walked along the path between the trees, taking branching paths as I found them.

It was cloudy, and the woods were dark. Between the interlocking branches, I observed trees stretching as far as I could see. There was no wind, and cicadas provided the only sound.

N** Mountain was much too large to find a single dismembered corpse on. I eventually decided my search was futile. I returned to the bus stop, covered in sweat and exhausted.

There weren't a lot of homes along the road the bus took, but there were a few. There had been one on the road toward the top, and I had asked the old man in the garden if any cars had gone up that road the day before. But he shook his head. He even called his family and repeated my question, but none of them had seen a car.

What had made Morino send that message? Had the killer forcibly taken her with him? She wasn't stupid and wouldn't be tricked easily.

Was I overthinking things? Had she not been captured at all?

I sat down next to the bus stop and read the notebook again. I was not skilled enough at profiling to glean anything about the killer from the descriptions of the murders.

My sweat dripped onto the pages, and the ink smeared, making bits of it unreadable. Apparently, the killer had been using a water-based ink.

Where had the killer written in this notebook? At home, after he returned from the killings? I doubted he'd written it during the crime. He had written it from his memory, colored by his imagination.

The bus arrived, and I stood up. Looking at my watch, I saw that it was after three. I was leaving the mountain.

There was still a chance the killer had not yet killed Morino but had only trapped her in his home. The only way to find out was to ask the killer himself. If he had already killed her, I would have to ask him where he'd left the body instead—because I wanted to see it. Either way, I had to leave the mountain and find him. I had every intention of doing so.

iv

The coffee shop Morino always went to was in the middle of the arcade near the station. She had given me directions earlier, but I had never actually been there.

As she had said, the lighting was low, wrapping me in comfortable darkness. Quiet music was playing, melting into the air without drawing attention to itself.

I sat down at the counter.

There was a sign for the bathrooms in back. I glanced at the floor in front of them, where Morino had found the notebook.

There was only one other customer: a young woman in a suit. She was by the windows, reading a magazine as she sipped her coffee.

The shop master came to take my order, and I asked, "Does that woman come here a lot?"

He nodded, and then he frowned, wondering what of it.

"Not important. First, do you mind if I shake your hand?"

"Shake my...? Why?"

"To mark the occasion."

The shop master had a very sincere face. He wasn't young, nor was he old enough to be called middle-aged. He had pale skin and wore a plain black T-shirt, the kind sold anywhere. His hair was neatly buzzed.

At first, he seemed to think I was just a strange customer— probably because I was staring too much.

He brought my coffee quickly.

"I'm friends with a girl named Morino. Do you know her?"

"She's a regular."

I asked if she was still alive.

He stopped moving.

He slowly put down the cup that had been in his hand, and then he turned to face me. His eyes were clouded, like two black holes bereft of light.

I thought the odds of this man being the killer were significantly higher than those of the other customers from that evening—and now I knew I had been right.

"What do you mean?" he asked, playing dumb.

I held out the notebook. When he saw it, he smiled, flashing dull white canines.

"Morino found this the other day."

He took the notebook and flipped through it.

"I'm impressed that you knew it was mine."

"At least half of it was nothing more than a gamble." I explained how I had gone to N** Mountain to look for her body and what line of thought had brought me here.

†

What had the killer been thinking?

I'd begun by imagining the killer after he'd dropped the notebook.

Why had he written the notebook? To help him remember? To keep a record? I was sure he had read it over and over and that he attached great value to it, so he must've noticed that the notebook was missing.

Where had he kept the notebook? Either in his pocket or in his bag. Considering he had dropped it, probably in his pocket. Maybe he had washed his hands in the bathroom and dropped the notebook as he pulled out his handkerchief.

So when had he noticed it was missing? Ten minutes later? A few hours after? I was sure he had noticed it before the day was out.

He would have tried to figure out when he had last read it, the last time he was sure he had it. Then he would have retraced his steps, figuring out where he was most likely to have dropped it.

And I was willing to bet he had narrowed it down pretty well—mostly because I imagined he looked at it quite often. Every time he felt his thoughts growing dark, he would calm himself by reading the notebook. And if he read it that often, he would be able to pinpoint a narrow range of places and times he could have dropped it.

Then the killer must have looked for it, staring at the ground trying to find it.

But he would not have found it there. So the killer must have thought that someone picked it up. If someone were to read the book, he was finished—the police would search for the third victim and find the body. That wasn't a problem in itself; the problem came if they managed to lift his prints from the notebook or match his handwriting.

If this had happened to me, what would I think? I certainly wouldn't kill a fourth victim. The police might be investigating nearby. After all, the notebook had been dropped someplace the killer went on a daily basis. The police would assume he lived nearby. He couldn't take that risk.

But a few days had passed, and Mizuguchi Nanami's body still had not been found—because Morino and I had not turned over the notebook to the police.

The killer had been watching the news every night, waiting for them to find her body. He would not kill again until he was sure it was safe... but Morino had gone missing.

Discounting the possibility that Morino's disappearance was just some sort of prank, I tried to figure out why the killer would act. If I were the killer, why would I choose a fourth victim?

* *I couldn't bear to wait any longer.*
* *I got overconfident, sure I wouldn't be caught, and underestimated the police.*
* *I didn't care if I got caught.*
* *I thought that nobody had picked up the notebook, that nobody had read it.*
* *I thought that whoever picked it up had not believed it.*

Or perhaps he had actually not noticed that he'd lost the notebook. These were all possibilities... but I decided to bet on another theory. I believed the killer had thought as follows:

* *Someone picked up the notebook but was unable to read it. That's why they haven't given it to the police and Mizuguchi Nanami's body has not been found.*

The shop master listened to all this, nodding with interest. "So why did you think it was me?"

I took the notebook back and opened it. I showed him where my sweat had smudged the writing, leaving it illegible. "You knew what kind of ink you'd used, and you knew that if it got wet, nobody could read it. I theorized that the killer had assumed he'd dropped it outside, not in the shop. Morino told me it was raining hard when she found the notebook; it seemed likely the killer knew he had dropped it while it was raining."

It was only natural that the killer would assume that if the notebook had been picked up in the shop, it would have been given to the police. But there were no reports of Mizuguchi Nanami's body being found. "So the killer must have concluded that he'd dropped it outside in the rain, I thought. In that case, the notebook would be wet, and it would be unreadable."

Morino had said the only person who had gone out in the rain was the shop master.

It was a tightrope walk based on pure speculation—but when I finished it, the shop master grinned.

"I did think I'd dropped it in the rain," he admitted. "Morino's upstairs."

The second and third floors of the shop were the man's home.

The shop master carefully placed the notebook back in his pocket. Then he turned his back to me, moved toward the entrance, and opened the door.

The clouds from earlier had cleared away, and the sun was beating down outside. It looked like pure white light to my eyes, which were now accustomed to the darkness inside the shop.

The man left the shop and crossed the road, vanishing into the light.

The regular customer stood up, coming to the register to pay her bill. She looked around the shop and asked me where the shop master had gone, but I merely shook my head.

†

The stairs were outside the building, and to get to the second floor, I had to leave the shop.

Morino was tied up on the third floor. She was still dressed like Mizuguchi Nanami, and she was lying on the floor with a rope tied around her arms and legs. She appeared otherwise unharmed.

When she saw me, Morino's eyes narrowed. That was how she smiled. She was gagged with a towel and thus unable to speak.

When I undid the gag, she sighed.

"The shop master pretended he was hurt, and he asked me to help carry something. Before I knew it..."

Getting the ropes off of her looked difficult. I left her there and looked around the room. Judging from the state of the place, the master lived alone.

There was white paper on the desk, with a number of tiny crosses drawn on it.

I found a set of knives on the shelf. It was easy to guess that these had been used to kill his victims—he had mentioned them often in the notebook.

Morino called out, angry with me for not untying her.

I selected one of the knives, using it to cut the ropes.

"We'd better run—he'll find us."

"No, he won't."

He would never come back. I was sure of it. Yes, there was a slight possibility that he might come back to kill the two of us— but for some reason, I knew he wouldn't.

When we had been talking at the shop counter, I'd felt as if the two of us had a lot in common.

He'd left the shop quietly precisely because he knew that I would never tell anyone.

Morino looked surprised that I seemed so sure the killer wasn't coming back. She stood up, adjusting her clothes.

"I managed to send you a message, but he noticed."

Her phone had been laid on the desk and switched off. Mizuguchi Nanami's bag was there too; after all, Morino had been carrying it around. Had the killer not noticed that the girl about to become his fourth victim had the same bag as his third victim? Or had he targeted her because it was the same bag?

Morino had been tied up for a full day, so she staggered a little as she headed for the stairs.

When I left the room, I took the set of knives and the paper on the desk—as mementos. When the police figured everything out and searched this room, the lack of weapons might cause problems, but I didn't care.

I went to the first floor and looked inside. Quiet music was playing in the empty shop.

I flipped the sign on the door, turning it to CLOSED.

Morino stood behind me, watching and rubbing her wrists— the rope marks were still there.

"It was horrible," she said. "I'm never coming here again."

"It wasn't all bad. You got to meet him."

Morino frowned. "Got to meet who? Why did the shop master do this to me, anyway?"

She had not realized that the shop master was a serial killer.

I looked down, staring at the tiny crosses on the piece of paper in my hand.

II
WRIST-CUT

prologue

As I was preparing to go home after school, I sensed someone standing behind me in the increasingly empty classroom. When I turned around, I saw it was Morino.

"Something I wanted to say to you before you left," she explained. We had not spoken all day, so it had been nearly twenty-four hours since I'd heard her voice. "I rented a strange movie yesterday..."

Apparently, Morino had been absolutely dying to talk about this movie with somebody, but I was the only person in the class she ever talked to—and she would only do that when I was alone, not when I was talking to any of our other classmates. Therefore, she'd been unable to speak to me until just before I went home.

A few girls to the side of the room noticed us and began whispering. I could tell they were talking about us. At first, people had wondered if we were a couple, but our body language was never at all intimate, our expressions remaining sullen throughout each conversation. So just how close we were remained a mystery to our classmates. But as far as they were concerned, Morino talking to anybody was remarkable in itself. She hid herself in the class, vanishing the moment school ended—she lived like a submarine, hugging the sea floor.

Unless wearing the summer version of her uniform, she always wore black—black from her long hair down to her shoes—as if she was doing her best to melt into the darkness, fleeing detestable light.

I once asked Morino *shibou douki*, or why she'd chosen this school to attend.

"The uniforms are black and very plain. That's the only reason... When you first said 'shibou douki,' I understood a very different meaning."

She wrote the homonym on the blackboard in white chalk: the kanji for "death wish." As she did, her thin wrist emerged from inside her uniform sleeve. Her skin was very pale, as if it had never been exposed to sunlight.

She had a pretty face, so a few boys had tried to chat her up—until something had happened to change everything: one of the teachers had done something to her that amounted to sexual harassment, and she'd produced an aerosol can filled with pepper spray, calmly attacking him with it before picking up her desk chair and beating him to the ground. I had been watching in hiding. After that, no boys dared approach her.

†

The story I am about to tell is not the story of how Morino and I made each other's acquaintance; it is the story I remember every time my eyes happen upon her pale wrists.

In spring of that year, the news shows were all excited about a case involving a number of severed wrists—a case I had secretly become involved in.

This was at the end of May, before I had ever spoken to Morino...

i

As he stared at his own hands, Shinohara thought: Hands, obviously, were the ends of vertebrates' forelimbs. His own hands had developed to grasp objects, with five fingers that could type on a computer keyboard or tilt a cup of coffee. It seemed self-evident that hands were the essence of humanity. That was why there were palm readers; palm readers said the lines on a person's palms allowed them to determine an individual's personality and destiny. Hands were a mirror that reflected the person's past and future.

Shinohara had liked hands even as a child—he had been so obsessed with hands that when his parents had taken him outside, he hadn't seen the crowds of people, only their hands. But the way hands moved was unfalteringly true. The tendons flexing on the back of the hands, the five fingers, the nails at the tips of those fingers, and the white crescents at the tips of them... Fingerprints, in particular, were critical to defining the individual.

In the lower years of elementary school, Shinohara had cut off the hands of a doll his sister had thrown away, making sure nobody noticed. The tiny doll hands had rolled around in the palms of Shinohara's own hands. He put them in his pocket, throwing away the handless doll. Whenever he could, he would rub those tiny hard hands with his thumb. The tiny grooves on the plastic hands told Shinohara so much more than the words his mother and teachers said to him.

He had cut the front paws off cats and dogs with pruning shears, as well. Pruning shears were very good for cutting through tiny wrists. Shinohara liked the hands of dogs and cats. Human hands did not have pads, which always struck him as funny—if you pushed the pads, claws came out, and there was hair growing between them. Paws could not grasp objects like human hands, but they'd evolved in their own unique fashion.

Shinohara was well aware that most people could not accept his belief that the essence of humans lay in their hands; he had observed the people around him enough to understand that the world was controlled by the empty words emerging from heads and mouths. When he grew older and started working, he knew to hide his ideas—but every now and then, he found himself thinking about hands again... that five-fingered design that only God could have created. Shinohara could not keep them out of his head.

Then one spring, he had severed his first human hand—a baby's hand. He'd found the baby sitting in a stroller, and he'd cut off its hand with pruning shears when the mother had left it alone briefly.

The baby's tiny hand was warm and soft. When Shinohara severed it, the baby had woken up and stared crying, and the warmth of its hand in his had begun to fade. Shinohara shoved the baby's hand in his pocket and took it home, where he kept it in the refrigerator.

The baby's hand was not the only one. Shinohara knocked out a child, cutting off its hand under cover of darkness. He cut hands off high school kids and adults, as well. Fully grown human hands were too thick to cut off with pruning shears, but a saw left the cut much too ragged for Shinohara's aesthetic sensibilities to accept. He could hardly carry around an ax with him, though—so in the end, Shinohara settled on a meat cleaver. Once his victims were unconscious, a single strong blow would cut right through the bone for a nice clean cut.

Shinohara had not killed anyone—he only wanted the hands, not to kill anyone. It mattered nothing to him whether the non-hand parts lived or died, as long as nobody saw him, so he simply abandoned the unconscious bodies.

The newspapers and TV news all said that none of the victims could identify who had attacked them once they'd woken up in the hospital, which was always a relief to Shinohara. He had worked carefully and in the dark, but he was still afraid of being caught.

Shinohara liked hands, and he enjoyed cutting them off. He felt a great sense of release when the hands were separated from the rest of the body—in his twisted view of the world, releasing those hands was actually heroic.

Even once at work he had cut the hands off a doll—a hand-sized, cheap cloth thing stuffed with cotton. It was so small that the hands were not very detailed—they had no fingers, simply a round part at the end of the arm. But they were hands neverthe-less. This was simply how hands had evolved in the manufacturing of dolls—evolved beyond fingers. Cutting those off had helped

Shinohara ease the tension between the world and himself. He put all the hands he had cut off in his refrigerator, including those of the cloth doll and the dog and cat paws. He never threw away any of them.

Shinohara lived alone, but his house felt full of life. Every time he opened the fridge, he saw the rows of hands inside. When he touched them, he felt like he knew the original owners' pasts, what they had lived through, and also what the future had in store for them. What he sensed by touching them became words speaking to him and telling him of the love the hands' parents had given them, as well as the pain the world had inflicted on them.

The news and the papers talked about Shinohara's crimes every day. They were calling it the Wrist-Cut Case now. Shinohara didn't care what they named it—but he didn't enjoy being hated, treated like a criminal. He didn't like having their value system forced on him.

As he watched the evening news, Shinohara explained his feelings to a child's hand, which he had taken out of the refrigerator and was holding in his own hand.

"Yes, exactly as you say," the child's hand's curves, indentations, and elasticity told him through Shinohara's palm.

Shinohara's anxiety and anger melted away. He could feel courage rising up within him once more.

ii

In his morning class, the chemistry teacher had said, "During lunch, I'm going to reorganize the chemistry office. If anyone can spare the time, I'd appreciate the help."

The teacher didn't seem like he actually expected anyone to do so, and most of the students completely ignored him—so when I showed up in the office at lunch, he appeared surprised.

It was a sunny day, and warm spring light poured down outside the windows, but the chemistry office was comparatively dark and a little chilly. In the distance, I could hear students laughing and playing.

The chemistry office was cramped and lined with cases, which were filled with chemicals and models of molecules and even a few organs preserved in formaldehyde. There were wooden desks by the windows, and these were covered in scientific books and papers about plants and space. There was also an old computer—and on the next desk, beneath a pile of books, a printer was hidden. Light filtered through the blinds, picking out clouds of dust in the air.

"Erm, then start by carrying the garbage into the lecture hall," the chemistry teacher instructed, as he pointed at a blue plastic wastebasket filled with balled-up pieces of paper. I nodded, picked up the trash, and headed for the lecture hall.

†

"Who the hell would waste his lunch on *that*?" someone next to me had muttered when the teacher had solicited help. I'd already forgotten what I'd said in response, but the other student had laughed, so I must've said something dull.

It was easy to act like my cheerier classmates. If I kept up with the most popular TV shows and variety programs and responded with the right words and expressions, it was easy to seem like I was following along. Everyone believed me to be an outgoing boy, and I was able to avoid any unnecessary trouble.

What kind of trouble? In kindergarten, I had once become obsessed with the idea of coloring in a doll's face with black marker and cutting off its arms and legs—and had done just that, which caused a great deal of concern from those around me. I could clearly remember the worried looks my mother and teachers gave me.

After that, I became good at lying. Like with the crayons we used for drawing. Until then, the black one had always been much shorter, but after that I was careful to wear all the colors down evenly. I don't remember drawing much of interest afterward, but the subject matter must have involved a number of rainbows or flowers or the like. This seemed to put the adults around me at ease.

By understanding the value system the world preferred, remembering and feigning it, I was able to convince others that I was free of problems. I simply had to participate enthusiastically in the boring conversations my classmates were having.

I didn't tell my classmates that I was helping to clean the chemistry office that day. The character I played in class would never do that sort of thing, and I wanted to avoid the impression that I was doing it to score points. Besides, I wasn't helping out of the goodness of my heart—I had a plan.

Rumor had it that the chemistry teacher for my class made the tests at his desk in the chemistry office. There was a chance his notes were in the garbage, and I was hoping to get my hands on those while I was helping out.

In my first year, I had randomly found myself helping this teacher to clean his office, so I knew where he would start: He would begin by having me carry the trash into the lecture hall next door. Then we would organize the office, and he would accompany me to take out the garbage. (The trash generated while cleaning took two to carry.) That was what had happened last year.

Herein lay the problem: there was no time to pick through the contents of the trash. I needed a plan. So I borrowed a wastebin from another classroom before I went to help the chemistry teacher, hiding it in the chemistry lecture hall. Then I went to the chemistry office and offered to help.

If things played out like last year, the first thing he would do was instruct me to carry the garbage into the lecture hall. If he did not, I would have to carry it out when he wasn't looking.

All the trash receptacles in the school were identical. The chemistry office wastebasket was the same blue plastic as every other one in the school—which meant I could switch the chemistry office trash container for the one I had hidden in the lecture hall without the teacher noticing.

The office wastebasket, where the test notes might be, would remain hidden under the desk in the lecture hall while I was helping him. When we were done, I would carry the other classroom's garbage to the incinerator under the teacher's watchful eye.

And when that was done, I would be free to go through the trash in the chemistry lecture hall at my leisure.

As I mentioned, before I entered the office, I had already borrowed the trash bin from the next class over and hidden it under the desk. As expected, the teacher had ordered me to carry the garbage into the lecture hall, just like he had the year before. Everything was going smoothly.

To keep him from noticing my plan, I followed his instructions as naturally as possible, carrying the trash into the lecture hall. There was a door between the rooms, meaning I didn't have to venture into the hall.

But at that point, something happened that I couldn't have planned for. The lecture hall had been empty a moment before, but that was no longer true. Someone was sitting alone at a large table in the corner of the room, reading quietly. She had long black hair, and she lurked like a shadow in the dim light of the lecture hall. Peering closely, I recognized her. It was Morino, who had been in my class since the start of the spring term.

She looked up, glancing at me as I entered from where she sat in the far corner, as far from the office door as possible. Then she immediately turned her attention back to the book, showing no interest in me at all.

At first I wondered if she'd come to help, but apparently that was not the case. I decided she wouldn't interfere with my plan.

I had never spoken to Morino, but her oddness had occasionally caught my attention. She didn't stand out much—but in not standing out, she attracted attention. There were people in class who were charismatic and filled with light and energy; Morino, however, seemed to be forging her way stubbornly in the complete opposite direction. She had mercilessly ignored anyone who attempted to speak to her until she was completely isolated—and she appeared to love that isolation.

And now she was reading in the corner of the lecture hall. I ignored her, exchanging the wastebin I had hidden in advance for the one I had just carried in. I hid the office trash under the desk. Morino did not seem to notice.

I left the trash and Morino in the lecture hall and went back to the office as if nothing had happened.

"There was a girl in there, right? She comes almost every day at lunch," the chemistry teacher said. The lecture hall was dimly lit and one of the quietest places in the school. I could understand why she went there. It was nothing like the bustling classrooms where we spent most of our time. It was silent, as if time had stopped and the darkness did not wish to be disturbed. It was steeped in a comfortable repulsiveness, like when one clinically observed things as they died.

Following the teacher's instructions, I lifted boxes down from the tops of shelves and checked what was in the bottles of chemicals inside.

Meanwhile, he took a can of compressed air and blew the dust out of the computer keyboard—a very finicky man, apparently. The whole time we were cleaning, he was working right next to me, and there would never have been time to look through the trash.

When we were finished, the two of us went into the lecture hall, carrying a big pile of garbage.

"You hardly ever see girls with long black hair like her anymore. Everyone gets it dyed these days," the teacher said, glancing at Morino. That was how black and beautiful her hair was. I told him my sister's hair was much the same.

Morino's slender, pale hands turned a page in her book. In the dimly lit lecture hall, they were so pale that they seemed to glow, the images burning themselves into my retinas.

The teacher and I carried the trash to the incinerator, and then we went our separate ways. I quickly headed back to the lecture hall; I had about ten minutes before afternoon classes started.

By the time I reached the hall, Morino was already gone, presumably headed to class. This was ideal for my purposes.

I pulled out the wastebasket I had hidden under the desk and rifled through it, keeping one eye out in case someone came in. Unfortunately, what I had been looking for was nowhere to be found.

Instead, I found something carefully wrapped in layer after layer of paper. I opened the package and found a doll—with the tips of its arms cut off.

It was a cloth doll, small enough to fit in the palm of my hand. The feet had not been damaged. From the design of the doll, it seemed safe to assume the severed hands had not had any fingers. It was a very simple thing, but the doll with no hands reminded me of something—the Wrist-Cut Case that was all over TV.

People of various ages and genders had, when walking alone, been knocked unconscious—and then their hands had been chopped off. Dogs and cats had also been found with missing front paws, and this was believed to be the work of the same person. All such incidents had happened not far from here.

Had the chemistry teacher, Mr. Shinohara, cut off the doll's hands? What for—some kind of game? No, I thought it was much more likely that he was the man behind the Wrist-Cut Case. I knew this was quite a leap from finding a doll with no hands, but the person who had cut all those hands off must be somewhere, and it was not all that unlikely that he was nearby. And when I considered the reasons why the chemistry teacher might have cut off a doll's hands, I could not deny the strong possibility that it was simply an extension of his enthusiasm.

†

After I found the handless doll, I thought about the Wrist-Cut Case every day in class. Midterms were coming up fast, but I hardly noticed. Out of all the gruesome incidents the news had covered lately, this was the most fascinating. Pondering the culprit's terrifying fixation with hands was exactly the kind of thing I liked to do. And I believed...that he was just like me. Obviously, the particulars were different, but I still felt a connection to the man behind the gruesome wrist cuttings.

After that, I often made my way to the lecture hall during breaks so that I could brush past Mr. Shinohara. He remembered me and would wave when he saw me. He was a young man, thin, with short hair. I spent a lot of time wondering if he was really the man behind the Wrist-Cut Case.

I once came across Mr. Shinohara talking to Morino outside the lecture hall. He had seen the book Morino was carrying and was telling her he had a copy of the follow-up. It was a nonfiction book about dealing with the mentally unstable. Morino simply replied, "Do you?" her usual blank expression never faltering.

In class, I continued to function largely through pretense. It was easy to live as an ordinary high school kid, never standing out—but my mind was occupied almost entirely with the latest reports on the Wrist-Cut Case, and it was exhausting to keep my slang current and to chatter happily with the humans around me about the latest celebrity gossip. I occasionally felt like an idiot for expending all that effort.

It seemed Morino spent as much time in the lecture hall as Mr. Shinohara had said. Almost every time I peeked in the doors, she was sitting in that quiet room alone.

She was always alone, but not because she was being bullied—it was more like she had deliberately cut off all communication with those around her. Her stony silence made it clear that her interests and passions had nothing in common with those of the other students.

"Apparently, Morino tried to kill herself in junior high," someone told me. With that in mind, I took a closer look at her pale hands. I didn't know why she had wanted to die, but I doubted the world made it easy for her to live.

If I stopped acting, I would end up like her. If the people around me discovered how merciless and unemotional I was, how much more difficult would my life become? I compared my current situation with that hypothetical and couldn't find much difference—I was isolated either way.

Three days after I found the doll, I decided to carry out a new plan.

iii

Mr. Shinohara lived on a quiet street in a normal house, two stories tall with thin white walls that shone yellow in the light of the setting sun. There was no one around, and the only sound was an airplane flying past far above me.

Mr. Shinohara was the homeroom teacher for a second-year class; I happened to know someone in that class who had been able to tell me the teacher's address and confirm that Mr. Shinohara lived alone.

I looked at my watch. It was Thursday, and all the teachers would be in a meeting, so I would have plenty of time before he got home.

After making sure there was no one around, I went through the gate and around the back of the house. There was a small yard with a clothesline, and that was all. Nothing in the garden but grass—no weeds or insects, just a flat, empty bit of ground. A large window faced into the garden, but it was locked, so I wrapped a towel around my hand to break it. Then I listened carefully, making sure I had not attracted any attention, before unlocking the window, taking off my shoes, and entering the house.

The culprit behind the Wrist-Cut Case was cutting off human hands and taking them away with him. Nobody knew what became of the victims' hands. Some people imagined the culprit enjoyed looking at them, whereas others suggested he ate them. Nobody knew the truth—but any which way, there was a strong possibility that the killer had left evidence in his house. My first goal tonight was to search Mr. Shinohara's house for such evidence.

I had broken the living room window, scattering glass across the floor, so I had to walk carefully to avoid cutting myself. The house was very tidy, with the magazines on the table and the remote controls all lined up neatly.

I made as little noise as possible. I was worried that Mr. Shinohara might return home suddenly, and I didn't want to miss the sound of the key in the front door. I would have to run before he caught me.

The floors were highly polished. Although the lights were off and it was dark, I could see by the small amount of still-lingering sunlight streaming through the windows.

I found the stairs. Careful not to touch the wall or handrails, I went up them. Even if I left fingerprints, Mr. Shinohara would not call the police if he were the Wrist-Cut Case culprit—but I still didn't want to leave any trace that I had been in his house.

On the second floor, there was a bedroom with a desktop computer and a number of bookshelves inside. The books were arranged by size, with the spines carefully lined up together, no dust anywhere.

There was nothing to suggest Mr. Shinohara was the wrist cutter.

I placed the middle and index fingers of my right hand on my left wrist to measure my pulse. It was faster than usual, evidence that I was tense. I took a deep breath, trying to relax.

I thought about wrists for a moment. When doctors want to test if someone is alive or dead, they always hold the wrist, feeling for a pulse. How would the doctors feel for a pulse on a victim from the Wrist-Cut Case without a wrist?

I looked at my watch. The teachers' meeting at school should have been ending about then. If Mr. Shinohara were to head directly home, I would need to hurry.

I looked at the other rooms on the second floor, two tatami-floored rooms with shelves and wardrobes. But there were no clues to suggest that Mr. Shinohara had hurt anyone.

Each time I left a room, I checked to make sure I hadn't forgotten anything, like my student ID, a uniform button, a textbook, or a sock. The worst blunder I could possibly make was to leave anything behind that could be used to identify me. Why? Because it could be avoided easily if I paid attention.

Certain I had left no trace behind, and still wearing socks, I went downstairs—into the kitchen.

Did Mr. Shinohara ever cook? There weren't many dishes, and everything was placed away neatly. There was nothing in the sink. It was as if the cups and cooking implements had been placed there decoratively the moment he bought them, never once used.

On the table, there was a rice cooker, which was a bit too big for someone living alone. I had no information on his family or background—perhaps he had formerly lived with other relatives, or perhaps there was no real meaning to the oversize rice cooker.

The stainless steel sink was polished, and it gleamed in the nearly horizontal light coming through the window. With no lights on, the house was growing steadily darker. The reddish glow from the sink was the only source of light. The only sound, the low hum of the refrigerator—the same silence as in the chemistry lecture hall. I could feel my emotions growing still.

In the center of the kitchen, I took my wrist, measuring my pulse again. Beneath the skin of my left wrist, my blood vessel throbbed steadily. My fingers felt it expand and contract. My pulse was normal again.

Then it abruptly sped up, pulsing violently, as if about to explode.

My nose had picked up an unnatural scent: something rotting, something being consumed by bacteria. The images that scent brought to mind sent my pulse racing.

I began tracking the source of the smell. There was nothing in the cupboards or drawers. My eyes fixed on the refrigerator.

I gripped the refrigerator handle through my handkerchief, careful not to leave fingerprints. As I opened the door, there was a distinctive tug as it came unsealed. The smell grew stronger, and I knew I had been right—Mr. Shinohara was behind the Wrist-Cut Case.

In the cold fridge air, lit by the lamp, were rows of hands—on the shelves, placed with their fingers toward the door, the fingers and nails lined up next to one another like piano keys.

In the back, there were several small dishes, on top of which were the front paws of dogs and cats. The hands of the doll I'd found in the lecture hall garbage can were in the door. They were just balls of cloth, but they were the same color as the doll, so I knew they were the doll's hands.

I had long been a proponent of the theory that the wrist cutter was preserving the hands. I had no basis for this—it was merely what I would have done. I had been right.

I picked up one of the hands, a woman's hand. Red nail polish was flaking away, and the hand was cold and heavy in my palm.

I was touching dead skin. No, not dead—all his victims were alive, each living with a missing hand...but it made sense to refer to the part that had been cut off as dead.

There were right hands and left hands. There were the hands with nails that had turned black and hands with skin that was still beautiful.

I stroked several of the hands. I felt like I was peering into the depths of Mr. Shinohara's heart. Regular people wouldn't have understood, and I was sure Mr. Shinohara was convinced that no one would ever understand him. But it was easy for me to picture him alone in this kitchen, stroking his collection of hands.

The hands were in his refrigerator, so Mr. Shinohara must be the wrist cutter—but I had no intention of telling the police. Perhaps I should have, but that did not interest me. I had a different goal in mind.

I too wanted a hand cut off of someone. Touching Mr. Shinohara's collection made me want it even more.

I looked around the refrigerator. There were all kinds of hands in there. I could take any of them. Not just any hand would do, though; I knew exactly whose hand I wanted. But I put all the hands in front of me into a bag that I'd brought with me.

†

It was dark by the time Shinohara arrived home from the high school where he worked. He had stepped into the house and was headed for the living room when he noticed something was wrong: the window had been broken, and glass was scattered across the floor. The window itself was open as well, and cool night air was pouring into the room. Someone had broken in.

The first thing Shinohara thought of was the hands in the refrigerator. He went directly to the kitchen, opened the refrigerator door—and couldn't believe his eyes. All of the hands that had been keeping cool in there that morning were now gone. Human hands, dog and cat hands, even the doll's hands—they were all gone, and the refrigerator was almost completely empty. The only thing left was the small quantity of food Shinohara had kept in there with the hands.

Something was nagging at his mind, but he couldn't quite figure it out. He knew he needed to clean up the glass in the living room, but his mind was full of the missing hands, so he couldn't think straight.

He went upstairs, turned on his computer, and sat down in front of it.

Someone had broken in and stolen his hands, taking all the hands away.

A clear drop of liquid fell to the surface of the computer desk. It had fallen from his cheek... Shinohara suddenly realized that he was crying.

His entire life, he had never exchanged words with any human as intimate as the contact he had felt with those severed hands. If anyone else had seen him with them, they would have thought he was simply sitting there in silence—but Shinohara knew he had been communicating with those cold, silent hands—through the bumps and grooves, the elasticity.

Anger washed over him in waves so intense that he couldn't breathe. He was too afraid to call the police, but his desire to get revenge on whoever had taken the hands from him was much stronger than his fear.

The thief who had taken his hands must be punished. He had never killed anyone, but he'd make this thief the first exception. He would catch this thief, Shinohara swore it. He would cut off the hands to save them, and then he would strangle the thief—or stab the thief through the heart until death came.

But how would he find the thief? Shinohara rested his elbows on the desk, thinking.

The keyboard was dirty. He reached for the can of compressed air he always kept next to it. Then he froze—his eyes had found something on the keyboard.

No doubt about it—the thief had dropped it. No other explanation made sense. It was very small and easy to overlook, so it was something of a miracle that Shinohara had even noticed it.

It was then that Shinohara remembered the inside of the refrigerator. Something had been bothering him, and he understood it now. The hand thief had made a mistake, a very careless mistake—one that had foolishly revealed the thief's identity...

iv

The next morning, Shinohara went to work with a meat cleaver, the same one he always used when cutting off hands. It fit neatly inside his bag. As he greeted the other teachers in the office, none of them guessed what was in his bag.

It was always hectic in the mornings. Outside the teachers' room, students hurried past. First semester midterms were coming up quickly, and tests were being constructed on a number of different desks.

One of the other teachers asked how Shinohara's test was coming along. He smiled back and answered. Shinohara often believed his life consisted entirely of these feigned smiles. They annoyed him immensely.

Hands. Hands. Hands were more important than the other teachers. First, there were hands, and then the human followed. There was no point in talking with the human.

He had morning classes, so he couldn't yet go to see the thief who had stolen his hands. But he knew who it was. He had to catch the thief and demand to know where his hands had been hidden.

Only one night had passed—he desperately wanted to believe the hands were somewhere safe. When he knew where they were, then he would have to cut off the thief's hands with his meat cleaver. It would never do to let the hands die with the rest of the body, so he'd have to make them his.

The last session he taught that morning was his homeroom class. All those hands copying what he wrote on the blackboard... There were forty-two students in his class—and eighty-four hands.

Shinohara explained what the midterm would cover, but his thoughts dealt only with the stolen hands. The thief had left his food, taking only the hands. Shinohara hadn't noticed it right away, and it didn't make any sense.

At last, the bell rang and class ended. All morning classes were over, and it was time for lunch.

Shinohara left the room. The bag with the meat cleaver was in the teacher's office, and he was going to get it. The halls were at their noisiest and most crowded—but to Shinohara, it was all a dim roar.

He waited in the teachers' room for a few minutes, and then he headed for the chemistry lecture hall.

†

I headed for the chemistry lecture hall as soon as lunch started. When I opened the door and checked inside, I found it empty, so I went in, closing the door behind me. Instantly, the noise outside was cut off; the air inside was completely still, as if time had stopped.

I measured my pulse: it was beating like I'd just been running as fast as I could. My skin felt taut. I was very tense.

What had Mr. Shinohara done last night after he had arrived home? What had he thought when he noticed the hands were gone? Had he been too angry to think? I could only guess.

I hadn't seen him that morning—and if I had, I would've pretended to know nothing. He couldn't notice me; if I did anything strange, there was a strong risk it would ruin everything. I was pretty sure he didn't know I had stolen the hands, but that might've been nothing more than wishful thinking.

It was possible that I had made some terrible mistake without realizing it—but there was no way for me to know. If I had, and Mr. Shinohara came after me looking for revenge, then there was a strong possibility that my life would be in danger.

As I stood in the dark, deserted lecture hall thinking, I heard someone standing outside the door.

†

Shinohara opened the door of the lecture hall. There was one student inside, and the moment he saw that student's face, a surge of emotion ran through him.

He wanted to beat the student to death, but Shinohara stomped down those emotions, forcing himself to call out a friendly greeting instead. He planned to pretend to know nothing.

The student looked up. "Hello, Mr. Shinohara."

It was like always, nothing out of place—yet Shinohara knew the student was laughing at him on the inside, enjoying the performance and being around him like this. Yes, the student had come to the lecture hall to watch Shinohara squirm, knowing that his hands had been taken.

Hiding his nauseous rage, Shinohara drew closer. He must not betray his plans. He must not reveal that he knew the student to be the thief.

The foolish thief suspected nothing and didn't try to run. Shinohara was able to stand directly behind the student without arousing suspicion.

The thief had taken away the doll's hands—but nobody should have recognized those as hands. The doll was too small, and there were no fingers on those hands—they were just balls of cotton covered by a half sphere of cloth. Yet the thief had taken them with the rest of the hands.

The only person who would've known those were hands and taken them...was someone who had accidentally found the handless doll. The moment that person found the doll, the thief must've guessed that the chemistry teacher was the one behind the Wrist-Cut Case.

Shinohara put his hand on the shoulder of the student in front of him. Her shoulder shook. She turned slowly around, looking at him. "What is it?"

She was good at acting, Shinohara thought.

He had placed the handless doll in the wastebasket in the chemistry office. There was only one person who would have had a chance to see it—Morino, the girl who had been in the lecture hall while he'd been cleaning the chemistry office, while the office trash was sitting in the lecture hall. The male student who had been helping him would never have had time.

"Please take your hand off me, Mr. Shinohara. You're interfering with my reading."

This girl was always reading in the corner of the lecture hall. Her eyebrows twitched—more expression than he'd ever seen from her before.

When Shinohara had noticed the dirt on his keyboard the day before, he'd also found a long black hair between the keys. It had been sheer coincidence that the hair had landed there, out of all the places in his house it could have been. Shinohara's hair was short, so it couldn't be his—meaning the intruder must have had long hair.

And the bookshelves... On his shelves was the follow-up to

the book the girl was reading. And it had been pulled out, ever so slightly. He always kept his spines aligned, yet this one had been jutting out a full five millimeters. This girl had found it and looked at it.

There was no doubt in his mind: she had stolen his hands.

Shinohara tightened his grip on her shoulder, squeezing as if to break it.

Morino winced.

"Tell me where you hid the hands," he ordered, as politely as he could manage.

But Morino just tried to push him off, complaining that he was hurting her. The book she was reading fell to the ground.

"Where are the hands?" he asked again, loosening his grip and making sure she heard him. Her usual, expressionless mask had crumbled, and she shook her head as if she had no idea what he was talking about.

Pretending not to know, Shinohara thought. Instantly, his hand wrapped itself around her slender throat, squeezing.

Morino's eyes opened wide, staring up at him in shock as his fingers sank deep into the soft flesh of her neck. He was going to kill this girl, but there was no help for that. His grip tightened.

In a minute, she would stop moving. As he mused on that, out of the corner of his eye, he spotted a small cylinder in her hand—some sort of spray. By the time he noticed, it was too late: the spray was aimed right at his eyes.

There was a hiss of compressed gas, and his eyes began to burn.

†

Morino had been carrying around a can of pepper spray. She unloaded it in Mr. Shinohara's face, and then she hit him in the head with her chair before she began shouting for help. She did not scream—she just called out, calmly but loudly.

A minute later, several students and teachers came running. Mr.

Shinohara lay at the center of the crowd, clutching his throbbing eyes.

I could not leave my hiding place beneath the podium until the crowd dispersed.

epilogue

Mr. Shinohara was arrested—but not as a culprit behind the Wrist-Cut Case. Instead, he was convicted by society for a much lesser crime. No one knows his real crime, even now.

He's no longer a teacher and has since moved away. There have been no new victims in the Wrist-Cut Case.

The hands I stole from his house are buried in my backyard. I didn't need them. I didn't care about hands the way he did.

I had wanted to convince him that Morino had stolen his hands.

When I saw the hands in the refrigerator, I knew he was keeping them all, just like I had predicted. Even before I entered his house, I had been planning on using that fact and the doll hands to lead him to suspect Morino. I was glad he was smart enough to figure out the clue about the doll hands. He simply didn't know that I had switched the trash bins, sifting through the contents afterward.

I also left behind a long black hair—the same type of hair Morino had. It was my sister's hair, which had come in handy. I had remembered Shinohara cleaning his office keyboard with compressed air, and so I figured the hair stood a good chance of being discovered if I were to place it on his computer keyboard at home.

Moving the book he had mentioned to Morino had been insurance.

If he had determined that Morino was the thief, causing him to cut off her hands and kill her, my plan would've been complete. I only would've had to wait until her severed hands were in his fridge, and then I could've gone to steal them. Of course, there were a number of holes in this plan: there was no guarantee he would've taken her hands home even if he had killed her...but there was a good chance he would've.

The only hands I had wanted were Morino's pale, beautiful hands.

"Will you teach me how to smile like that?" she asked me the next day. It was the first time Morino had ever spoken to me.

Whenever I talked to someone else, I smiled. But inside, I had no expression—and Morino had somehow picked up on that. The performance that no one else had ever seen through was no match for her.

After that, we each had someone to talk to. Our relationship was a little too cold to call friendship—but when I spoke to her, it was the only time I could stop acting, letting my face remain devoid of expression. It gave the muscles of my face a well-earned respite. There was a comfortable disinterest to our relationship that allowed me to express the inhuman and unemotional sides of myself.

†

The world had long since forgotten the Wrist-Cut Case by the time summer vacation ended and second semester began.

The light in the classroom was yellow as the sun began to set. A breeze came in the open windows, toying with Morino's long black hair as she stood in front of me.

"So this movie used real freaks as actors, but the story was even stranger: the freaks were carrying around some sort of shrine..."

As she spoke, I murmured the movie's name. Morino looked ever so slightly surprised. Her expression barely changed at all, but I could tell.

"Right."

It was a movie directed by a German woman. Of all the people I knew, only Morino and I would be interested in something so strange.

"Do you remember the Wrist-Cut Case?" I asked.

"The one from last spring?"

"If you had been one of the victims, what would you be doing now?"

Morino stared down at her hands. "It would be very hard to put on a watch. Why do you ask?" she said, looking puzzled.

She didn't know the man she'd grappled with had been the wrist cutter . . . and I still stared at her hands from time to time. Perhaps it was better that Mr. Shinohara had not cut them off. Perhaps they were more beautiful alive—and Mr. Shinohara might have cut them in the wrong place.

"No reason," I said, and I stood up to leave.

The reason I wanted her hands was because she had those beautiful scars, from when she had tried to kill herself.

III

DOG

i

Dripping blood, my opponent attempted to flee into the grass—but it was easy for me to circle around in front of it. The four-legged animal was covered in wounds, and it was already too exhausted to move quickly.

I thought it was time to put it out of its misery. It no longer possessed the will to fight back.

I took the animal's throat between my upper and lower jaw. I felt its neck bones break in my mouth. The sound and sensation traveled up my jawbone. The animal slumped, hanging limp in my mouth.

I showed no mercy. I didn't want to do this, not really—but Yuka wanted me to, so I killed my opponent.

I opened my jaw, and the animal's dead body fell from my mouth, slumping limply to the ground. There was no light in its eyes, and it had gone completely quiet.

I howled.

Yuka and I had brought the four-legged animal here, under the bridge. Yuka had stopped in front of a house as we'd passed, gazing through the gate and sizing the animal up. When I followed her gaze, I'd seen the animal looking back at us.

Yuka had looked at me and said, "This is tonight's prey."

It was not as if I understood the words Yuka spoke—yet I knew what she was saying.

This ritual happened occasionally at night. I'd lost track of how many times. We would find our prey in town, taking it to the secret place under the bridge that only Yuka and I knew about. And then Yuka would make me fight.

I obeyed her orders. I ran across the ground as she commanded. I leapt on my opponents, knocking them down. The four-legged animals I fought were all smaller than me, so if I slammed into them, they would fall over, hurt. Blood would splatter their fur, and their bones would break.

When I won, Yuka would smile, looking very happy. We couldn't communicate with words, but her feelings flowed through me like river water, so I always knew when she was happy.

Yuka had been my friend since I was very small. When I first met her, I was with my brothers, who had been born with me. I was sleeping nestled up against my mother, and Yuka peered down at me with interest. I can still remember that now.

Half my howl vanished into the night sky. The other half echoed low under the bridge. The bridge was right overhead, blocking most of the sky—and when I looked up, I could see nothing but inky darkness.

The river was wide and the bridge large. On the riverbank around the bridge, there was a sea of tall grass, which you had to push your way through to get anywhere. But below the bridge, there was a small clearing without grass. The sunlight didn't reach here, which left a circular clearing—where we were.

Yuka and I had found it one summer day, discovering that you could stand in the middle and be surrounded by walls of grass. It had been our secret place to play ever since.

But now it was where Yuka made me fight.

I didn't want to bite and kill the animals, but Yuka wanted me to. When she gave me those orders, her eyes were dark as night, with no light at all.

Yuka had been sitting at the edge of the circle, watching me fight. Now she stood up.

It was time to go home. I knew what she was thinking. We had a connection that was beyond words.

I picked up the corpse in my mouth and went to toss it in the hole that was in the grass a little way from the clearing. When I dropped it in, the tiny body tumbled down along the edge of the pit. It wasn't that deep a hole, but the bottom was dark and hard to see. I could hear the body hit bottom.

The hole had been there when we found this place. Someone might have dug it, planning to bury something. It was too dark to see, but the bottom of the hole was now filled with the corpses of animals Yuka had made me kill. If you stood near it, there was a horrible stench.

The first time we carried out this ritual under the bridge, Yuka had ordered me to throw the body in the hole after. I hadn't yet learned to fight, and I was almost as badly hurt as my opponent in the end. When I'd faced my opponent, my mind went blank, and I had no idea what to do. But now I was good at fighting. I could kill my opponents calmly. Yuka was satisfied with how strong I had become.

The hair that had been ripped out when I bit my opponent filled my mouth. I swallowed it and then headed for the water, pushing my way through the grass until it opened up before me.

The forest of grass abruptly gave way to a vast expanse of running water. The water was so black that it looked less like a river than a giant pool of darkness. The lights on the bridge above cast reflections in the water from there to the opposite bank.

I washed the blood off my mouth in the river, and then I returned to where Yuka was waiting.

"Time to go." Yuka uttered speech that held that meaning as she headed for the stairs.

The stairs led diagonally up the bank to the bridge. To get to the stairs from the clearing, we had to push our way through grass. I ran to her side, and we walked together.

As we neared the stairs, I saw some grass move—the tips of the long grass stalks swayed slightly. For a moment, I thought someone was standing there, and tensed. I listened closely, but it seemed it was just the wind.

Yuka had already reached the top of the stairs, where she was waiting for me. I bounded up the stairs after her, leaving our secret place behind.

†

When school let out for the day, I met my classmate Morino in front of the station. There was a big bus terminal nearby and a square with fountains and flower beds. There were also a number of benches and a number of people sitting on them, killing time.

Morino was sitting on one of those benches, away from the road, in the shade of some bushes. She would always read when she had time—but not today. Her book lay closed next to her on the bench.

Morino was leaning forward, her head down and her face hidden behind her hair, which acted like a veil.

As I approached, she raised her head and gazed at me. Her skin was pale as porcelain, untouched by the sun. There was a small mole just under her left eye. Her features were as lifeless as a doll's. All she had to do was stop moving, and she could easily work as a mannequin.

She pointed silently at the ground. There was some dirt at her feet, on the white paving stones. When I looked closer, I saw that it was moving.

Ants were taking apart a butterfly and carrying it away. In the ants' jaws, a butterfly wing stood up like a yacht sail, casting a shadow on the stones. Morino had been staring fixedly at that.

There was no particular reason why we arranged to meet here. It would have been equally convenient to leave school together, but Morino was a little too well-known. The way she looked and acted, and the rumors that swirled around her, meant that people often turned to look as she went past. She stood out, and I didn't want to be seen in her company too often.

But Morino never worried about anyone around her, treating everyone like so much static. It was as if her nerves that were responsible for worrying about what people thought had burned out long ago. Or perhaps Morino simply didn't notice how much attention she attracted. She could be a little oblivious sometimes.

"Let's go," she said, standing up and walking away.

I headed in the same direction. She had promised to guide me to a used bookshop she frequented.

"It's a very small shop. I'm the only customer."

When I'd asked the name, she'd told me—but I'd never heard of it. She had given a general description of the shop's location, but that had not helped much either. So I had had her draw a map on the board—but the lines she had drawn resembled no place on Earth and were impossible to parse. And as she'd added yet another line of chalk, she'd been at a loss to explain how the bookstore had come to be constructed in the middle of a river. Therefore, we'd agreed that she would take me there directly.

As we walked, the shops gave way to rows of houses. The sky above was clear, and the sun beat down on our backs. The road ran straight ahead of us, middle-class homes on either side of us. Morino strode forward unwaveringly; she must've walked this way often.

"Have you heard about the pet kidnappings?" I asked.

"Pet kidnappings?" she echoed. Apparently she had not.

As we walked, I explained. Neighbors of ours had noticed their pet dog was missing that morning, and I'd heard my parents talking about it at breakfast.

"Not the first time," my mother had murmured. I always watched the news, paying close attention to any strange cases, but my mother knew more about the local gossip.

According to her, about twice a week—on Wednesday and Saturday mornings—people had been discovering the animals they kept outdoors were missing, meaning that the animals had been stolen late Tuesday and Friday nights. All the stolen pets had been dogs. As the rumors spread, more and more people began keeping their dogs inside at night.

Morino listened with obvious fascination. When I'd told her

everything I knew, she asked, "Anything else?" I shook my head, and she began to mull it over.

I was a little surprised that pet kidnappings were a source of interest to her. She had never once mentioned dogs, cats, or even hamsters, so I'd assumed she had little affection for animals.

"What does the kidnapper do with those things?"

"Those things?"

"You know, the stinky things with four legs that make a lot of noise."

Did she mean the dogs?

Morino stared into the distance in front of her, muttering, "I can't understand why anyone would gather a bunch of those things together. Is he training some sort of army? Baffling."

It sounded as though she were talking to herself, so I didn't respond.

"Wait," she said, suddenly stopping dead in her tracks.

I stopped as well.

There was still a fair amount of ground ahead of us before the road ended in a cross street. I looked at her, waiting for some explanation for our abrupt halt.

"Quiet," she said, holding up one finger.

Apparently, her feelers were so attentive right now that just my looking at her was enough to draw that response. I could see her ears perking up, trying to catch a sound.

I couldn't hear any unusual noises—just a dog barking somewhere. Otherwise, it was an ordinary, quiet afternoon. I could feel the warmth of the sun on my back.

"Nope, we can't go any farther in this direction," she declared.

I looked ahead of us. There didn't appear to be any construction blocking our way, and an old man on a bicycle was even pedaling past us.

"So much for the bookstore. This road used to work..."

I asked about her reasoning, but she only shook her head ruefully in response. Then she began heading back the way we had come.

Morino had a strong tendency to follow her own instincts, regardless of what anyone else said to her. She didn't blend in with the rest of the class and paid no attention to anything people said to her. She spent the bulk of her time alone, without expression, so for her to look so upset and defeated ... it must've been something significant.

I glanced down the road again. There were houses on either side of the street, and just inside a gate up ahead, I could see a doghouse—a brand-new one. Had they just bought a dog? I could barely make out the sound of the dog breathing inside. I listened closely for other sounds, never dwelling on the dog at all.

It took me a long time to work it out.

In that time, Morino had quickly placed a good twenty yards between us. I turned to follow her, but she had stopped again, raising one hand to signal me.

"Danger! We can proceed no farther." Gazing directly ahead, she bit her lip. "We're surrounded," she moaned, tension in her voice.

A little girl with a big dog was walking toward us.

The dog was a golden retriever with beautiful fur. Holding a leash attached to its collar was a short, thin girl, probably in the third grade, with hair down to her shoulders, which shook with each step.

As she passed us, her dog met my eye, and as it walked, I could see my own reflection bobbing up and down in the dog's eyes— dark-black, wise eyes. They stared up at me as if sucking me in.

Then my reflection vanished from its eyes; the dog had looked away from me to gaze up at the girl.

The girl and dog passed us by, turning into a nearby house, one story with a red roof.

"I'm home," I heard the girl call out. The golden retriever went in the front door with her. There was no doghouse in the yard, so it must've lived inside.

When the girl and the dog were gone, Morino peeled herself off the wall and began walking away as if nothing had happened. I assumed she would have something to say for herself, but she said nothing. Her expression and manner were just like always, so I knew dealing with such circumstances must have been something of a daily ritual for her.

"I had no idea this road was so fraught with danger," Morino said bitterly.

I asked if it was possible to get to the bookshop using some other road, but apparently that would involve a rather extensive detour. Morino had already abandoned the idea of taking me there.

Following along after her, I thought about the missing dogs again. Why twice a week, on Tuesday and Friday nights? What fate lay in store for the kidnapped dogs?

Morino and I found strange cases—and the people involved in them—darkly fascinating. Tragic human death ought to have torn our hearts in two—deaths so unfair that they made people want to scream. But we cut those articles out of newspapers, looking down the deep, dark well at the hearts of the people involved.

Most people wouldn't understand such interests—but it bewitched us like magic.

This time, it was not an especially strange case, nothing more than some missing dogs. But it was happening very close to home. A small disturbance right next door was much more interesting than a huge fire in some other country.

"Are you at all curious to know who's kidnapping those dogs?" I asked.

"If you find out, tell me," she said without expression. I took this to mean that she was hiding her own reluctance to have anything to do with this case... or with dogs.

†

Yuka and I lived in the house with Mama, but Mama was never home. She left in the morning and came back late at night. During the day, only Yuka and I were at home.

I had been with Yuka since I was small. My brothers were taken away right after I was born, and I had been with Yuka alone ever since.

Yuka spent most of her time sprawled out in front of the TV. I would go over to her, lie down on the newspapers spread out on the floor, and rest my head on her back.

When we were bored with TV, we stood up and stretched. Yuka would wander around the kitchen and bathroom, and I would follow after, trying to keep up.

Then we would go for a walk. I liked walks—Yuka and I, walking together. There was a string tying us together during walks. If I started to go the wrong way, Yuka would frown at me.

Sometimes a stranger would come to the house, a big man Mama brought home with her. When he was in the house, the air smelled bad. The comfortable house where Yuka and I lived would vanish.

When he came in, he always patted my head, smiling at Mama as he did—but he never met my eye. When I felt his hand on my head, I always wanted to bite him.

Yuka and I hated him because he would always hit Yuka when Mama was out of the room.

When I first saw it, I thought I was imagining things. Mama had left for the kitchen, leaving Yuka and me alone with him.

Yuka was next to him when he'd suddenly jabbed her with his elbow. Yuka looked surprised, gazing up at him.

He smiled, leaned over, and whispered something to her.

I was watching from the corner and couldn't hear what he said, but I could see Yuka's expression change.

I felt a terror run through me. Yuka and I were sitting far apart, but deep down, our hearts were connected. I could feel her shock and confusion flowing into me.

Whenever Mama came back into the room, the man would stop whatever he'd been doing. Yuka would look at Mama anxiously, but Mama never noticed anything wrong.

Yuka looked to me for help, but all I could do was pace back and forth.

Every time he came over, his treatment of Yuka got worse. He even kicked her in the belly sometimes! Yuka would groan in pain and fall to the floor coughing, and I would run to her, putting myself between them, to the man's great annoyance.

He always came over on the same nights of the week. Those nights, Yuka and I would always huddle in the corner to protect ourselves. The house always felt very sinister when he was around. We could never tell when he might open the door and come in a room, so Yuka was always too frightened to sleep.

Eventually, we could stand it no longer, and we began fleeing the house.

Yuka started making me kill animals after the man began visiting. She cried a lot after he began coming over, and her eyes had a new kind of darkness inside them. That darkness made me very sad.

ii

"We first noticed at eleven o'clock at night," the young house-wife explained as she clutched her sound-asleep child to her bosom. We'd exchanged a few pleasantries at the beginning of the conversation, and she'd mentioned that the child had been born only three months earlier.

"Before bed, my husband went to check on Pavlov, and he wasn't in his house..." Pavlov was the name of their dog, which had gone missing on a Tuesday night two weeks ago. It was a purebred dog, but of a breed I'd never heard of before.

The housewife and I were facing each other in the front door of a small home of Western construction, which was not much more than a mile from my house.

On the way home from school, I'd decided to make inquiries at the homes where dogs had been kidnapped.

I'd explained to the woman that I worked for the school news-paper and was investigating the series of pet kidnappings that had been occurring in the neighborhood. When I suggested that my work might lead to the capture of the individual responsible, the housewife had become extremely cooperative.

"Thinking back on it, I remember Pavlov barking a lot around ten. But he often barked when people walked past, so we ignored it."

"And that was the last time you heard him?" I asked.

She nodded.

From here, I could see a tiny yard to one side with an empty doghouse—a fairly large one, with a metal hook out front for attaching the dog's leash.

"The kidnapper unhooked the leash and pulled the dog away?" I asked.

She shook her head. "They left the leash—and there was a half-eaten chicken nugget."

The kidnapper must have dropped the chicken, the woman explained.

When I asked if the nugget had been store-bought, the woman was unsure but thought it had looked homemade.

The kidnapper had brought something a dog might like from home to tame the dog and then taken it away. Using a bit of chicken made the whole crime seem rather prosaic—a very common sort of crime, not at all related to professional dog thieves or evil spirits.

I bowed my head and pretended to be grateful for the woman's help.

She looked sadly at the doghouse, remembering her beloved pet. "I hope you find out who did this." Her voice was quiet, but there was murderous fury hidden within it.

When the child in her arms began to sniffle, I said goodbye and turned away. As I did, I realized the house across the street had a dog as well. Through the gate, I could see a black dog—a big dog, about half my height.

"Its name is Chocolate," the housewife said from behind me.

I mentioned that I hadn't noticed it was there.

"Yes, it almost never barks."

Chocolate's house was in a much more visible position than

Pavlov's—but the dog was so quiet that the kidnapper might have simply overlooked it.

I went home, where my sister, Sakura, and my mother were making dinner. My mother was hovering over the pot, stirring, while my sister chopped vegetables.

My sister was two years younger than me and getting ready for her high school entrance exams. She was normally in cram school at this time of day, but she said the school was closed today. Until the spring, she'd worn her hair long, but she'd cut it boyishly short over the summer.

Her personality was the exact opposite of mine, and she helped out around the house a lot. She could never turn down a request for help. For example, if my mother was sitting in front of the TV snacking and she turned toward my sister, clasping both hands together and saying, "Sakura, do the dishes for me?" Sakura would refuse at first.

"Aw, no! Do them yourself!"

But my mother would hang her head and look forlorn—as if it was the end of the world. The moment Sakura saw that, she was done for. She would look totally shocked and hurriedly splutter, "Okay, okay! Don't cry!" as if she herself were about to.

Then Sakura would jump up and race into the kitchen. As soon as this transaction had been completed, my mother would return her attention to the TV and her *senbei*. I frequently wondered if Sakura knew how much of what my mother did was a performance. Was Sakura really that naïve? It seemed she was doomed to look after my parents in their old age.

Sakura had a very special talent—at least, that was how I viewed it, although she seemed to think it was more a curse. Most of the time, however, she appeared to be a very ordinary person.

"Did you go by the game center again?" my mother sighed when she saw me come in. I wasn't a big fan of video games, but that was my usual excuse when I returned home late.

I sat down on a chair in the kitchen and watched them as they cooked. They operated in silent harmony. As my mother stir-fried vegetables, she could hold out one hand silently, and my sister would know exactly what she wanted, silently handing over the saltshaker. My mother would taste the stir-fry, and before she could even ask for mirin, my sister would be bringing it over.

They were both talking to me, so I responded appropriately. They laughed. Sakura laughed a little too hard and gasped for breath.

"Stop making us laugh and set the table. So what did the teacher do?" Sakura asked.

Apparently I had been talking about school. I would occasionally lose track of what I'd been talking about or why people around me were laughing. Everything I had to say to them could be conducted by reflex alone, and the stories were invariably improvised, made up on the spot. Strangely, this did not seem to create any discrepancies.

It must have looked like I was part of a warm and joyous family. My family seemed to think I was an outgoing boy—good at making people laugh but not much good at school.

But to me, there had been no conversation between me and my mother and sister. I forgot what we said as soon as it happened. It was as though I were sitting there in stony silence while everyone around me cracked up for no reason at all, as if I were living in some surreal dream.

"Kiri's dog is still missing," Sakura said, washing the cooking implements. My ears had been muffled, barely able to hear anything around me, but suddenly they were picking up every noise. "She was sure it would come home on its own, but..."

I asked for details.

Sakura explained that her classmate's dog had vanished on Wednesday of last week. There were rumors the pet kidnapper had taken it.

"And when they found the dog missing, it seemed like they'd used a bit of sausage to nab it."

"My," my mother muttered, adding that she had forgotten to buy sausage at the store.

"What kind of dog? A big one?" I asked.

Sakura frowned at me, alarmed. Apparently, there was a look on my face I usually hid from my family.

"W-what?" I stammered, covering.

"The dog was a mutt, but a pretty small one."

Abruptly, I realized I had forgotten to ask Pavlov's owner the same question. I broke off the conversation as naturally as I could and ran back out the door, still in uniform, my mother calling out after me that it was almost time for dinner.

When I reached the house where Pavlov had once lived, it was getting dark out. I rang the bell, and the same young housewife I had spoken to a couple of hours before appeared. She looked surprised to see me again, and she was no longer holding her child.

"Sorry to bother you again, but there was something I forgot to ask. How big was Pavlov?"

"You came all this way for that?" she said, puzzled. Then she explained that Pavlov had not been full-grown and was still on the small side.

"Only a little bigger than a puppy?"

"Right. But his breed can get very big, which is why his house is so large."

I thanked her and left.

When the kidnapper had taken the dogs, the leash had been left behind. So how were the dogs transported? Did the kidnapper bring a leash? It would've been easier—and faster—to simply unhook the leash from the doghouse, if that were the case. So the kidnapper had taken the leash off the dog's collar and carried it away.

Now, why had the pet kidnapper chosen Pavlov and not the quiet dog across the street? I would have chosen the one that barked less simply because it would probably be easier to kidnap. But whoever was behind the pet kidnappings had not done that. My best guess was that Pavlov had been taken because he was smaller and thus easier to carry. The dog my sister's friend had owned was also on the small side. It seemed likely that all the dogs the kidnapper had taken were small ones.

But why pick dogs that were easy to carry? One possibility was that the culprit didn't have a car or any other vehicle large enough to carry a dog, which would explain avoiding large dogs and choosing small ones. From all the information I'd managed to gather, I knew that the area from which dogs had gone missing was not very large. Someone with a car would have avoided carrying out the crimes in such a confined area, instead collecting dogs from all over the city.

I remembered reading about a kind of analysis used when investigating killings done without motive, purely for the fun of it—it focused on the basis for the killer's choice of victims. The killer in that case had unconsciously chosen targets that were weaker than himself. For example, all his victims had been less than five feet tall, not a single one of them even close to five foot three. In that case, they were able to speculate that the killer was between five feet and five feet three inches tall. Such a method of thinking might prove helpful in the missing-dog case.

When I got home, my father had returned from work, and my family had started eating already. I told them I'd gone to the convenience store and joined the conversation, smoothly working it around so that I could ask about houses that kept dogs in the neighborhood.

"The dog over there is really cute. I can't imagine why they don't keep it indoors, as small as it is," Sakura said, somewhere in the middle of the list.

"It must bark a lot," my father said.

I asked for the address. It was Tuesday night, so it was possible the kidnapper would target the house that evening.

†

The house in question was on the corner, an old building of Japanese construction. I looked over the wall and spotted a large garden with a doghouse at the far end. The doghouse looked hand-made, like a wooden box, and there was a stake driven into the ground next to it, around which the dog's leash was tied.

The dog had big eyes, and the moment it saw me, it began barking furiously, jumping around. It was small enough that even a child could carry it easily.

I moved away from the house, hiding myself in a thicket a safe distance away. There were no lights near me, and I was surrounded by darkness.

I checked my watch. It was dark out, but when I pressed the button on my watch, a light inside it turned on so I could read the display. It was ten, the same time they had last heard Pavlov bark two weeks ago. If the kidnapper was coming here tonight, it would be soon.

The ground beneath me was covered in leaves, and the slightest movement shook the branches of the bushes around me. It was early fall, so it was still warm during the day, but come night, it was a little chilly.

I reached into my jacket pocket, touching the hilt of the knife inside, which I had brought with me just in case.

If I did catch a glimpse of the kidnapper, I had no intention of turning the criminal in. I intended to simply watch from a distance, unseen—so it was unlikely I would need the weapon, yet I had brought one of the knives from the knife set with me anyway, without really thinking about it. The naked blade made it easy to cut myself, so I carried it in a leather case I had bought for it.

I enjoyed watching people carry out unusual crimes. This hobby had once led me to encounter a man who had killed several women. I'd stolen a set of twenty-three knives from that man's apartment, which I now kept hidden behind a bookcase in my room. When I was at home, I often gazed at the reflection of the ceiling light in the metal of the blades—the white light gleamed like it was wet.

Occasionally, my reflection in the blade would transform into the faces of the women those knives had killed. I knew this was just a trick of the mind, but I felt like their suffering and despair had stained the knives forever.

The knives were a little too much for me. I should never have brought them home. I felt like the gleam in that metal surface was telling me to use them.

I checked my watch again, turning the light on and reading the display. It was Wednesday now. Not a single person had passed the whole time I'd sat in the bush.

I wondered where the kidnapper lived. If I knew that, I might be able to narrow down the list of places to wait. At any rate, it seemed obvious I hadn't seen the kidnapper that day.

Ten minutes later, I left the thicket and returned home.

My parents were asleep, but Sakura was studying for exams. When she heard me come home, she came downstairs, asking where I'd been. I told her I'd been to the convenience store.

†

I'd known the man would be coming today, so I should never have fallen asleep.

I was torn from my slumber by Yuka's scream, her voice coming from the living room.

I ran toward her.

She had been hiding in back with me, but he must have taken her into the living room. Mama was out of the house, so the man was alone with Yuka.

Yuka was lying in a heap, groaning. She sounded very sad, fighting against the pain.

The man was standing next to her head, staring down at her without expression. He seemed so big, like his head was touching the ceiling. And Yuka seemed so small. All she could do was moan in pain, powerless.

Anger boiled over in my mind. I howled, the voice tearing out of me.

The man turned toward me, eyes wide in surprise. He took a step back, moving away from Yuka.

She lay there groaning, but her eyes were on me, eyes filled with love. From the bottom of my heart, I knew I had to protect her.

I heard the front door open and someone call out. Mama had come home from shopping. That was where she had gone when she'd left him there.

I tried to bite the man's hand, but Mama grabbed me from behind. My jaws snapped shut a few inches too short.

But that was long enough for Yuka to stand up. As Mama shouted angrily, Yuka ran for the door. I ran after her, and we both fled the house.

Outside, we both ran as fast and far as we could. I heard Mama calling after us, but we didn't turn around. We fled into the depths of the night.

Rows of lights lined quiet, dark roads, but the only thing they really illuminated was the ground beneath our feet. Our two small shadows flitted from one lamppost to the next.

The night stretched as far as we could see in every direction—but I was with Yuka, so I wasn't scared. Still, thinking about her made me very sad.

Yuka wasn't crying, but I could tell she was hurt. I felt it too. Occasionally, the pain was too much, and she had to stop for a moment. It hurt me to see that, but there was nothing I could do but stand by her side.

The animal we had found that afternoon was tonight's prey—that's what Yuka said. That day on our walk, we'd found an animal that looked easy to take away. We headed for that house.

I was sure Yuka had noticed it too—it was getting harder to find animals we could steal easily now. More and more houses were keeping the animals inside. They were beginning to take measures against us.

I was always anxious now, afraid that someone would see what we were doing…and I was always on guard, startled by every shadow.

I wasn't afraid of Yuka, of course, nor Mama, nor even that bad man. I was afraid of strangers. There was someone after Yuka and me because we were taking the animals. And that someone would eventually discover what we had been doing underneath the bridge. It was easy to guess what would happen. If everyone knew what Yuka and I were doing, we would be separated. Without me, there would be no one to protect Yuka, and I couldn't let that happen.

We could see tonight's house up ahead. The top of the roof caught the streetlight, but everything else was dark, swallowed by the night. The house was on a corner; when we'd walked past that afternoon, there had been a small dog in the yard.

"Come," Yuka said, and we stepped forward.

But then something caught my eye. I called out to Yuka softly, and we froze. She looked over at me, puzzled.

A moment ago, there had been a small gleam of light in the thicket across from the house. It had been just a tiny point of light, which had soon vanished—but I knew someone was there. All my nerves stood on end, focused on that spot. I couldn't be sure, but I felt as if someone was hidden there, watching the house where Yuka and I had been headed. It was possible that my mind was playing tricks on me and there was nothing there—but I felt sure.

Not today, I told Yuka with my eyes. She looked at the house again and agreed.

That night, we did not steal any animals. We spent some time under the bridge, and then we went home. Yuka wanted me to kill something, but I was relieved that I didn't have to.

Still, I was anxious. The shadow chasing after us had taken form and shown itself. It was not just a figment of my imagination—it was real.

iii

My Tuesday night stakeout had passed without the kidnapper showing. The next day, Wednesday, I casually quizzed my classmates and family, trying to figure out if any dogs had gone missing.

But it seemed the kidnapper hadn't stolen anything that night—or perhaps a dog had been stolen somewhere beyond the reach of my information network.

"Do you know what kind of person is behind this?" Morino asked me, looking up from her book as she sat in the corner of the chemistry lecture hall Wednesday at lunch.

I shook my head. I had no idea.

"Why would anyone steal *that* animal in the first place? To sell them to pet shops for money?" Morino asked, as if it was utterly incomprehensible that anyone would ever want that particular kind of animal.

"I doubt the kidnapper's after money—even the purebred dogs they sell in pet shops tend to get put down once they're fully grown. Almost nobody buys them."

If someone was in the market, it'd be for research test subjects, not pets. Pet dogs trusted humans, making them easier to handle than wild dogs. I'd heard they would fetch a good price on the black market.

"The only reason I can think of to kidnap dogs is to hurt them. There are people who claim abandoned dogs and cats from Internet sites for that reason."

"So the kidnapper is killing the stolen pets for fun? That's pretty crazy," Morino said.

But something about this seemed off to me. If that was true, *where* was the killer hurting the animals? Not at home. When the news occasionally mentioned animal bodies discovered in parks, discussions about animal abuse usually followed, but I hadn't heard about any such discoveries recently.

†

On my way home from school that Wednesday and Thursday, I made inquiries at homes where pets had gone missing, covering one house each day. The homeowners didn't seem to suspect that

I didn't actually work for the school newspaper, and they were helpful.

But I found no real new information about the culprit. Both the stolen animals were small, and both were mutts. One of the pet owners had found partially eaten food left behind, the other had not.

On Friday, I once again got on a bus, heading for a home with a missing pet. According to the information I had managed to gather, this was the earliest disappearance, and the farthest from my home and school. It was one of the houses along the river.

Comparing my map with the addresses, I found the house I was looking for. It was newly built. I rang the front doorbell, but it seemed nobody was home.

There was a small garden with a bed of tulips, along with a dog food dish in front of an empty doghouse. The dish was made of plastic; it was a bit dirty, and it had "Marble's dish" written in marker in a childish scrawl.

I left the house and got back on the bus, this time getting off at a stop near home.

It was Friday; another pet might well vanish tonight. As I was thinking about that, someone called out to me. I turned around and saw Sakura, wearing her junior high school uniform and pushing her bike toward me. She jogged a little until she caught up with me.

She always stopped at cram school on her way home, studying for a few more hours, so I asked her what she was doing there so early.

"Something came up, and I couldn't go to cram school today," she said listlessly. She looked a little pale and downcast, and she could barely keep her bike going in a straight line.

"You saw something again?" I asked, taking her bicycle.

She thanked me and nodded.

Sakura was born under an unusual star, giving her what I called a gift but what she detested and called a curse: Sakura frequently discovered corpses.

The first time was on an elementary school field trip to the mountains. She had been in the first grade, and she'd become separated from the others. She ended up at the edge of a pond, where she found a human corpse floating in the water.

The second time was four years later. Sakura had gone to the sea with a friend's family, and she'd once again been separated from the others. This time, she found a man's body washed up on the rocks by the shore.

The third time was three years later, in her second year of junior high, at her volleyball club camp. After taking a wrong turn while out jogging, she'd found herself in a deserted area. Then she'd tripped over something—a human skull.

Every time she found a body, she came home looking pale. Then she would run a fever and spend the next week in bed.

"Why is it always me?" she cried.

The gaps between her discoveries were getting shorter, and a quick estimate suggested she would find her fourth body this year or next. When she got old, she might very well find them every minute or two.

"So what did you find today?" I asked, as the wheels of her bike squealed at my side.

"On the way to cram school, I saw something…and then I felt sick and decided to skip."

Between the junior high and her cram school, there was a river with wide banks—broad, shallow, and slow moving. Crossing the river was a big concrete bridge, which lots of cars used. There was a separate lane for bikes and pedestrians.

"I had my bag and a towel in the basket of my bicycle."

The towel was a blue and white one she used often. A truck had zipped by, and the wind had sent the towel into the air. Before she could catch it, it had flown over the edge of the bridge, dropping out of sight.

With cars zipping past behind her, she had leaned over the railing, looking down. Fortunately, the towel had not fallen into the river. Rather, it was caught on the grass along the riverbank far below.

"I went down to the bank to get my towel."

At the end of the bridge was a set of stairs made of concrete that led down to the bank. When Sakura reached the bottom of those steps, she'd found herself in a sea of grass with pointy green leaves as tall as she was. She'd pushed her way through them—the grass was thick, but not too thick for a person to pass through.

"I couldn't tell from up above, but there was a space under the bridge where the grass stopped." There was a circular patch of dry ground surrounded by a wall of grass. It was like being inside a cage.

The massive bridge loomed overhead like a roof; when Sakura had looked up, half the sky was filled with the underbelly of the bridge.

"I looked around for my towel, but..." She'd heard the buzzing of insects—a great number of flies. Looking closer, she saw the swarm clustered over one spot.

"I pushed my way toward it because it was in the same general direction as my towel..."

As she walked, Sakura smelled something rotting. She parted the grass, and just as she neared the swarm of flies, a black pit opened beneath her feet. It was more of a depression than a hole, only about three feet across and three feet deep. She almost fell in. Then, heaving from the stench, she looked down, and she saw what was in the hole...

†

The hole was filled with an alarming number of lumps. They were torn to bits and shapeless, so at first I didn't know what they were, just black and red lumps.

Trying to ignore the stench, I bent down, looking closer.

Jaws, tails, and collars—dogs. Beneath the torn fur and flesh, maggots wriggled. There was layer after layer of lumps piled up in the hole. All of them had once had life and frolicked about beneath the sun. It was a strange feeling, the lure of death and destruction.

The hole was filled with rot and stench. Staring down into it, I found myself remembering images of World War II. The hole of death had a lot in common with those images.

I stood up and looked around. Like Sakura had said, there was nothing here but grass: the pointed tips of the grass against the red light of the setting sun and the flies buzzing around them like black specks. The flies must have thought me a friend, as they kept crashing into my uniform and cheeks. Everything was tinted red by the fading sunlight.

When Sakura told me about her discovery, I'd immediately guessed there was a connection between the hole and the pet kidnappings. I figured there was a strong possibility that the place she'd found was the place I'd been looking for.

I sent her home alone and headed for the bridge. I took the concrete stairs from the end of the bridge down to the riverbank and there found the clearing in the sea of grass. There was a cloud of flies a short distance away.

I looked down into the hole at my feet. Marble and Pavlov were among these corpses.

I turned away from the hole, leaving the bridge, and I went home, waiting for night to fall.

When the clock showed ten, I put a knife in my pocket and emerged from my room.

Sakura was still in shock from seeing those dead animals, and she was sprawled out on the sofa in the living room. When I passed in front of her, heading for the front door, my mother looked up from her TV show, asking where I was going. When I answered, "The convenience store," Sakura muttered, "The midnight convenience store warrior!"

I returned to the space under the bridge. It was Friday, so there was a strong chance the kidnapper would show.

As I walked, I tried to imagine what someone who killed animals for fun would be like. I could almost picture the kidnapper tossing the dead dogs into the hole.

If I could, I wanted to watch the killer work. I was curious about the kind of ritual that preceded the disposal of the corpses.

Things that were merciless and cruel always captivated me. The conversations my classmates enjoyed and the warm words I exchanged with my family never really resonated with me. They were just static, like a radio that wasn't tuned properly.

At night, the river turned black, like a universe without stars but spread across the ground. The lights on the bridge barely managed to illuminate the water. There were no signs of anyone else around, so the kidnapper must not have arrived yet.

I cautiously descended the stairs and went into the grass. As I pushed my way through it, I remembered what Morino and I had said on the phone before I left the house.

"I'm going to see someone who likes dogs. Do you want to come?"

"I'd love to, but I have so much homework."

"There wasn't any homework."

"My mother's illness took a turn for the worse. She's at death's door."

"No need to force an excuse. If you're afraid of dogs, I won't insist," I said, and I got a response well beyond what I had expected.

"W-what are you talking about? Afraid of dogs? Don't be silly! I'm not afraid of those things!"

She'd sounded earnest—not the kind of person who was fun to tease. I apologized and, for the sake of her pride, hung up pretending not to know the truth.

Now I hid myself in the grass.

My knees on the ground, I pulled a digital camera from my pocket. The lights on the bridge above were the only illumination, so it was questionable whether I'd be able to capture anything. I opened up the aperture and set the shutter speed to the slowest setting, trying to get an image without resorting to using the flash. If I used the flash, the kidnapper would know I was there, and I hoped to avoid that.

I did not intend to report the dog killer to the police, preferring to keep the kidnapper unaware of my existence. It was a rule of mine not to get involved. I was a third party, just watching from the sidelines. If I didn't report the criminal, more pets would be kidnapped, and more people would be sad and would cry, but that did not bother me at all. I was that kind of person.

From where I was hiding, I could see the stairs leading down from the bridge and the clearing. I figured the kidnapper would cross the clearing on the way to the hole, and that was my chance to get a photograph.

The river carried massive amounts of water downstream. Hidden in the grass, I could hear the water moving past. I remember how black the river surface had been. It was a very quiet image.

A chilly wind blew past, rustling the grass around me. One blade poked me in the cheek.

When my watch showed twelve, a shadowy figure appeared on the bridge above. As it came down the stairs, I lowered my head, breathing quietly to keep my presence a secret.

The shadow reached the bottom of the stairs and vanished into the grass. The faint light spilling over the edge of the bridge was just enough to let me make out the swaying grass as the figure pushed its way through before emerging into the clearing. The figure had been hidden in shadow as it came down the stairs—but in the clearing, I could see it clearly.

Emerging from the grass was a girl with a dog. The girl was very short, with hair down to her shoulders. She was very thin. The dog was a golden retriever. It was the same girl and dog that had passed us when I'd been out with Morino.

A smaller dog was in the girl's arms. The dog was struggling and whining, but the girl was used to holding dogs, so she didn't drop it.

I got the camera ready.

†

When Yuka and I first found the clearing under the bridge, it was a very hot summer day. There were no clouds in the sky, and the sun beat down on the sea of grass around the bridge.

Yuka and I were on a walk. We'd played like we always did, running until we could run no farther. At last we were too out of breath to run, and we'd stopped on the road by the river.

We leaned against the concrete railing, resting, staring down at the sea of grass below. There was a gentle breeze, and the grass shifted like invisible hands were moving it.

Yuka called me. When I turned toward her, I saw that she was looking at the stairs leading down from the end of the bridge.

As we went down, I could feel her sense of adventure; it was almost dancing. At the bottom of the stairs was a world of green. We moved forward through it, our noses filled with the grassy scent.

Yuka must have decided it was boring walking normally, because she glanced back at me and then suddenly ran forward. Clearly, she was signaling me to give chase. We forgot how tired we were as we chased each other around in the grass.

It was a hot summer day, and I was soon roasting. Still, I followed Yuka through the grass. When I lost sight of her, I'd soon hear her laughing, and I'd surge toward the voice, causing her to run again.

Suddenly we came out into a clearing. It was like the world opened up before us. The powerful scent of grass faded, and a gentle breeze wrapped around us. We were in a circular area that had remained free of grass.

Yuka had found it first, and she was standing in the center of the clearing, appearing surprised. She looked around, and then she saw me come flying out of the wall of grass. At first, it confused both of us, but soon we began to feel like we'd found something special. I could see her eyes glittering with joy.

How long ago had that been? It seemed like a distant memory.

Shortly after we found the clearing, he'd started coming. And then Yuka and I had begun our midnight walks. The wind grew colder every day. We no longer felt the warm light that had enveloped us that summer day.

Even if we did take a walk during the day, we no longer ran or chased each other. We no longer played; we just went looking for homes with dogs. Doing so made it easier to find prey at night.

Yuka told me to do so. I didn't know why, but I knew it wasn't for fun. Yuka's eyes never smiled. Her sadness and hatred overwhelmed all other emotions. I had to do as she asked.

The wind was a little colder than it had been last time. It was still early in the evening, and there were still plenty of cars racing by on the bridge. Their blinding lights raced toward us, our shadows spreading out before shrinking and zipping past us, then vanishing into the darkness.

We looked down at the grass from above. Most of it was lost in darkness. The wind rustled the grass, waves traveling through darkness. We could only make out a small portion of it from the faint light of the streetlights on the bridge.

Yuka and I went down the stairs and into the clearing.

I looked closely at the wall of grass around us. Was anyone hiding there? Could I smell any stranger's scent in the air?

Just as my nerves were all standing on guard, Yuka called me. It was time to begin.

We placed the dog we'd brought with us in the center of the circle. It was not as small as a puppy but not as big as a grown-up, either—it was a young dog, almost finished being a child. It looked up at us, surprised. We'd kidnapped the dog on our way there.

When we took the dogs, they always called loudly for their owners. When they did that, we would calm them down by giving them my food.

Yuka moved to the edge of the clearing, leaving me with the dog. She always sat there and watched the carnage.

I stared into my opponent's eyes, and I got ready to jump on

him. The dog was cowed by my stare, and it lowered its head. My
nerves were on end, waiting for Yuka's signal.

My opponent had no idea what we were about to do. It looked
up at me anxiously, whining—looking for its owner.

A gust of cold night wind rattled the grass like the roar of the
surf and then vanished. Silence fell. The stream of cars on the
bridge seemed to have died out, and I could no longer hear them.
In the silence, I tensed. The air crackled. The little hole waited
for destruction and death. I strained my senses, waiting for the
moment to begin.

The dog in front of me looked around nervously, cowed by the
mood in the air. It whined again plaintively.

As it did, Yuka called out, short and sharp: "Fight!"

I sprang forward, closing the distance between the baffled dog
and myself instantly. Our shoulders crashed together. The dog was
knocked aside, rolling. I growled. My opponent bared its teeth,
still a little confused. Its eyes filled with confused hostility.

My heart began beating faster. I could feel the ground beneath
my feet and the flow of air past me so clearly. My mind was occupied with figuring out just how long it would take me to cover the
distance between my opponent and me. Every little move the dog
made had me guessing which direction it would go. I had been
through many fights, so I was getting good at this.

But my heart was always filled with sadness. How long was Yuka
going to make me do this? I didn't really want to kill anything. All
my life, I'd never thought my jaws were meant to be used this way.

The dog moved to the right, as I knew he would, and I was there
ahead of him. The dog's fur scattered in the air. Blood spilled, and
the dog staggered. Darkness surrounded us.

We fought awhile longer, and then Yuka stood up.

"Bite!" she shouted, her voice charred with hate. Those feelings
were all for that man; she had started making me do this after he'd
started coming. The suffering locked within her was all released
here when she made me kill.

I regarded the wounded dog in front of me, and then I looked at

Yuka screaming. I howled. My shrill cry echoed under the bridge. My head felt hot. Why was this happening? Why couldn't we play and laugh like before?

The dog shivered, trying to hide itself in the darkness. It no longer had any will to resist. It could barely stand, and it was terrified of dying.

I would end it now.

I whispered to myself, advancing on the four-legged animal. I opened my jaws wide and bit it on the neck. My teeth pierced its skin, sinking deep. Blood gushed out, filling my mouth.

That summer day had been bathed in the light of fortune. Yuka and I had found the clearing in the grass while running around. I had jumped on Yuka, and she had fallen over. For a moment, I was worried I'd hurt her, but she lay there looking happy, so I flopped down on the ground next to her, and we gazed up at the sky together. The sun had warmed our bodies, and our noses had been filled with the smell of grass and the faint odor of our sweat...

The animal in my jaws stopped convulsing. Blood dripped off my chin. The body was getting cold. All sound around us had ceased.

I was good at killing now. I didn't know if it was a good thing, but Yuka had taught me that my jaws could become a weapon.

All warmth had left the dead thing now. All that remained was a cold lump of flesh.

She had taught me, I thought again.

I took the dog that had been in my mouth and placed it on the ground, looking up at Yuka, who stared silently back at me.

I knew what she wanted. I could feel the strength of her will flowing into me.

Why had she made me kill all of these animals?

I had never known before—but now I finally understood: Yuka had been training me.

She had made me kill all these animals so I could experience death that many times, honing critical parts of me. My experience with death would prevent me from hesitating and failing when the time came.

Yuka could not fight that man, but I could become the fangs that would protect her.

Yuka nodded. She knew I understood now. She had been waiting for me to work it out.

I didn't need any more training, I told her.

The man was sleeping over tonight. We would settle this in the morning. Yuka whispered this to me.

I tossed the dead animal in the hole, washing my mouth in the river and swallowing the animal's fur. Now we would go home—and wait for morning.

Yuka and I turned to leave the clearing under the bridge. But just as we were about to push our way into the wall of grass, I stopped. Yuka was already in the grass; she stopped too, turning back.

"What?" I could feel her asking.

I looked at her, and then I searched the grass behind me. For a moment, I thought I had seen it move oddly.

Nothing, I thought. Let's go. I looked back at her and ran to her side.

There may have been someone there. I was sure there had been—the same one who'd been after us, trying to catch us. And at last, he had hidden and watched what we were doing.

Until now I had been afraid of getting caught. Not anymore. I knew what I had to do now, and I was no longer anxious.

We didn't need to kill animals again. I was done with my training. We no longer needed to fear the shadow that had chased us.

We climbed the stairs. I looked back one more time at the sea of grass, which was shrouded in darkness. I wanted to tell whoever was hiding there what Yuka and I had really been doing. I wanted him to know what had happened to Yuka and why she had decided to do this.

I still think that.

iv

"Hello...?" Morino's sleepy voice came from the other end of my cell phone. Her tone indicated she found it completely incomprehensible that anyone would call this early in the morning.

It was starting to get bright outside the window. I had slept only three hours, but I was able to regulate my sleeping patterns at will, so I hadn't had much difficulty rising early.

I told Morino that I'd found the kidnapper.

"Oh," she said, hanging up. I didn't have time to tell her that the kidnappers had been the girl and the golden retriever we'd passed on the street. Apparently, sleep was far more important to Morino than the identity of the pet kidnapper.

My phone rang. It was Morino. I answered, and she got right to the point.

"You took pictures?"

I explained that I'd brought my digital camera the night before but had been unable to get anything usable. There wasn't enough light under the bridge. The pictures were too dark to see anything.

"Oh," she said, and she hung up again.

I changed clothes and left my room. My parents and sister were still asleep, and the house was quiet. At the entrance, I put on my shoes, and then I went outside. The sky was red to the east, turning the lampposts into silhouettes.

"Tomorrow morning," I had heard the girl whisper last night under the bridge. Just after the ritual of death, that tiny little girl had whispered those words into the golden retriever's ears.

From where I'd been hiding, I couldn't work out the rest of the sentence. Was something going to happen that next morning, Saturday morning?

Would they do the same thing? I headed for her house, armed with my camera. I knew where she lived. I had seen her go in the gate with her dog the other day. That must be her home. My plan was to quietly follow them and then watch them as they worked.

Shortly after I left the house, I realized I'd forgotten something.

I had my wallet and the camera. I checked my pockets, and then I looked up at the second-story window, my room. I'd left the knife in my room.

Was it worth going back for a knife I wouldn't even use? Or should I head straight for the girl's house? I didn't want to waste any time. It would be easier not to go back.

But even as I thought this, I found myself climbing the stairs again. I took a knife from the set behind my bookcase. There was a white sheen on the blade's surface, and I had to fight off the urge to cut the tip of my finger. When the urge passed, I slid the knife into the leather sheath.

I left the house, my fingers on the sheathed knife in my pocket. It was thirsty, I thought. The blade of the knife was as parched as the desert sand.

I looked to the east, and the sky had turned the color of blood.

†

It was morning.

Yuka and I had woken as one when the light hit us. A single beam of sunlight had slid through the curtains and then across the carpet, the bed, the futon, and our faces. For a moment, we stared at each other.

It was fun to wake up with Yuka. Kicking each other, we wondered how we would play today. I never wanted to forget this moment. Even if we were separated, I always wanted to remember her like this.

Gazing at the dust in the sunbeam, we made up our minds and got out of bed.

We opened the door and looked around.

We could hear him snoring in the room where Mama slept. He always slept in there when he came over. Mama always went to work very early, which meant he would usually sleep in there alone all morning.

Yuka and I quietly walked down the hall until we stood at the entrance to the bedroom. Mama slept in the room at the very back of the house, and there was a sliding door between the room and the hall—but that morning, Mama had forgotten to close it, so it was open wide enough for me to slip inside.

I poked my nose through the gap, checking the room.

There was a futon laid out on the tatami. There the man was sprawled on his back, sound asleep—his mouth half-open, his throat exposed. He was a giant standing up, and I could never have reached his throat to bite, but when he was asleep, the man's throat was right under my nose.

I slid my body through the gap in the door, entering the room without a sound. The tatami creaked softly as I walked. Yuka stayed at the door, watching. She looked worried.

I was right next to his head now. He didn't sense me coming, and it didn't look like he was going to wake up. His eyes stayed shut. The futon was half over his belly, which rose and fell as he breathed.

Something moved in the corner of my eye. I looked and thought I saw a shadow across the window, behind the curtains.

Yuka noticed my look, and she shot me a puzzled frown.

Was there someone outside the window? Or had the curtains moved on their own? Perhaps it was simply the shadow of the tree. I shook my head and put it out of my mind. I had to concentrate on the man before me.

I looked at the man's face, and when I remembered how he had hurt Yuka, my heart filled with rage.

I turned back to Yuka, staring into her eyes.

We did not need words. I knew what she wanted, what she wanted me to do. I could see it in her eyes.

I slowly opened my jaws.

I would not hesitate. I had done this many times under the bridge.

I bit down.

My teeth sank into the man's throat. His skin broke, and blood came out. I intended to bite deep, to tear out his throat, but human throats were much stronger than I had expected. My teeth hit something hard, and they would not go deeper.

The man's eyes opened and he sat up, but my teeth were still in his throat. My body was pulled upward as he moved.

The man looked at me and shrieked in surprise, but not very loudly—critical parts of his throat were already damaged. He hit me in the face with his fist, but I didn't let go.

Now the man stood up. I hung from him by my teeth, and he shook himself, trying to knock me loose.

I fell to the tatami and rolled.

There was a moment of silence, like time had stopped.

Red drops were falling toward me where I lay at his feet. I looked up, and he was gingerly touching his throat, looking stunned. Part of his throat was torn away, and a lot of red stuff was falling away from the hole. The man clapped his hand over his throat, but the blood seeped between his fingers.

I stood up and spat out what was in my mouth. It fell into the pool of blood on the futon, the piece of flesh I'd torn from the man's throat.

When he saw that, his eyes widened, and he fell to his knees, scooping it up. He tried pressing it to the wound, but the red stuff kept gushing out. Soon his hand began to shake, and he dropped the chunk of flesh I had bitten off. The man did not pick it up again. Instead, he looked at me, his face a wreck. He looked furious but also like he was about to cry. His mouth opened wide, and he howled. There was a strange whistling sound mixed in with the noise, but it was still loud enough to echo through the room.

Then the man attacked me. He was very strong, and I almost passed out when he kicked my belly.

Yuka screamed in the entrance, frozen there. She didn't know what to do.

"Run!" I yelled, but she wouldn't leave me behind.

The man wrapped his hands around my throat. He pushed me

down against the bloodstained tatami, spitting horrible words. Blood and spit flew from his mouth in shocking quantities, splashing on my face.

I bit the man's hand, and he pulled back instantly, giving me enough time to get up and slip through the gap in the door. Yuka and I ran away together.

The man was bleeding a lot, but it didn't appear as if he was about to die. A dog would have given up by now, but the man did not crumple. Not only that—he was attacking ferociously.

As Yuka and I ran down the hall, a thunderous noise sounded behind us. The man had flung the sliding door open so hard that it had almost broken.

I was scared. There was no way I could kill him. He was so much stronger than me. I could bite him over and over, and he would just stand up and hit me. And if he killed me, then he would go for Yuka after. I didn't know what to do.

We ran toward the entrance. The man was right behind us, his footsteps getting closer.

From Mama's room to the entrance, there was one turn, and then the hall was straight. We could be at the entrance in no time at all—yet that time seemed so very long.

We were almost at the door when Yuka shrieked. Her feet slipped, and she went tumbling. She lay in a heap on the floor.

"Yuka!" I cried, and I tried to stop. But I was running too fast, and my body couldn't stop so quickly. I knocked aside the shoes in the entrance, slamming into the door. Only then did I stop.

I tried to turn around and scramble back to Yuka's side—but froze in my tracks.

He was standing next to Yuka, blood running from his throat, glaring down at me. He looked so terrifying. He was saying something, but the words were not intelligible.

He took a step toward me, both hands forward, making sure I could not get away.

I couldn't move. I just stood there, my back against the door. I couldn't open the door and leave Yuka there alone.

What should I do? Thinking wasn't getting me anywhere. Rage and regret rampaged through me. He wouldn't let me attack him again.

I began to give up.

He had hated Yuka and had done terrible things to her, but I had been too weak to save her. No matter how I went up against him, I was powerless, and things always turned out the way he wanted them to. If I had been stronger, maybe then I could have protected Yuka...

His hands were almost on me.

On the floor, Yuka looked up at me.

"Sorry," I whispered. All I could do was hang my head, turning my eyes away from poor Yuka and waiting for the man's hands to close around me.

The lights were off, but the morning light came in through the windows, dimly illuminating the room. My head down, I watched the shadows of the man's hands coming toward me, down the step from the hallway into the entrance, closer and closer.

I'm sorry I couldn't save you...

Following the shadows of his hands was a line of blood dripping from his throat. It dripped down the step and into the shoes.

I wish we could play together again...

The shadows of the man's hands reached my shadow. I kept my head down, not moving, but the man's palms were on either side of my face. I could see his red-stained hands out of the corners of my eyes. His shadow fell over me, like the sun had set and darkness had come.

Yuka...

Tears fell from my eyes.

As they did, I heard something behind me. There was a door behind me, and I heard the sound of shoes on the other side of it. There was a squeak, and then something metal fell onto the floor at my feet.

With my head down, I could see it clatter into view. It gleamed, even covered by the man's shadow.

The hands on either side of me stopped, taken aback by the sudden noise. There was a silence, like time had stopped.

The sound of shoes came again, but this time, they were moving away. There was a slot in the door for newspapers, and the thing at my feet had been dropped through it. The squeak had been the slot opening.

I knew it was the one who had been following Yuka and me, the shadow I had seen through the window earlier.

I had been dimly aware of his presence, which was why I moved before the man did now. That momentary advantage determined our fates...

†

Eventually, the girl and the dog burst out of the gate and ran off, heading away from the corner where I was hiding. They never noticed me there.

When they were gone, I went back to the house. The front door wasn't locked. Inside lay the man's body. He was sprawled on his back, and I could clearly see the knife handle sticking out from his heart. There was a trail of blood leading down the hall, and there were red stains all over the entrance. I examined him, being careful not to touch anything. I didn't know who he was, but I guessed he was the girl's father. Did she have a mother? I took a photograph and left the scene. I considered taking the knife, but then I decided to leave it there—it seemed like this was where the knife belonged.

As I left, I wiped the door handle with my sleeve, not wanting to leave fingerprints.

I went home, where I found Sakura watching television and doing homework.

"Where'd you go?" she asked.

I told her the convenience store, and then I ate my breakfast.

After, I went back to the girl's house. As I got closer, I could feel a buzz in the air. When I turned the corner and came in sight of her house, I knew why. Someone had called it in, and the police were there, with a crowd around them, watching.

The red lights on the patrol car shone on the wall of the house. The people in the street were pointing at the girl's house and whispering; they must've been neighbors—housewives in aprons and middle-aged men in pajamas. I stood behind them, looking up at the house, listening to their hushed voices.

It sounded like the woman who lived there had come home to find a man she knew lying in the entrance with a knife in his chest. From this information, I learned that he had not been the girl's father after all.

Casually, I struck up a conversation with a woman in an apron. I asked about the people who lived there. Even though she didn't know me, she answered happily, her excitement overcoming her suspicion.

Apparently, a woman lived there with her daughter and a dog. There was no father; there had been a divorce. The girl refused to go to school, instead spending all her time alone in the house with the dog.

According to the woman in the apron, the girl and dog were missing, and nobody knew where they were.

I turned my back on the crowd and walked away. A block away, I passed some kids on bikes, pedaling toward the crime scene like they were on their way to a festival.

†

A set of concrete stairs led from the bridge down to the bank of the river, which was covered in a sea of grass.

It was a beautiful day, and I could see my shadow clearly as I went down the stairs. The grass shone green in the sunlight, and the wind sent ripples across its surface.

When I reached the bottom of the stairs, all I could see was grass, as tall as me. Looking up, I could see the underside of the massive bridge and the blue, cloudless sky.

I pushed my way through the grass until it suddenly opened up before me, and I came out into the clearing. A golden retriever was sitting in the center of it.

The girl was nowhere to be found.

The dog wasn't tied up or anything. It just sat like a statue, surrounded by the wall of grass, as if it had known I would come. It had distinguished, wise eyes. A beautiful dog, I thought.

I had thought the girl and her dog might be here, but I had been only half right.

I went over to the dog, putting my hand on its head. The dog didn't seem scared, and it allowed me to touch it.

There was a piece of paper stuffed in its collar, which I pulled out.

"To the person who gave me the knife," it said.

Apparently, it was a letter from the girl to me. The girl had noticed me, and she had guessed I might come here.

The letter was torn out of a notebook and written in pencil. It must have been written on the stairs, and the letters were hard to make out.

I read it. It was scattered and incoherent, but I could follow the general idea. She mentioned why they had been kidnapping pets and why they had been doing what they did under the bridge. She explained about the man's violence and thanked me for giving her the knife. It was a very childish letter, but I could tell she had worked hard on it.

At the end, she asked me to take the dog. It must have taken her a very long time to write that. It had been erased several times, and it must have been hard for her to write. But I knew she had guessed the dog would be put down if she took it with her.

I put the letter in my pocket and looked at the patient retriever. It had a collar but no leash. I wondered how I would get it to come with me or if I should just leave it there.

Yesterday, the girl had beckoned to the dog and it had come, so I tried the same, and the dog obediently followed me.

It followed me all the way home, walking right behind me. I figured I'd forget about it if it turned away, but it never did.

My parents weren't home, but Sakura was in front of the TV doing homework. When she heard the dog come inside, she turned around and yelped. I told her it was ours now. She was surprised, but she got used to the idea quickly; it was far less shocking than finding corpses. She began thinking up names for the dog, but I stopped her. I had heard the former owner call the dog by name under the bridge, and the same name had been written in the letter. I told her the dog was named Yuka.

I remembered peering in the window of the girl's house that morning. I had done so just as the girl bit down on the man's throat. At first, I had no idea what was going on—but now that I'd read the letter, I understood. The dogs the girl had fought and bitten to death under the bridge had all been practice, preparation for killing that man.

I left Yuka with Sakura, sat down on the sofa, and read the letter again. It was written in pencil, and she had pressed very hard, like most children did. I had to puzzle it out one letter at a time. It was clear she worshipped her dog.

I thought back on the night before. That girl had occasionally looked at the golden retriever before acting. Not wanting to get them dirty, she'd removed her clothes before fighting the dog.

She talked about the dog like it was the voice of God. In the letter, she claimed to understand Yuka's words clearly.

"How did we get this dog?" Sakura asked.

I told her it had belonged to a friend of mine, but the stepfather had hated dogs and had been mean to it, so the friend had asked me to take it in. It wasn't far from the truth. The girl's letter had described how her mother's boyfriend had hurt the dog and how she had been driven to kill him because of it.

"Who could be mean to a dog like this?" Sakura exclaimed, indignant. Yuka tilted her head, looking up at Sakura with deep black eyes. I couldn't tell if Yuka knew as much as the girl said she did. That girl might simply have been seeing her own reflection in Yuka's eyes.

My cell phone rang. It was Morino. I left the dog with my sister and went upstairs. Morino told me about a murder that had happened right in our neighborhood.

"We were on that road the other day! It happened right where we were! The wife found the man just inside the entrance."

"Yeah," I said. I explained how there had been teeth marks on the man's neck, a trail of blood from the bedroom to the entrance—and how the knife that had ended the victim's life had been handed over to the killer by someone else.

"How do you know all that?"

"You see, the girl we passed that day is the killer," I said, and I hung up.

I liked watching criminals, but I had a rule: I was always a third party, and I never got involved. I had broken that rule this time. I'd seen the girl and dog run toward the door, the man coming after them. And before I'd known it, I'd given the knife to the girl.

I didn't consider this a bad thing. It didn't bother my conscience at all—presumably because it hadn't been my will. I believed the knife had seen the future, and the knife just wanted it to happen.

†

A few hours later, the missing girl was found wandering aimlessly, and she was taken into protective custody. There was blood on her mouth and clothes, and she'd been found alone, in the middle of nowhere.

I learned of this via a message to my phone from Morino, a message I read in my darkened room. My room was quiet—I never listened to music—and I could hear Sakura happily playing with the dog down below.

I closed my eyes and imagined how the girl must have played with the dog under the bridge, on a hot summer day, with the green grass all around them.

IV
MEMORY/TWINS

i

I have a classmate with the family name Morino whom I talk to occasionally. Her given name is Yoru. If you read the names together, you get Morino Yoru, or "the woods at night." Her hair and eyes are both jet-black. Our school also has black uniforms, and Morino always wears black shoes. The only color anywhere on her is the uniform's red scarf.

The name Yoru matches Morino's black-clothed figure perfectly. Her commitment to the color is so great that I imagine if the darkness of night were given human form, then it might well look like her.

In direct contrast to all that black, her skin is pale like the moon, as though it's never known the sun. There's no flush of health; she seems to be made of porcelain. There's a small mole under her left eye, and she has a mystic air, like a fortune-teller.

I once saw a girl with a similar air in a movie, a movie that opened with a couple drowning. The rest of the film depicted their attempts to adjust to life after death. The leading ghosts were invisible to normal humans—but eventually, they found a girl who was able to see them. That girl was the heroine of the movie, and her name was Lydia.

"I'm basically half-dead myself," Lydia had said, explaining why she was able to see the ghosts. "My heart is filled with darkness."

Lydia wore all black and was sickly pale. She preferred staying indoors and reading to playing outside, and she seemed very unhealthy.

Some people began calling people like her "Goths." Goth refers to a culture, a fashion, and a style. If you search for Goth or "gosu" online, you'll find any number of pages. Goth is short for Gothic but has little connection with the European architectural style. It has much more to do with the Gothic horror novels popular in Victorian London, like *Frankenstein* or *Dracula*.

It seems fair to call Morino a Goth. She frequently expresses an intense interest in torture methods and execution devices, and a fascination with the dark side of humanity is a common characteristic among Goths.

Morino rarely exchanges words with anyone else. She has nothing fundamentally in common with our healthy, overenergetic classmates. If classmates smile and speak to her, Morino will simply stare back at them, her blank expression never crumbling—and she'll say, "Oh." Even if classmates wait for her to say something else, nothing will happen: Morino will react no further.

Most people who speak to her end up feeling ignored. The girls in class have said as much. Ever since, they have begun looking down on her.

This attitude only helps complete the barrier around her that keeps everyone else away. While everyone else is laughing and talking, Morino alone remains utterly silent, as though she is in some other dimension, as if there is a shadow cast on the spot where she sits.

But Morino doesn't intend to ignore anyone. After talking with her awhile myself, I became convinced of this. It isn't out of spite that she doesn't happily respond; rather, it is simply because she is that kind of person. She has nothing against the others, and she is equally distant with everyone.

After carefully observing such interactions, what I sensed was confusion. When someone spoke to Morino, she couldn't figure out how to respond, and she was unable to think of anything to say. But this was all speculation on my part, as I didn't know what she was actually thinking. Most of the time, her emotions didn't register outwardly, and it was hard to tell what she felt.

For a while after we first spoke, I thought she was like some sort of doll. The impression she gave off was one more like an object than something animate.

†

One Wednesday in October, just after the leaves were changing from green to red, Morino came into the classroom with her head down, and everyone fell silent. Her long black hair was hanging down, obscuring her face, and she was walking slowly, dragging her feet in a very creepy fashion. Most of the students must have thought she looked like a ghost—but her air was much more dangerous, like some sort of wild animal.

The barrier around her had transformed from its usual transparent sphere into something covered in spikes; she seemed like she might attack anyone who got too close to her. She was silent, as always—and nobody ever spoke to her, anyway—but you could see just how different her mood was by the tension on the faces of those sitting near her.

I was not all that intrigued. I simply assumed she was in a bad mood. That day, we didn't have a moment to speak, so I didn't learn the reason why. (Morino would never approach me to speak when I was talking to any of our other classmates.) I learned the reason the next day, though, after school.

When homeroom ended, the other students stood up and left the room. Eventually, the class was empty—and so quiet that it was hard to imagine how noisy it had been a few minutes earlier. Only the rows of empty desks, Morino, and I remained.

A pleasantly cold breeze drifted in through the windows. The class next door had not been dismissed yet, and I could hear the teacher's voice from down the hall.

Morino was sitting low in her seat. Both her hands hung list-lessly at her sides, and she looked exhausted.

"I'm not sleeping much," she said, yawning. There were shadows under her eyes. Her eyelids were half-closed, and she stared past them into the distance.

I was in my seat, preparing to head home. Her seat was over on the other side of the room. There was no one else there, so I could hear her well enough, and it didn't occur to me to move closer to her to talk.

"Is that why you were so strange yesterday?"

"I get like this sometimes. No matter how hard I try to sleep, I can't. Insomnia, I guess."

She stood up. Still looking very sleepy, she staggered toward the chalkboard.

There was an outlet at the front of the room, and an extension cord plugged into it, which was connected to the eraser cleaner. Morino unplugged the cord, which was a good sixteen feet long. Leaving the other end connected to the eraser cleaner, she wrapped the cord around her neck. She stood there that way, motionless.

"No, doesn't feel right," she said, shaking her head and dropping the cord. "When I can't sleep, I always wrap something around my neck, close my eyes, and imagine myself being strangled to death. Then I can fall asleep—it feels like sinking deep underwater."

I was disappointed: she hadn't yet gone mad from lack of sleep. "If that helps, you should try it before you're this far-gone."

"Not just any bit of rope will do."

Morino was after a certain type of rope, and the extension cord had not proved an effective substitute.

"I've lost the one I used the last time. I'm trying to find a new one, but..." She yawned, looking around blearily. "I don't really know what I'm looking for. If I could figure that out, goodbye insomnia."

"What did you use last time?"

"No clue. It was just something I found, and I tossed it out as soon as I could sleep without it."

She closed her eyes, fingering her throat. "I just remember how it felt…" She opened her eyes, as if she'd just had an idea. "Right, let's go rope shopping. You should buy some rope or cord yourself; it might come in handy. You might need it when you kill yourself."

The class next door had finished, and I could hear the sound of all those chairs being pushed back at once.

†

We left school and headed for a large general store on the edge of town. It was a fair distance, but it was on a big road with a lot of buses, so it didn't take us long to get there. The bus was about half-full, so Morino sat down while I stood looking down at her, hanging on to a strap above me. She put her head down and tried to sleep, but even the bus's comfortable sway was not enough, and we arrived without her having slept a wink.

The large store was filled with wood and metal for construction, as well as any number of tools. We wandered through the aisles, looking for anything like a rope. AV cables for connecting TVs and video players, clothesline, kite string… they had everything.

Morino picked up each one, feeling it with her fingers—carefully, as if she were choosing what to wear.

She seemed to have fairly strong opinions about what sort of rope should be used to hang oneself, and she explained them, looking haggard. "First, thin string would just snap. Electric cords are strong, but they lack in beauty."

"What about plastic?" There was a big ball of plastic string on the bottom shelf, and I only asked because I happened to see it.

She shook her head, expressionless. "It stretches. Ruins everything. I'm done here."

We found a number of different chains in another section of the store. From two-centimeter-thick heavy chains to delicate chains only a millimeter or two across. They were on the shelves in rolls, like toilet paper. There was a machine nearby that allowed you to cut the chain to the length you needed.

"Look at this—so thin, but it says it can hold up to a hundred pounds," she said, holding a thin silver chain between her fingers. She pulled it out, pressing it to her neck. The chain in her hand caught the light, glittering. "Nice color—would make even a dead body look beautiful...but when you hanged yourself, the links would probably bite into your skin."

She let it drop. It wasn't a match for her ideals.

She'd spent a lot of time thinking about what kind of rope she'd want to kill her.

If I were going to strangle somebody, what kind of rope would I use? I pondered this as we wandered the store.

"I don't want it to tickle my neck," she said, when I pointed to a rough woven rope. "Old-fashioned rope like that was all over the house in the country where I used to live. They use it on the farm a lot."

She had lived somewhere else until the fourth grade—in the mountains, a two-hour drive from here.

"Where my mother was born and raised, my grandparents have a little farm. My father used to drive two hours to and from work every day."

But they had eventually moved to spare him that drive. All this was news to me.

"I always thought that when it came time to kill yourself, you'd slit your wrists, not hang yourself," I said.

She held our her wrist. "You mean this?"

On her wrist was a thick white line, like a welt. The skin was slightly raised, and it was clearly a scar left from a slashed wrist. I'd never asked about it, so I didn't know why she'd cut her wrist.

"That's not a result of trying to kill myself—it was just a sudden impulse."

She went through her life without expressions, but she apparently did have emotions strong enough to produce that kind of reaction. Her lack of outward expression was similar to the way a thermos is never hot on the outside: No matter what was going on inside, it never affected the surface.

But when emotions get too strong, humans have to do something. Some people encase their emotions by playing or exercising, whereas others calm their emotions by breaking things. People in the latter group could let their feelings out just by breaking furniture or the like. But Morino was unable to direct those feelings outward, so she'd directed them at herself.

Suddenly, a familiar voice called out to me.

I turned around to find my sister, Sakura, standing a short distance away and looking at us in surprise. There was a big bag of dog food in her arms. She'd just happened to be here shopping.

Morino looked over sleepily. She saw the picture of the dog printed on the bag, and her cheek twitched.

Sakura remarked on how surprised she was to see me there, and then she regarded Morino.

Morino looked away, not because she was avoiding Sakura's gaze but because she was avoiding the picture of the dog. She would never even go near a shelf with the word "dog" on it.

"And your pretty friend?" Sakura asked, curious. I explained politely that this was probably not the kind of person Sakura imagined her to be. She didn't appear to believe me.

"Okay. Mom sent me out here. I have to get the dog food and pick up some clothes at the dry cleaner's."

Sakura pulled a note out of her pocket and read it. Her character was a lot better than mine. She was supposed to be busy studying for exams, but she still couldn't refuse a request to do someone else's work.

"Then I have to pick up some tofu and tangerines from the woman next door and walk the dog when I get home."

She waved at Morino, grinning.

Morino was too busy not looking at the dog food to notice. She had one hand on a shelf for support, denying the existence of the picture on the dog food with all her might.

When I was sure Sakura was gone, I said, "You can look up now."

Morino straightened up, turned toward the shelves as if nothing had happened, and began examining a roll of wire on the shelf.

"Was that your sister?" I nodded.

"I had a sister—a twin sister. She died a long time ago." I had not known this.

"Her name was Yuu. Yuu..."

As she explained this, she ran her fingers along the long silvery wire, white teeth showing between her bluish lips and her quiet voice emerging through both.

Yuu had hanged herself and died, Morino Yoru told me.

She had wrapped any number of ropes around her neck today, but Morino had not found anything that would solve her sleeping problems. I left without buying anything, either.

We crossed the parking lot, heading for the road. With the heavy lines under her eyes, Morino looked as if a strong burst of wind would be enough to knock her over.

There was almost nothing around there except the massive general store: fields and vacant lots covered in dry grass and the newly paved asphalt road running through them. The area would be developed in time, though.

On the side of the road, there was a bus stop with a bench, where Morino sat down. One of the buses that stopped there must go to her house.

The sun was getting low in the sky. The sky was still blue, but the undersides of the clouds were turning pink.

"May I ask about your sister?" I said, glancing at her. She sat in silence, not answering.

There weren't a lot of cars on the road in front of us. One would pass every now and then, but for the most part, there was only the wide expanse of asphalt, along with the empty plane of dried grass beyond the guardrail. In the distance, there was a single iron tower, like a speck on the horizon.

"Go ahead," she said eventually.

ii

"Yuu died when we were in the second grade, so I only remember her as a child, not even eight years old... At the time, we lived in the country—nothing but farms all around."

Her house had been on the slope of a mountain. There was a forest behind it, and they could constantly hear the sound of bird wings flapping.

"Yuu and I slept next to each other in the same room. When it got dark and we tried to go to sleep, we could hear owls in the darkness outside."

It was an old wooden house, with floors and pillars that gleamed darkly. There was green moss growing on the roof tiles, and there were a number of broken tile fragments on the ground around the house. It was a comfortably large house, and all the rooms had tatami floors—except for the kitchen, which had been added later. The twin girls, Yoru and Yuu, lived in that house with their parents, grandmother, and grandfather.

Morino's father drove two hours into town to work every day. Her grandparents were often out, checking the water in the rice fields or carrying different farming tools from the shed. The fields and paddies were a five-minute walk from the house. All the daikon and cabbage they ate came from those fields.

"But the daikon we grew were not shaped as nice as the ones in shops, and they were a little bit yellow."

There were a number of trees in the yard. The ground was bare earth, and it would turn to mud when it rained, forming pools of muddy water. If you went outside after it rained, the ground would stick to your feet and try to trip you.

There was a shed on the left side of the house—a small one built right up against the side of the house. They kept the farming tools in there. The roof had been broken during a typhoon, but rather than fix it, they had just spread a blue tarp over the top. It leaked a little, but there was nothing more than tools inside, so it wasn't really a problem.

"I played with my sister all the time."

When they entered elementary school, they walked hand in hand to the school in the valley. The road was thin and winding. On one side, the mountain sloped sharply upward, and it was covered in trees. The other side also had trees, but it was possible to glimpse the view below through the leaves. Piles of brown leaves would gather on either side, and the path got slippery in the rain. The branches on the tall trees blocked the sun, and the road was always gloomy and damp.

"It was downhill all the way to school, and easy. But it was uphill all the way home, and exhausting."

Yoru and Yuu had identical faces, down to the location of their moles. And they both had long hair down to their waists. They always chose similar clothing. I could easily imagine the two identical girls running down the tree-covered mountain road.

"We looked the same. Even our mother couldn't tell us apart. Sometimes, before we took a bath, we would both take off our clothes and stand there silently."

When that happened, their mother could not begin to guess which was the elder sister and which was the younger.

"But our expressions and behavior were different, so if we started talking, everyone knew who was who."

Even as a tiny child, Yuu always found it funny when their mother stared at them in confusion. And the moment it struck Yuu as funny, their mother could point right at them and say, "This is Yoru, and that's Yuu."

Yuu had always shown her emotions more easily than her older sister. When she was talking with her parents, she always smiled.

"At the time, our favorite games were drawing pictures and pretending to be dead."

During summer vacation, the elementary school pool was open, and they could swim all they wanted.

"It was a small school, and there were only about a hundred students. There were fewer than twenty students per grade, but the pool was packed every day, all summer long."

Under the blinding white sunlight, the children splashed around. If you were to lie on your back in the pool, your ears underwater, the cicadas in the mountains would sound like walls tumbling down.

"There were always a few adults around the pool, making sure the children didn't do anything dangerous. Sometimes they were teachers, sometimes students' parents. Most of the time nothing happened, and they would sit on a bench in the shade, gossiping."

One day, the twins decided to surprise the adults watching by pretending they had drowned. They floated facedown in the water, lying limp, competing to see which of them could hold out longer and look most like a corpse.

They must have made an eerie contrast with the children playing noisily all around them, the two girls floating quietly in the water, their hair spread out like seaweed, only their backs above water, immobile as long as they could hold their breath. When they could no longer stand it, they would lift their heads slightly, take a breath, and then die again.

"The reaction was bigger than Yuu or I had anticipated."

The women watching the pool were two of their classmates' mothers. When they saw the girls lying motionless, one of them jumped up on the bench and screamed. All the children in the pool turned toward the bench. The little kids splashing around, the older kids practicing swimming—everyone knew something had happened. The mother who had not screamed stood up and ran to try to save the drowning girls...but running next to a pool is very dangerous.

"She tripped and hit her head, knocking herself unconscious. The mother who had screamed saw that, and she went to call an ambulance. Yuu and I got out of breath and stood up, only to find everyone around us in a state of panic. It was like hell on earth. The younger kids were crying, scared and confused. There was a boy next to the unconscious woman, shaking her shoulder and shouting, 'Mommy!' He was one of our classmates."

The twins had looked at each other and, without another word, they'd quickly gotten out of the pool and fled, without even changing clothes.

"We went out the back gate, each with a bag holding our clothes and towels in one hand and our shoes in the other. As we ran along the path through the rice paddies in our swimsuits, ambulance after ambulance screamed along the distant road toward the pool. How many bodies had that women seen? There were at least five ambulances."

The school was at the bottom of the mountain, and rice paddies stretched as far as the eye could see on the side away from the mountain. Green rice stalks covered the ground, making the world appear completely flat. The girls walked along the path among the paddies.

"The grass pricked our feet."

They didn't know what had happened after the ambulances reached the school. They didn't think about it much—just went home, ate some shaved ice, and went to sleep.

"That wasn't the only time we played dead. We also spread ketchup on each other's faces and pretended it was blood."

They stood in front of the refrigerator, squeezing ketchup on their fingers and dabbing it on each other's faces. Their pale skin was soon red.

"The ketchup started dripping down, and we had to lick it off. Eventually, we got bored with the taste of ketchup, so we wiped it off with sausages and ate those."

Another time, they had left the house with a can of meat sauce.

At a corner not far from their house, there had once been a traffic accident. A kindergarten boy had been hit by a car and had died. Yuu laid down in the same place and closed her eyes.

" 'Go ahead,' she said, and I emptied the can of meat sauce on her face. It looked just like her brains were coming out. I told Yuu not to move, no matter what happened. She kept her eyes closed so the sauce wouldn't get in them, and she nodded."

Yoru had hidden in the bushes, waiting for someone to come by and scream. When children saw them, they wouldn't be surprised the way the grown-ups were—they'd come over assuming it was some sort of game.

"Even the people who screamed soon realized it was just meat sauce, and then they laughed. We had done this kind of thing before, and our neighbors knew all about it."

"No cars went past?"

If there had been a traffic accident there, then cars must have gone by there sometimes. And Yuu was lying in the street; she might've been in danger.

When I asked this, Morino explained without expression, "A car did come. Yuu had her eyes closed and didn't notice. It slammed on the brakes, stopping right in front of her. The noise made Yuu sit up, wipe the meat sauce off her face, and turn around—only to find the bumper right in front of her. The bumper was polished silver, and her face was reflected in it..."

"You didn't call out and warn her?"

"No. I watched in silence. I wanted to see what would happen."

I searched her voice for any trace of guilt, but there was none. It must not be a quality she possessed. In this sense, she was a lot like me.

"We were twins, so we looked the same. We thought alike too. But our personalities were a little different. My sister was weak."

A bus passed in front of the bench where we were sitting. It stopped and waited for us to get on, but Morino didn't move, so it pulled away, leaving the stench of its exhaust behind.

The sun had reached the horizon, and the sky in the east was dark. A wind was blowing, shaking the dry grass beyond the guardrail.

Morino sat low on the bench, her hands clasped tightly together on her knees.

"We spent a lot of time thinking about death. Where would we go when we died? What would happen to us? We found these ideas fascinating. But I think I knew more about death than Yuu, and I was a much crueler child."

With no expression, Morino told me how she'd ordered Yuu to do all kinds of things.

"At the time, we kept an animal in the shed. It had four legs, drooled a lot, and stank—you know the type I mean."

Presumably, it had been a dog. I was surprised to hear she had once had a pet dog.

"I ordered Yuu to mix bleach into its food. I wasn't trying to make it turn white or anything dumb like that. I just wanted to see it suffer."

Yuu had begged Yoru to stop.

"But I didn't listen, and I forced her to put the bleach in the dog's food. She didn't want to, but I didn't let her stop."

Eating bleach didn't kill the dog, but it was very sick for two days. Morino's parents and grandparents had nursed the dog, looking worried. It had convulsed and moaned in pain all day and all night, its howls echoing across the mountain sky.

Yoru observed it all, but Yuu had been too scared; she'd stayed in the house, her hands over her ears.

"Yuu cried a lot."

Yoru had observed her sister just as she had the dog. Rather than give the dog the bleach herself, she'd placed all the guilt squarely on Yuu. Yoru's experiment had allowed her to observe both the dog and her sister suffering.

Yoru and Yuu had played at hanging themselves too, but only once.

"To be more accurate, our game stopped one step short of hanging ourselves. It was raining out. We couldn't go outside, so we were playing in the shed. This was a month or two before Yuu died."

The sisters each had placed a wooden box on the floor of the shed, piling a second box on top of the first. They'd stood on top of the boxes, placing their necks in a loop of rope hanging from the beam overhead. All they had to do next was jump off the boxes and die.

"I said we would jump on the count of three—but I was lying:

I wasn't going to jump. I was going to watch Yuu as she was strangled to death."

One...two...three. On the count of three, neither one did anything. Neither girl jumped, and there was a long silence.

"Yuu had guessed what I was thinking, so she didn't jump. When I asked her why she hadn't jumped, she just stood there looking terrified."

Yuu couldn't point out how unfair it was, so she stood and took Yoru's flood of insults.

"You bullied Yuu?"

"You could call it that. But I wasn't conscious of it at the time. Most of the time, we got along fine. And Yuu did her own share of awful things. She was better at pretending to be dead and scaring people than I was."

"Did your family know what your relationship was like?"

"No."

Morino fell silent, staring at the road in front of her. A car passed by. It was getting dark around us, so the car had its lights on. For a moment, her profile was caught in the light. The wind was blowing her hair around, and several strands were stuck to her cheek.

"Yuu died during summer vacation when we were in second grade. It was sunny that morning, but it got cloudy quickly, and by noon it had begun to rain..."

Shortly after noon, their mother had gone shopping. Their father was not at home, and their grandparents were out as well. Only the twins were home.

At first, the rain was barely more than a mist, tiny drops on the window, but it gradually grew stronger, and the drops on the window swelled and began trickling down the pane.

"At about twelve thirty, I saw Yuu go into the shed. She didn't say anything to me, so I assumed she wanted to do something alone, and I didn't follow."

Yoru sat reading alone.

About an hour later, she heard the front door open. When she went to see who it was, Yoru found her grandmother with a bag of pears.

As her grandmother closed her umbrella, she explained, "Our neighbor gave me these. Shall I peel one for you?"

"I said I would go call Yuu, leaving my grandmother in the entrance and running to the shed."

Yoru opened the shed door—and saw it. She screamed at once.

"Yuu was hanging from the ceiling, a rope around her neck. I went back to the front door, where my grandmother was standing with the pears in her arms, surprised to see me panic-stricken."

She told her grandmother that Yuu was dead.

Yuu had hanged herself. It was a suicide, but an accident. The rope around her neck was not the only one; around her chest, just under her arms, there was a second rope—a rough, heavy rope, the kind used in farming. One end was tied around Yuu's body, and the other end was hanging behind her like a tail. The same kind of rope was hanging from the ceiling beam. It had all been part of one rope originally—but it had broken.

"My sister hadn't meant to die. She'd meant to hang from the rope around her chest and pretend she'd hanged herself, to scare everyone else. But the moment she jumped, her weight had been too much, and the rope broke."

Yuu's funeral had been a quiet one. And that was the end of the story.

I had one more question, but I didn't ask it. I just watched Morino's tired face, listening to her sigh.

The sun had set by now. The lamps along the side of the road were on, and a light in the side of the bus stop illuminated the time schedule. We sat on the bench, bathed in the glow of white light around the bus stop.

In the distance, I could see a pair of headlights. The big square shadow behind them must be a bus. Soon I could hear the engine, and then it stopped in front of us.

Morino stood up and stepped through the open door. I left the bench as well.

We didn't say goodbye; we didn't even look at each other.

iii

It was a Saturday, two days after Morino Yoru had told me about her sister's death. It dawned cloudy.

There was no school, so I boarded a train early in the morning. The train took me away from the city, into more and more remote areas. As we swayed from side to side, the crowd of passengers got off one by one, until only I was left. I looked out the window, watching the sunless, dark-green farms slide past me.

I got off the train at a station near a few remote farmhouses. I got on the bus outside the station, riding it for a while, until it started up a slope and the trees began to thicken. We were high enough to look down on the village now. The road was thin, barely wide enough for the bus to pass. On both sides of the road, the trees were growing over the guardrails and tapping on the bus windows.

I got off at a stop in the forest. When the bus had driven away, there were no vehicles on the road. I checked the schedule. There was only one bus an hour. There were no buses going back in the evening, so I would have to leave before then. There was nothing around me but trees, but I walked awhile, and it soon opened up so that I could see a few houses ahead.

This was where Morino had been born, where she had lived as a child.

Once, I stopped and looked around me. When it was sunny, the autumn leaves must've made the mountains look red. But under these clouds, everything looked drab.

I began walking toward the house where Morino had lived. As my feet carried me forward, I remembered the conversation I'd had with her the day before, at school.

Friday at lunch, the library had been almost empty. There were bookshelves lining the walls, and the rest of the space was filled with desks and chairs for reading. Morino was sitting in the back, the most deserted part of the room. When I found her, I went over and spoke.

"I want to see the house where you used to live."

She looked up from the book she was reading and frowned. "Why?"

"Have you forgotten that I like to visit places where people died?"

Morino looked away from me and back to the book in front of her. As I stood next to her, I could only see the curve of her neck. She was attempting to ignore me, focusing on the book.

I looked down at the book she was reading. On the corner of the page, it said, "Chapter Three: You Are Not Alone...How to Live Positively." This came as something of a shock to me.

Her head still down, Morino corrected my assumption. "I thought this book might put me to sleep."

There was a long, uncertain silence, until finally she looked up. "I regret ever telling you about Yuu. If you're going, go alone."

The house and shed were still standing. Her grandparents lived there, farming.

I asked why she didn't want to go, and she said lack of sleep meant she was just too tired.

The next day was Saturday, and there was no school, so I decided to go to the country then. I had Morino give me the address and directions. It looked like I could make it out there and back in the same day. I gave Morino a notebook to have her draw a map.

"They'll be surprised if a strange high school boy shows up out of the blue," I said. She nodded, and she promised to call them and tell them I was coming. We decided to say I was going to take some photographs of the country.

"Is that all?" Morino asked, as expressionless as always.

I looked at the map she had drawn. "Your maps always give me goose bumps," I said, and then I turned my back on her. I could feel her staring at me all the way to the library doors. It was as if she wanted to say something, but the words were caught in her throat.

Blackbirds flew against the low, ashen clouds. I looked down at the notebook in my hand and the map Morino had drawn. According to the map, the road went through the middle of a kindergarten. I found it hard to believe any parent would send their children to a school like that.

Deciphering the map, I headed in the direction of Morino's old home. I had the house number and several landmarks, so I was sure I could get there even if the map proved unhelpful.

As I walked, I ran over the story Morino had told me on the bus bench again, the story of a girl with a cruel mind and her twin sister.

Yuu had been found hanging from a rope.

But there was one thing that didn't make sense about Morino's story—namely, the part where she found her sister's dead body.

Yoru had opened the door to the shed and screamed at once. Then she had run to her grandmother and told her that Yuu was dead.

Why had Morino known instantly that Yuu was dead? They were always pretending to be dead and surprising people, so why didn't she assume her sister was simply faking it?

Shrieking in surprise when you saw something like that was only natural, and a real corpse probably looked much more horrible than someone pretending...but the fact that she had never even considered the idea that it was a prank, instead instantly running to tell her grandmother...that seemed very unnatural to me.

I compared the map and the road again. There was a deep river valley in front of me. According to the map, this was a dry cleaner's. The clothes would get wet as soon as they were cleaned, I thought.

As I crossed the bridge, I looked up at the sky. The clouds were hanging low around the mountaintop, and the trees up there looked very dark.

After walking awhile longer, I found the house where Morino had once lived. Built in the mountain's embrace was an old building, the roof covered in moss, just as she had said. There was nothing around but trees and fields, and it must have been pitch-black at night. No gates or walls—I simply followed the road until I found myself in their yard.

As I headed toward the front door, I noticed the shed on the left. This must be the shed where Yuu's body had been found. The walls were of dry, white wood. There was a blue tarp over the top, tied in place with plastic string. It was very old and leaning to one side.

Glancing sidelong at the shed, I stood at the entrance. The door was made of glass set in a wooden frame, and it slid open to one side. I rang the doorbell, and someone called my name from behind.

When I turned around, an old woman was standing there, a hoe in one hand.

Her back was curved, and she was wearing loose work trousers, with a towel around her neck. I decided she must be Morino's grandmother.

The hoe in her hand had dirt stuck to it. She was standing a fair distance away, but I could smell the earth on her.

"Yoru called last night. I was worried you weren't coming!" she said. The grin on her wrinkled face made it hard to see any resemblance to Morino, who always seemed as if she had already died, sharing nothing of the vitality and sunny disposition her grandmother radiated.

I bowed my head and explained that I would leave as soon as I had a few good pictures. But Morino's grandmother ignored me, hustling me into the house.

There was a shoe box inside the door and a number of what looked like souvenirs placed on top of it. The hall led away into the house, which smelled of air freshener and strangers.

"You must be hungry!"

"Not really."

She ignored me, sitting me down at the dining room table and placing a dish laden with food in front of me. Eventually, Morino's grandfather appeared. He was a tall old man with white hair.

The two of them seemed to think I was engaged to Morino.

"You must marry Yoru someday," her grandfather said suddenly, bowing his head as I reluctantly ate. I glanced out the window, wondering if I would be able to see the shed and get back before it started raining and the final bus left.

There was a picture on the side of the kitchen cabinets. In the picture were a pair of doll-like little girls. They both had long black hair, and they were staring directly at the camera, not smiling at all. They were dressed all in black, and they were holding hands. It looked like the picture had been taken out front. I could see the door to the house behind them.

"Yoru and Yuu," the grandmother said, catching my gaze. "You heard about her twin sister?"

I nodded.

"That was when they were six," the grandfather said. Neither one of them had anything else to say about the picture.

After I had eaten, I was allowed to clasp my hands in front of the shrine. I knew that showing my manners like this allowed a number of other things to move forward smoothly.

Looking at the photograph of Yuu in the shrine, I imagined that her death must seem like only yesterday to her grandparents. It had been nine years ago. Nine years to Morino or me was more than half our lives—but to people her grandparents' age, nine years was probably not much different than one or two to us.

After I had clasped my hands, Morino's grandparents sat me down in the living room and asked what their granddaughter was like at school. Before I could begin to answer, they were telling stories about what Morino had been like as a child. I assumed they had no interest in anything I had to say.

"Oh, right, we have some pictures she drew in elementary school!" her grandmother exclaimed happily, standing up and vanishing into the back.

The grandfather watched her go, and then he bowed his head to me apologetically. "My wife's getting a little carried away, I'm afraid."

I shook my head—a generic reaction seemed appropriate.

"Yoru has never really brought any friends home, you see. When we heard you were coming, she got excited."

Morino's grandmother came back in carrying a paper bag, which she set down on the table before pulling from it a number of pages of old drawing paper—pictures Morino had drawn in elementary school using paint and crayon. I had guessed as much from her maps, but Morino appeared to have no artistic talent at all.

On the back of the pages were names and grades.

Some of these were drawn by Yuu. Their drawings had been kept together. There were drawings with Yoru's name from first through sixth grade, but Yuu's were only for first and second. This fact really drove home the truth that there had been a girl here named Yuu who was no more.

I compared drawings the two of them had done in second grade.

"You can hardly tell what either one of them was trying to draw, can you?" the grandmother said, beaming. There was no difference in the twins' artistic ability. But they had been attempting the same subject, and they had produced similar drawings.

Both pictures featured a symbolic representation of a cross section of a house, in the middle of which two girls with long hair stood next to each other. Presumably, those girls were themselves.

"I wonder what they're doing," the grandmother said.

"Standing in the house?" the grandfather replied.

"I suppose," she laughed.

I said nothing, but I knew what they had been drawing. There was a red line around each of the girl's necks, connected to the ceiling. These were drawings of them playing at hanging themselves in the shed.

"They drew those pictures during summer vacation in second grade, for homework. Yuu was supposed to take that picture to school when vacation ended, but...they drew it just a few days before Yuu died." She smiled fondly at the memory.

There was not much difference between the pictures, but Yuu's was a little more detailed. In hers, a red line wound around the beam above, boxes were stacked on top of each other, and the sun shone above the house. And there were the shoes they wore.

In Yoru's picture, none of this was drawn in any detail; it was colored very simply, or possibly boldly. The legs were flesh colored all the way down, with no attempt at shoes. The background was all dark gray.

My attention focused on the shoes in Yuu's picture. One girl was wearing black shoes, and the other was wearing white ones. I wasn't sure if there was any meaning to that, but I decided to make note of it.

I put the picture back down on the table.

"I'd better take those photos," I said, and I went outside, carrying my digital camera.

When I opened the door, though, everything looked white. At first, I thought it was mist, but it was merely drizzle—tiny drops all over the mountains. It wasn't the kind of rain that made it worth using an umbrella, so I wandered around in it, snapping pictures at random. After I'd done that for a while, it started to rain harder.

Eventually, I pretended to randomly find my way to the shed.

The shed door was made of wood. It was closed, and I couldn't see inside. I could hear rain pounding on the tarp on the roof. I grabbed the door handle and opened it. It was a little stiff, but it opened.

The light slanting in through the entrance lit the interior hazily. It smelled of dried plants.

It was about six and a half feet tall and about ten by thirteen across. The floor was dirt, almost clay.

There was a beam near the ceiling, under the half-broken roof. There were a number of holes in it, and I could see the blue of the tarp though them. A single light hung down.

In the story, there had been a dog here, but there wasn't anymore. It must have died. There was a small door cut in the wall next to the door, presumably for the dog. The dog must have been tied up next to that.

I stepped inside. The air in the room seemed to quiver. It was slightly damp and a little chilly.

Once, Yuu had been there, hanging from the ceiling beam. It felt like the dead little girl was still hanging there.

There was a switch next to the entrance. I flipped it, and the light turned on. It was a very dim bulb that illuminated very little.

I remembered everything Yoru had told me: two boxes piled on the ground with the girls on top, about to hang themselves...the bleach they had mixed into the food for the dog they kept in there.

I had my doubts about Yoru's version of how Yuu had died.

Yoru had known her sister was already dead when she'd opened the shed door; she'd only pretended that she'd just discovered it at that moment.

Why had she needed to do that? What would make her want to hide that? The more I thought about ir, the more I felt like she must have had something to do with her sister's death.

"We found Yuu here."

I turned around and found Morino's grandmother standing in the entrance. She peered gravely into the shed, gazing slightly upward.

"I heard she died trying to surprise everyone."

I turned to look at the same place her gaze was fixed. That must have been where Yuu was found.

It was raining really hard now. I could hear it pounding on the ground. But inside the shed, it felt like all the sounds outside were muffled, even the rain hitting the tarp above us and the wind rushing past.

Drops of water slipped through the hole in the roof, which had been broken in a storm and had never been repaired. But there was almost nothing in the shed, so the water did no harm.

To one side were farming hoes and spades, even a scythe leaning against the wall, plus pruning shears and a thick roll of coarse rope.

There were several different kinds of cord next to the dog's door, left there even after the dog had died. There were several different colors, but my eyes were attracted to the red one.

"I remember it so clearly," Morino's grandmother said quietly. "I came back from a neighbor's, and I was putting my umbrella away. Yoru was standing in the entrance..."

Her version was the same as what Yoru had told me. When Yoru had seen the bag of pears, she'd gone to call her sister. She'd opened the shed door and screamed. There was one thing about the story that bothered me; before I could ask about it, though, I felt something strange underfoot.

My feet were sticking to the ground. The floor was made of clay, so when it rained, the water leaking from the ceiling moistened everything, making the ground soft and sticky.

I lifted my foot and felt my shoe peel away from the ground. A film of mud remained attached to my sole.

It had been raining the day Yuu died. The ground must have been like this. But the footprint I'd left behind was not very deep, and the twins had been children, weighing a lot less than I did. Were they heavy enough to leave footprints?

I looked out through the open door. It was raining hard. If it had been raining longer than it had today, the floor of the shed would have been wetter still, so the girls might have left footprints.

It had started raining around noon the day Yuu died. Yuu had gone into the shed shortly afterward, and Yoru said she had stayed inside. When she found the body, Yoru said she had seen it from the shed door.

If Morino's grandmother had seen Yoru's footprints inside the shed, then the story I'd been told at the bus stop was a lie. If Yoru's footprints had been in the shed, then that would prove she'd been there before she supposedly found the body.

"When you found Yuu, were there any footprints on the ground?"

It seemed unlikely the grandmother would remember such a trivial detail, but I asked anyway.

"Yuu's footprints, yes," Morino's grandmother said. The box she'd been standing on had been knocked on its side; when the grandmother had gone to pick it up, she'd seen child-sized footprints on the ground.

Oh well, I thought. It was only natural that Yuu's footprints were on the ground.

"You could tell they were Yuu's footprints at a glance?"

"Those girls looked exactly the same, so we told them apart by their shoes. Yoru wore black shoes, and Yuu wore white. They had different soles, and the ones on the floor of the shed were definitely Yuu's."

I remembered the picture Yuu had drawn. It made sense. They must have been Yuu's shoes then. Yuu had been found hanging from the ceiling, barefoot, with her white shoes placed on the ground next to her. As with many suicides, she had lined her shoes up neatly next to her.

"There were no signs of Yoru's footprims?" I asked, just to be sure.

Morino's grandmother nodded, wondering why I had even asked. Yoru had not stepped inside after finding the body. Her footprints were nowhere to be found. Only one child's footprints were in the shed.

"Is the rope that was tied around Yuu's chest still around?"

Morino's grandmother shook her head. She seemed to have forgotten all about it. "Anyway, you'd better stay here for the night. It's raining very hard."

I thought about it and nodded.

We left the shed and went back into the house. Morino's grandmother told me a number of places that would make for good photographs.

"I hope the weather's better tomorrow," she said.

As I took off my shoes, I noticed a little plastic toy among the objects on the shoe box. When I picked it up, I discovered it was a little flower brooch, the kind you get as a prize in a candy box, of a very cheap color and design.

Which of them had owned this? Looking at it, I was reminded again that they had lived here when they were very young.

The brooch in hand, I looked down the long hallway into the house. Morino's grandmother had already gone into the living room and was out of sight.

I stood there thinking.

In my mind's eye, the two doll-like twin girls from the photograph were walking down the hallway toward me, whispering to each other and gravely thinking about how they could next pretend to be dead. In my imagination, they went all the way to the end of the hall and turned the corner. Trying to follow them, I took off my shoes and stepped up into the house. I looked around the corner where they had vanished, but of course, there was nothing there—just a quiet, dark space at the end of the dimly lit corridor.

iv

On Monday, Morino was clearly glancing sideways at me, wondering. She obviously wanted to ask what I'd been up to in the country. But I spent the entire day pretending not to notice her gaze.

I didn't speak to her until all the other students had left the room after the final class of the day. A few students had suggested I walk home with them, but I ignored their requests—which is not to say that I didn't respond. Without any conscious participation on my part, my mind created some believable excuse, smoothly deflecting their invitations. I had no idea what excuses I'd made. I had no interest in my classmates whatsoever, and such interactions were always carried out automatically, allowing me to live without making waves.

Finally, the sound of my classmates' footsteps faded, and the hall outside the room grew quiet. Only Morino and I remained. She was hunched over in her seat like a sinking ship, glaring side-long at me.

I slowly crossed the quiet classroom toward her seat. She sat three rows from the window, three rows from the back.

"I hear you spent the night in the country. My grandmother called to tell me about it," Morino said sleepily. The lines under her eyes had grown worse.

"She's a good cook."

I sat down in the seat in front of her, sideways, with the row of windows in front of me. It was still light out, and the sky was only slightly yellowed. In the distance, I could hear some sports team running and calling out as they did. The lights in the room were off, and the only illumination in the room was pouring through these windows.

"I heard a number of things at the house where you once lived."

"For example?"

"The pranks you and your sister pulled as children. That Yoru would never cry no matter how much they scolded her, but that Yuu always cried instantly, hiding behind her sister."

"She always depended on me."

We sat in silence for a long moment. There was a quiet tension in the air. I looked at her again.

"I've figured out a number of things about Morino Yuu. I'm not sure about every detail, but…"

Morino stopped glaring at me. She slowly looked away, closing her eyes. Her lashes seemed to tremble above the dark lines under her eyes.

"I thought you might," she said bitterly. She asked me what I had figured out.

"Yuu died when she was eight, nine years ago now," I said. Morino did not open her eyes. "Nine years ago, that day, you found her body hanging in the shed, and you went to tell your grandmother. But you'd known there was a body in there already. You'd been waiting in the entrance for someone to come home so you could pretend to discover your sister's death while someone was watching."

I stopped, waiting for Morino's reaction. She was silent for a moment and then she asked if that was all.

"You already knew your sister was dead. But you were acting, trying to hide that fact. When I try to imagine what would make you do something like that, I always come to one conclusion. In other words, you had something to do with your sister's death."

Morino nodded.

I continued. "Yuu had tied two ropes to the ceiling beam, one around her neck and the other under her arms, supporting her body."

The little eight-year-old girl had jumped off the wooden box. For a moment, it must've looked like she was hanging from the rope around her neck. But in fact, the rope around her chest was keeping her from falling too far.

Then another girl appeared, a girl with the same face. That girl took the pruning shears from the wall and went over to the girl hanging from the ceiling. She cut the rope around the girl's chest with the shears.

The rope broke, and this time the girl was hanging from the rope around her neck.

"You killed her."

Morino opened her eyes a little, not looking at me—not looking at anything for long.

"Didn't you hear about the footprints? My footprints were nowhere in the room."

I imagined the girl hanging there barefoot. The ground in the shed had been softened by the rain.

"No, you left footprints all over the shed. But nobody knew the truth. After you cut the rope and killed her, you saw your own footprints on the ground. And you knew you couldn't just walk away without arousing suspicion. You had to do something…"

Morino had looked up at the hanged corpse she'd made and down at the footprints on the ground, knowing she was in trouble.

Then she saw the shoes that were placed next to each other on the ground, and she made up her mind.

She took off her own shoes, stepping onto a fallen box. Careful not to leave any more footprints, she put on the shoes that had been placed under the corpse, replacing them with her own.

Now the footprints belonged to the dead girl.

"All you had to do then was slip out through the dog door. The ground was still dry there, and you wouldn't leave any footprints."

Morino finally opened her eyes and looked at me. "And my motive?"

"Hatred," I said.

Morino looked very sad. "When you said you'd 'figured out a number of things about Morino Yuu,' I knew you'd caught me."

I nodded.

It had baffled me: Why had her grandmother been so sure it was Yoru standing there when she'd opened the front door? They were twins, and they looked exactly alike—nobody could tell them apart at a glance.

But if she had been wearing black shoes, then it would've been obvious.

"It must've been hard to go nine years without telling anyone, Morino Yuu." That was Morino's real name.

†

A group of girls went down the hall laughing merrily.

Morino Yuu listened to them for a moment, until their voices faded and the hall was silent again.

"You're right," she said. "I'm the younger sister. I was the one who was always crying, always ordered around." She frowned, looking at me. "How did you know?"

"Yuu didn't know that people take off their shoes when they hang themselves. That made it all clear. When you were playing at suicide, Yoru might've told you, but I imagine you forgot."

I told her about the pictures I'd seen in the house, the pictures they'd drawn of themselves playing at hanging.

"Those pictures were drawn during summer vacation nine years ago, just before Yoru's death—which means whatever can be gleaned about the artist's personality at the time is also true about her personality on the day Yoru died."

Yoru and Yuu had drawn the same thing, but there had been a number of differences: In Yuu's picture, both girls had been wearing shoes. But in Yoru's picture, the girls' legs had been flesh toned all the way down. At first, I'd thought Yuu had drawn more details—but later, I changed my mind.

I began to think that Yoru had drawn the picture correctly, from memory. Yuu had drawn the sun, but Yoru's picture had a gray background—further evidence. At the bus stop, Morino had told me the hanging game had happened on a rainy day. It was not that Yoru had forgotten to draw the shoes—it was simply that they had both been barefoot.

"You said it yourself at the bus stop: you knew more about death than Yuu did; you were much crueler than she was. You were saying that as Yoru; so as a child, Yoru must have known about the strange custom of people taking off their shoes before hanging themselves."

When the twins had played at hanging themselves, they'd probably taken off their shoes and placed them aside. Yoru had known that was what you did, and she had probably insisted on it. That knowledge was reflected in her drawing.

But not so with Yuu: She had taken off her shoes when they were playing and then forgotten all about it. She didn't know the custom, and so she'd drawn herself hanging with shoes on.

The corpse in the shed had been barefoot, though. If Yuu had been playing at being hanged all by herself and had died when the support rope broke, then her body would've been wearing shoes.

Yuu was silent, listening carefully to nothing. Then her lips parted slowly and she spoke. "My sister with the black shoes died. And maybe I did hate her a little. But your guess isn't completely accurate." Her voice was very quiet. "You didn't see the rope around her shoulders, did you? I didn't cut it. It broke on its own."

At around noon that day, her older sister Yoru had suggested they pretend to have hanged themselves, to surprise everybody.

Yuu had agreed, and the two had set to work in the shed just as it began to rain.

The dog was alive then, and it watched them work, looking puzzled.

"My sister piled up the boxes and wrapped the ropes around the beam. I stayed below, making sure the boxes didn't fall over.

Yoru was on the boxes before the rain turned the ground soft, so her footprints were not in the shed.

Yoru alone was going to pretend to be dead, and Yuu was supposed to guide someone to the shed. Their preparations continued, and soon Yoru had both ropes around her body.

"And then my sister jumped."

Yoru had kicked away the boxes and fallen. The moment it looked like she was hanging from her neck, though, she was actually caught by the rope around her shoulders.

She had looked down at Yuu and smirked.

"When she was tricking people, she always had a little twisted smile. She never used any expressions when she was talking with our family; when she was tricking people was the only time she seemed to be enjoying herself."

But a moment later, the rope around her shoulders broke.

"I didn't do anything. The rope simply wasn't strong enough for my sister's weight. It broke close to the ceiling. If you had seen the rope or had been told more about it, you would've guessed correctly. It broke much too high for me to have reached."

Yoru hung there for a moment.

"I quickly tried to help. I wrapped my arms around her body and held her up. I was holding her in midair, trying to keep her from dropping any lower."

In the shed, there had been a girl hanging from the ceiling by a rope around her neck, desperately supported by a girl who looked just like her. The hanging girl struggled, kicking her legs wildly in the air. The dog had been tied up next to them, and it began barking furiously. The sound of the dog barking and the girl suffering was deafening in the tiny room. It seemed like that moment lasted for eternity.

"I tried to stop my sister from dying. I wasn't very strong, but I held her up. She kept screaming, though, her heels slamming into me."

Morino sat hunched over in her chair, staring at the wall across the room, seeing nothing but the events of that day. The girl's memories were nothing but a nightmare to her now.

If Yuu's grip were to slip, her sister's body would fall, and the rope would tighten.

Yoru's eyes had been wide open in terror as she screamed at her sister—but she hadn't been screaming encouragement.

"She said, 'Hold tighter, stupid.'" Morino closed her eyes tightly, holding her emotions in check. "When I heard that, I stopped trying to save her. I let go."

Yoru's body had fallen.

Her toes had stopped just above the ground. Yoru had not been wearing shoes; she was barefoot. Her toes were spread wide, all the muscles contracted, shaking at first. The dog barked furiously, hurting Yuu's ears. The convulsions and that barking seeped deep into her mind.

"Finally, her strength ebbed away, and her toes stopped moving."

Yuu had stepped backward and felt the ground stick to her shoes. She'd left footprints.

"If it had been my weight alone, there wouldn't have been footprints." Her sister's shoes had been placed on the ground next to her.

"I remember seeing those and deciding to lie to everyone. In that little shed . . . my sister's body still swaying slightly, like the pendulum of a clock."

The little girl's immature brain had thought desperately and seen a path before her. She had changed into the black shoes, putting her own white shoes in their place.

Walking on dry ground, she had slipped out through the dog door. Her shoes were black, and black shoes identified her as Yoru. She had to call herself Yoru and act like Yoru.

"I could no longer smile like I used to. I had to keep my face blank, like my sister's. We were always together, and I knew what my sister was like. I could imitate her. For nine years, no one ever guessed that I was Yuu."

She gave a long, weary sigh.

At eight years old, she had watched her own funeral. She had lived most of her life never saying her real name. Nobody knew what was going on inside her, and those emotions had built up until she had slashed her wrist... all because of her sister and the name that had been buried with her. The road the young girl had decided to follow was one of sadness and isolation, one on which her entire existence depended.

The light from the windows was fading, turning gold. The pale yellow curtains were half-drawn, dimming the sun. I could hear the sound of the baseball team at batting practice echoing through the air. Time in the empty classroom ticked by in silence.

At last, Morino opened her mouth, still not sure if she should say it. "Do you remember where and when we first met?"

I believed it was in this classroom, at the beginning of our second year of high school. She looked a little disappointed to hear that.

"In junior high, I saw you at the museum, looking at a human body cut into slices. Then, in the spring when we entered high school, I saw you in the library reading a medical text on autopsies. I recognized you at once."

That's why she had known I was acting in class. It made sense. We each had detected what the other was hiding from those around us.

"I find it hard to believe that you used to laugh and smile when you were Yuu."

"I know. I once was like that, but ever since I left the shed, I thought people would know I was Yuu if I smiled. I spent nine years trying not to have any expressions, trying to be my sister. Now I can't smile, not even if I want to."

She seemed ever so slightly forlorn; I doubted anyone else would have noticed it. She looked away from me as she continued, "I thought you might be the first to call me by my name."

I stood up. "I have something for you. I took it with me from your home in the country."

I removed it from a bag on my desk. "What?" she asked, not getting up.

"The rope you were looking for. I think it will fit nicely. Close your eyes—I'll put it on you."

Morino sat still, closing her eyes. I stood behind her, and her tiny shoulders stiffened; she was more than a little tense.

I wrapped a red rope around her neck. It was a dirty rope. I had found it in the shed, where it had been used to tie up the dog.

"I also know why you hate dogs so much."

I gently tightened the rope around her long black hair and her pale slender neck.

As the pressure tightened, her shoulders shook. For a moment I stood there like that. Then I tied the rope, letting the ends of it hang down behind her.

"Yes ... that's it ..." she sighed. All the tension poured out of her, everything inside her softening, releasing.

Yoru had died hanging from the dog's rope, a fact that had been sealed away deep in Morino's memories. She had never realized the rope she was looking for was the same one that had killed her sister.

"I never hated my sister. She did horrible things sometimes, but no one could ever replace her ..."

I picked up my bag and went home. When I passed her seat as I left the room, I turned back to look at Yuu one more time. She was sitting in her chair, her legs stretched out in front of her, her hands folded in front of her chest, the red rope around her neck tumbling down her back to the door.

Her eyes were closed, her lashes lowered. There was soft downy hair on her cheeks, like on a rabbit's back. It glistened in the light of the setting sun, as though she were clad in light. A tear ran down her check, falling from her chin onto her uniform.

I left her alone, closing the classroom door behind me without a sound.

V
GRAVE

i

Kousuke was calling Saeki. The boy always sounded innocent and full of fun, but today he sounded downcast. Kousuke was a little neighbor boy who had just entered kindergarten.

"What is it?"

Saeki was in his garden, tending to the morning glories. It was summer, early in the morning. There was a faint mist in the garden, making everything glitter. Children were walking past the wall around his garden, heading for their group exercises. Saeki couldn't see the children over the wall, which came up to his chest, but he could hear their footsteps and their chattering.

"Is my daddy still angry?" Kousuke had shown up at Saeki's house the night before, crying, and he hadn't gone home since.

When Saeki asked what had happened, Kousuke explained through his tears that he'd knocked over an antique his father had prized, breaking it. Kousuke had been told countless times never to touch the antique, but curiosity had gotten the better of him.

"No, I don't think he's angry anymore."

Saeki told the boy how the child's parents had come looking for him the previous night. When Saeki had met them at his door, they'd asked if he'd seen their Kousuke, looking very worried. Saeki had shaken his head, playing dumb. Then he'd helped them search for Kousuke.

"He's really not angry?"

"Really."

In front of Saeki, the stems of the morning glories were wrapped around bamboo poles that were sticking out of the ground. The bamboo had been dried, so it was light brown.

Saeki lived in an old house, with a garden larger than those of the homes around his. The property was an almost perfect square, with the house and garage flush against the east side. The rest of the grounds was open space, and Saeki had filled that space with trees. In the middle of summer, like today, the grounds were covered in leaves.

Saeki had always enjoyed gardening, even as a child. He'd raised the morning glories that bloomed along the wall around the garden himself.

That day, it was sunny. The sun was rising steadily into a cloudless sky, sunbeams slipping past the wall and the trees, and the bamboo poles supporting the morning glories cast long shadows across the ground.

He could hear Kousuke crying.

When Kousuke had knocked on his door the night before and begged Saeki to hide him, Saeki had let the boy in at once, peering out into the street to make sure nobody had seen the boy come in.

"You're sure you didn't tell anyone you were coming here, Kou?" Saeki asked again. The boy wiped away his tears, nodding. How reliable was a child's word? It occurred to Saeki that it was already too late for such concerns.

In the past, when he'd caught cicadas with Kousuke or watched him play with a cardboard box, an idea had been lurking in the corner of Saeki's mind, a fantasy he could never allow himself to entertain. He hated himself for thinking about such horrible plans. But yesterday, it had been like there was a fog across his mind...

"Do you think I should say I'm sorry?"

Saeki felt his heart breaking. Kousuke didn't even understand what was happening to him. He felt so sorry for the boy.

He didn't hate the child. Saeki himself lived alone, his family long since gone, so he'd always thought of Kousuke like a little brother. He'd often babysat when Kousuke's family was out, and the two had taken any number of walks together. Saeki was sure he loved the child as much as Kousuke's own parents did. So why was he doing this? There was no turning back now.

"You can't go home again, Kou," Saeki said, his voice shaking despite himself. The morning glories in his garden were each wrapped around a single bamboo shaft. Two of the bamboo shafts were marginally larger than the others.

Kousuke's voice trembled. He must've sensed that something was wrong. "Why not?"

His voice came from the thick bamboo shaft stuck into the ground. It was hollowed out, allowing sound to travel from the coffin buried underground up to Saeki's ears. Kousuke didn't know that he'd been buried alive. How sad.

The day before, when Kousuke had come into his house, Saeki had made up his mind. He'd led the boy into a back room. "Hide inside this box," he'd said, pointing at a box in the center of the room. It was just big enough for Kousuke to lie down inside.

Kousuke almost always did exactly what Saeki told him to. And he was too scared of his father's anger to suspect anything, so he climbed right inside the box.

Kousuke hadn't noticed, but that box was a coffin Saeki had made just for him.

Saeki put a lid on the box, nailing it shut. There were two air holes in the lid of the coffin, one over Kousuke's head and the other at his feet. Even though he was nailed inside, the boy could still breathe.

He left Kousuke's coffin in the room and went out to the garden, where he'd been digging a hole opposite the porch, in front of the wall. He only had to make it a little bigger, and it would be large enough to bury Kousuke's coffin.

When Saeki was finished with that task, he went back to the room, carrying the coffin out to the hole. He told Kousuke he was putting him somewhere his father would never find him. It was a struggle getting the coffin off the porch into the garden, but Saeki had managed, and he'd lowered it down into the hole.

He fit the hollowed-out bamboo into the holes in the lid. Then he scooped dirt on top until Kousuke was completely underground.

Saeki thought it looked strange to have two bamboo poles sticking out of a patch of bare ground, so he transplanted some morning glories he'd been raising elsewhere, along with the bamboo stalks he'd been using to train them. He'd carefully transferred two of the morning glories from their original poles to Kousuke's breathing tubes, disguising their primary function so they wouldn't arouse suspicion.

"What do you mean? I want to go home!" the bamboo pole cried.

Poor Kousuke, buried alive, Saeki thought, calmly holding the bamboo pole steady while he packed the earth around it, making sure it would stay upright.

What was wrong with him? He knew he loved this child. He had once seen Kousuke about to be hit by a car. The boy had been chasing a ball, and he never saw the car coming. When the car had braked just in time, Saeki had been so relieved that his legs had gone out from under him. So how could he do this to the boy now?

Saeki had grown up in this house. At first, he'd lived with his parents and grandmother. Both his parents had worked, so he'd spent most of his time with his grandmother. While the other children were playing basketball or making models, Saeki had spent his time gardening with her, filling pots with dark earth and planting the flower seeds inside. Saeki's classmates often had made fun of him, telling him he was like a girl. He was a frail boy, and strangers occasionally thought he was female, which always stung. But when he was with his grandmother, watering the flowers, she always told him he was a gentle child. Whenever his spirits were down, he remembered her words, and he promised himself he would live a good life, never letting her down.

Then, somehow, the fantasy of burying someone alive had

taken over. Before he knew it, that was all Saeki could think about.

He liked watering his garden, often doing so on sunny days—a hose in hand, his thumb over the mouth. The pressure built up, and the water sprayed quite a distance. A fan of water aimed at the trees, glittering in the light. When Saeki saw that, or when his grandmother smiled, he was so happy that it was as though the world grew brighter.

But at the same time, there was a dark place inside him where that light could never reach. He thought about putting his grandmother in a box and burying her in the ground. Every time the thought crossed his mind, he was instantly horrified.

How could he imagine such devilish things? There were times when he couldn't even bring himself to look at his grandmother, terrified that she would guess what he'd been thinking.

Was there some fatal scar inside his heart that had made him like this? He could think of nothing, but perhaps he had simply forgotten. Or—and this was his greatest fear—perhaps he'd simply been born that way.

A few years after Saeki had come of age, his parents and grandmother had died in an accident. Saeki had been informed of it at work.

Until then, his family had always been around at home, and his contact with them had been a constant reminder of his position in society. But after that, he'd been alone in the house, and there was nothing to keep his fantasies in check. Every day, he left work and came home; with no one to talk to there, he found himself thinking about the same thing, those same ideas that had been in his head since childhood. He tried to shake them off, though, telling himself that even thinking such things was unforgivable, and this served to increase his interest in gardening.

When his family had been there, he'd grown a few plants in pots and weeded the garden. But now he brought in better dirt, improving the quality of the earth in the garden, and the number of plants along the wall began to increase in number.

Saeki spent the whole year digging holes to plant trees. That was all he did outside of work. He showed no interest in anything other people his age did, instead spending all his time making holes in his garden and planting trees in them.

At last, there were trees all around the house: inside the garden walls, every inch was covered. If you poked your head over the wall, you were barely able to see the house through the forest. Only one part of the garden was left unforested, the area he could see from the porch. There was nothing blocking the line of sight from there to the wall. That ground was filled with flowers, and it was in bloom all year long.

At first, Saeki believed he was digging holes to plant trees. But along the way, he realized he was planting trees to justify the holes he dug. Eventually, he starred digging holes only to fill them in again. The garden was covered with trees, so close together they could barely grow branches, and there was no more room to plant, yet Saeki kept on digging, because that was the only thing that seemed to clear away the fog of his fantasies, his desire to bury someone—in the ground. When he was digging, Saeki forgot everything else—but only for that brief moment when the tip of his trowel bit into the earth.

Digging holes only to fill them in again had begun to feel empty and meaningless. Digging the hole cleared away the fog—but when he was done, the fog came back, stronger than ever. Saeki had to keep digging anyway, though; that was why there had been a hole ready for Kousuke the night before.

His neighbors didn't seem to find his activities sinister, even when they heard him digging late at night. Everyone bowed when they saw him, and they asked him for advice on their own gardens. Everyone knew he liked to garden, and no one thought it was odd. They all sympathized with him; he had lost his family, and only his hobbies remained.

He had grown friendly with Kousuke two years after his family had died, a year ago now. The boy had gotten lost in Saeki's garden, and they had soon become very friendly. Saeki had even gone on picnics with Kousuke's family.

When he'd known Kousuke for nine or ten months, Saeki had run across some wood just about Kousuke's height in his garage. He instantly thought it would be ideal for coffin making.

Saeki had shaken off the thought, even becoming furious with himself—but the next day, he'd started making the coffin, all the while grimacing at how stupid he was being. He would never actually use it, he told himself. Yet his hands hammered nails into the wood without his conscious guidance, working almost automatically, turning the wood into a box.

"I want to go home! Let me out!" Kousuke was crying now. Saeki could hear the boy's sobs from the bamboo pole. The inside of the hole was dark. The childish voice echoed inside it, the sound muffled.

Saeki didn't know what else to say to Kousuke. He felt so sorry for the boy, so very sorry. Although he pitied him, there was nothing else he could say.

Saeki's hands were holding a hose now. It was attached to the faucet on the side of the house.

The summer heat was getting stronger, and the sound of cicadas came from all around him. The heat spread from his back down, until it embraced his whole body.

A trickle of water lapped against the tip of Saeki's sandals; it was coming from the place where Kousuke was buried. Water was gushing out of one of the bamboo poles, dripping down the morning glories and forming a puddle on the ground. It was coming from the pole that had been an air hole.

The hose was sticking in the other pole. When Saeki's gaze rested there, only then did he clearly understand what he had done. However, that did not mean he had been acting unconsciously.

He had knowingly turned the valve on the end of the hose, filling the box in the ground with water. He had just felt like he was dreaming the whole while. The conscience that would have bothered anyone else didn't seem to function in him.

Water had filled the coffin—and with no other place to go, it had come back up the ocher bamboo pole. The summer sun glittered on the water pouring out of the pole. Saeki thought it was beautiful. The cicadas' song was joined by the sound of the children returning from their exercises. They came from the opposite direction this time, passing along the length of his wall. He couldn't hear Kousuke's voice anymore. And the morning glories were wrinkling, starting to fade.

†

Before he knew it, three years had passed.

The police had not come to arrest him. Kousuke's parents had moved away, looking very sad, and Saeki was the only person who had seen them off. Nobody imagined that Saeki had killed Kousuke; indeed, they all thought the boy's disappearance had left him stricken with grief.

He hadn't done any acting; he really did mourn the boy. But pangs of conscience left him unable to look directly at the boy's parents as they shed tears for their lost child. The purity of their tears only drove home the sheer horror of what he had done.

For three years, Saeki had been terrified that someone would find out what he had done. In all that time, Saeki had never once gone near the patch of land where Kousuke was buried. It was covered in weeds now. The morning glories had faded away, scattered seeds, and grown again, mingled among the weeds. A new family had moved into the house where Kousuke had lived.

At the beginning of summer, a housewife brought the neighborhood newsletter around to Saeki's house. At the door, she spoke about the serial killer targeting girls, a story that was all over the talk shows. Eventually, the conversation touched on Kousuke's disappearance.

"Three years since Kousuke vanished... You were friendly, weren't you? You must miss him."

Saeki tensed, but then he remembered Kousuke's little face smiling, and he felt a wave of sadness. He had drowned the boy underground with his own hands, but his twisted mind still had the nerve to feel grief over the loss. How horrifying.

Saeki nodded gravely. But when he looked up and saw the woman's face, he noticed something strange: she didn't seem at all sad, and she had already moved on to talking about how loud the cicadas were getting as the days grew hotter. The world already considered Kousuke part of the past.

A few days later, Saeki found himself buying new wood and nails and making another coffin. He had to make the coffin inside, so that no one would see him working over the wall. As he sawed the boards down to size, tiny bits of wood littered the tatami floors of the room.

The summer flew by. Saeki could feel his conscience trying to stop him from doing something horrible again, could feel it battling a crazed darkness inside him that was searching for new prey. But this inner struggle never showed outwardly, and the world around him seemed to think Saeki was just like he'd always been. Like a machine functioning automatically, he went about his daily life without any trouble at all.

Then, one Friday late in October, Saeki left work, got into his car in the parking lot, and started driving home. It was already dark out. As he joined the rows of cars with headlights on, his eyes naturally glanced sideways at someone walking by the side of the road. A moment later, he was shaken by the realization that he had looked at the person with an evaluating eye. He could not make out any expression on his face as he peered at its reflection in the rearview mirror; it was like the dark parts of his eyes had turned into little holes.

At work, he had always been taken for a very quiet man. He brought in flowers from home to decorate with, and he did the work he was assigned without complaint. People thought well of him, and he was trusted. None of them knew that Saeki had murdered a child.

As he neared home, he turned left onto a street with little traffic. And there, Saeki saw the girl.

She was walking by the side of the road. He could see her back in the glare of his headlights. She wore a black uniform, and she had long black hair hanging down her back.

As he passed her, Saeki unconsciously slowed down. The girl's hair burned into his eyes. It was like her long black hair was drawing him in.

He looked up through the windshield and saw the full moon hanging in the night sky. There were no clouds, and the area was faintly lit by quiet moonlight. It was a residential area, in front of a park. The trees around them had lost half their leaves already.

Saeki turned right at the next intersection and stopped his car. He turned out the headlights, checked his mirrors, and waited for the girl.

If the girl went straight or turned left, he would drive home. He had the day off tomorrow. He could spend his time relaxing around the house.

But if the girl turned toward him...

A single dry leaf drifted down, tapping against his window and landing on the pavement below. He remembered the neighborhood newsletter he'd read the day before. There had been an article about cleaning up the leaves on the roads, and they were to have cleaned this evening. There were a few leaves on the road now, but it had been covered in them that morning, so he supposed they'd already finished work here. Another leaf drifted silently down, settling against his windshield wipers.

There was no sound at all. Saeki sat in the car, his knuckles clenching the steering wheel tightly. In the mirror, he could see the corner he had just turned. Finally, the girl appeared in the pale light of the moon.

ii

Saeki parked in his garage and quickly closed the large metal door, which shut with a loud screech that echoed through the quiet residential streets. He stood outside the garage, staring down at the piles of dry leaves. The trees he had planted grew right up next to the garage, and they were wrapped in branches, so when their leaves fell, they nearly buried his garage. He would have to rake away the leaves soon.

Since his parents and grandmother had died, Saeki was alone in the house. He had to do all the cleaning and laundry himself. And every time he did so, it reminded him how alone he was.

His recently married colleague showed up at work wearing starched shirts now, and Saeki's boss had pictures of his children on his desk.

"Will you ever get married, Saeki?" a female coworker had asked once.

That would never happen, Saeki thought. Lovers, friends, family...all those things seemed very far away, out of reach. Saeki could manage casual conversation at work, but he didn't feel comfortable forming any deeper bonds.

The secrets and anxieties he harbored had built an unconscious wall between him and other people. There was no one he could ever confess these horrors to.

A chilly breeze brushed against his neck. It was colder than the day before, and Saeki shivered as he watched the leaves blow across the ground. But the chill he felt was not entirely the fault of the coming winter. Saeki realized he was standing outside without his suit jacket on. His white dress shirt was covered in wrinkles, which reminded him of his newlywed colleague's marital bliss. That man's shirts were always ironed.

He shook his head. This was no time to be thinking of other people. He stepped inside the garage. There was a door on the side of the garage, and he walked through it, making his way over to the car and opening the back door. As he picked up his suit jacket, he noticed the stain on the back of the cloth. It must be blood. Saeki looked down at the girl lying on the backseat, bleeding from her mouth and nose. He hadn't wanted anyone he might pass as he approached his home to see the girl lying back there, so he'd covered her with his jacket, hiding her.

The girl was still unconscious and didn't move. She was curled up, her long hair falling over her face like a veil. If she hadn't resisted, he wouldn't have had to hurt her, Saeki thought, rubbing the back of his hand, a red line marking where the girl's nail had broken the skin.

She had screamed as they grappled, her voice shaking the silent night air. Everyone around must have heard it.

He didn't clearly remember what had happened after that. Before he knew it, he'd hit the girl in the face several times. She had slumped over and was no longer moving, but his hands were still flying, pounding into her cheek. He'd shoved her into his backseat, thrown his jacket over her, started the car, and sped away.

Saeki had almost never done anything violent, not even as a child. When he saw news reports on child abuse, his head was filled with loathing. But now he had punched a girl in the face. He could still feel the impact on his hand, which tingled as if insects were crawling all over his fist. He shook his hand in terror, trying to get them off, but the sensation wouldn't go away.

He picked up the girl, carrying her out of the car and into the room at the back of the house. He left the lights off so that their shadows wouldn't show on the window or shoji screens. In the moonlight, the girl's arms and hair hung down, swaying as he walked. In the makeshift workroom, he laid her down in the freshly made coffin.

It fit her perfectly. It was like he had made the box specifically for her. But Saeki couldn't look at her face, not with the blood running from her nose and lips, not with the skin changing color where he'd hit her. The darkness inside him was branded onto her features, and he could not face up to it. He quickly put a lid on the coffin, nailing it closed. There were two small holes in the lid where the breathing holes would go.

There was an open hole next to Kousuke's grave, waiting for the girl. He had guessed that the events of the day would happen, and the hole lay waiting in the moonlight. The dirt taken from the hole formed a small hill next to it.

Saeki pulled the coffin out of the house, moving it directly from the porch to the ground below. An occupied coffin was very heavy.

He placed the coffin in the hole, fitting the pair of bamboo breathing poles into the holes on the lid. Then he filled the hole, scooping dirt onto the coffin. At first, there was a wooden tapping sound as the dry earth hit the coffin lid—but soon the lid was covered, and the task was silent. It took longer than Saeki expected to fill the hole. He was covered in sweat, and since he hadn't changed after arriving home, he had dirt all over the legs of his work suit. At last the grave was full, and he patted the earth flat with his trowel.

He had buried Kousuke in summer, placing morning glories on the bamboo poles. Bur that was impossible at this time of year. Morning glories were originally tropical flowers, and they didn't take well to cold. That left several unused brown bamboo poles in the weeds along the wall, but that would not arouse any suspicions. All he had to do was explain that he grew morning glories there in the summer, and all doubts would vanish.

So the freshly dug soil wouldn't stand out, he brought some straw he had laid on the flower beds and scattered it around the bamboo poles. When he was done, it looked like the ground had never been disturbed at all.

Saeki put his trowel away and sat down on the edge of the porch. For a long while, he stared at the bamboo poles along the wall. The girl was buried there.

The area between the porch and the wall was the only part of the garden not covered by trees. There were several flower beds, a line for hanging laundry, and the bamboo poles. But on either side of the porch, the trees crowded close, looming like black walls in the night. When the wind blew, the looming shadows shifted.

Saeki rubbed the spot on his hand where the girl had scratched him as he'd shoved her into his car. The numbness left over from having hit her had almost vanished. When Saeki touched his face, he found himself grinning broadly.

He went into the house and looked through the girl's bag. There, he found a can of pepper spray and a student ID. There was a picture on the ID: a girl with a beautiful face.

Below her picture was a grade and class, a seat number, and the name Morino Yoru. Saeki stood on the porch again, gazing at the bamboo poles by the wall and whispering that name to himself.

The person he had just buried had a name—such an ordinary thing to just now realize. The girl in the ground had parents, who had given her a name and raised her with love. And he had just buried alive the target of that love.

Sweet intoxication filled Saeki's mind, like sugar water seeping into a cotton ball. Aboveground, the girl he had beaten was terrifying—but underground, out of sight, he felt his fear changing to bliss.

Then Saeki heard a voice, faintly—the wind almost drowned it out, it was so small.

Saeki looked at the bamboo poles again. The pale moonlight picked them out of the shadows around them, sending black lines across the garden to the porch where Saeki was sitting. Four of the bamboo poles were thicker than the others.

The tiny voice he had heard came from two of those thicker poles. Saeki stood up, slipped on his shoes, and stepped directly from the porch into the garden. He walked across the garden, feeling like he wasn't moving at all, like he was a sleepwalker drifting through an unreal world. There was no light save that of the moon, and the trees around his garden loomed like dark shadows on either side, staring down at him.

He stepped onto the scattered straw, approaching the bamboo poles, which came up to his chest, and peering down into them. There was nothing inside but darkness, darkness like his hollow heart, across a diameter as wide as his thumb. He could just make out the girl's trembling voice, carried up the pole to the world aboveground. Her voice was very weak, and the wind snatched it from the end of the poles, scattering it like smoke.

One of the poles was louder than the other. There were two poles in the coffin, but one was at her feet. The other was near her face, and when she spoke inside the coffin, the pole near her face carried her voice better.

"Hello?" she said feebly. Her cut lip must've made it hard to speak loudly. "Let me out..."

Saeki went down on his knees, his palms against the earth between the bamboo poles. He had just buried her, and the earth under the straw was still soft.

The girl's voice was coming from under his hands. He knew it was just his imagination, but the ground felt warm, as if he were feeling the body heat of the girl buried there.

Poor thing. How helpless she was, trapped down below his soles, breathing through a pole in the ground. He pitied her. Knowing she was buried beneath him, unable to do a thing, he felt so superior. He felt the same as he did when looking at a puppy or a kitten.

"Can you hear me?" he asked, standing up. His voice traveled through the darkness inside the poles, reaching the girl.

"Who...who's there?" he heard her say. Saeki said nothing, and her voice rose up again. "You shut me in here, didn't you? Then you buried me underground."

"You know you've been buried?" Saeki asked, taken aback. If she had just now woken up inside the coffin, there was no way she should know anything but the fact that she was trapped in a small, enclosed, dark place.

The girl said nothing for a moment. Then, "I heard the dirt hitting the lid."

"You were pretending to be unconscious?"

He had thought she'd been sleeping since he'd knocked her out. When had she woken up? He had never tied her up. If she had been awake before he put her in the box, she would've tried to run.

"Are your legs injured? Is that why you didn't run?" he asked. The girl said nothing. Maybe his guess was right.

"Let me out!" she said angrily.

Her sudden anger took Saeki by surprise. She didn't cry and plead—she was giving orders. He couldn't see her underground, but he could sense how strong she was. But even in her strength, she was powerless.

"No, I'm afraid not. I really am sorry," he said, shaking his head, even though the buried girl couldn't see him. "If I let you out, you'd tell everyone what I did to you. I can't let that happen."

"Wh-who are you? Why are you doing this?" Her questions echoed in his heart.

Why had he buried her? He could find no exit from that question. It led him directly into a dead end. But he decided there was no reason to be polite and answer her, so he stopped thinking about it.

"That doesn't matter."

"Where am I? The mountains?"

"No, you're in my garden. This is your grave."

The girl fell quiet. He tried to imagine what her face must look like in that tiny, dark space.

"Grave? You've got to be kidding. I'm still alive."

"Burying dead people isn't as much fun," Saeki said, feeling like that was extremely obvious.

It seemed to leave the girl speechless for a moment. Then she growled, "If you don't let me out, you'll be in trouble."

"You think someone's coming to save you?"

"I know someone who will find me!" she suddenly roared. Then she yelped in pain and fell silent again. He could hear her breathing heavily. Maybe her ribs were injured and they hurt every time she spoke. Saeki thought there was a surprising passion in her words.

"This friend you trust so much . . . a boy?"

"Yes," she said, but with a confidence that made it clear she was talking about her boyfriend.

"May I ask his name?"

"Why do you want to know?"

"Curiosity."

There was a long silence, and then the girl said the boy's name. Saeki branded that name into his memories but privately wondered if she was lying. There was a possibility that no such person existed, but Saeki had no way of verifying the truth.

"I'm going to have to buy some binoculars."

The night sky was filling with clouds drifting across the face of the moon. Tomorrow it might well be overcast.

"Do you know why?" Saeki asked. The girl remained silent. "To watch him mourn your loss from a distance."

He was sure his voice had reached the girl's ears, yet she said nothing at all. Saeki said a few more things, trying to draw a response, but she reacted to nothing. She just lay there silently in the dark.

Assuming he had made her mad, Saeki left the garden. Her mood would change in the morning.

He went to the garage and cleaned the backseat of the car. He could leave no trace of her presence there. In the car, he always kept a small pillow, which he'd placed under her head when he'd laid her down. All her blood had soaked into it, so there were no stains on the seat. Saeki took the pillow out of the car and gathered up all the long black hairs from the floor.

When he was done cleaning, he went inside, checked the clock on the wall, and discovered that it was already past two. He went up to his room, laid down on his futon, and tried to sleep. He lay there with his eyes closed, searching for the entrance to the land of dreams, his thoughts on the girl locked in tiny, isolated darkness.

†

The next day, it was almost noon by the time Saeki woke up. It was Saturday, but where he worked, weekends meant little; he often had to work on Saturday and Sunday. But this week, he'd been lucky: Saturday was his day off.

He opened his window and looked outside. When he was a child, he'd been able to see the city from there, but now the trees were in the way. Above the treetops, he could see a gray sky. A cold wind shook the trees, brushing past Saeki's cheeks.

Wondering if the girl had simply been a dream, Saeki went downstairs and out onto the porch. He looked toward the wall, and only then was he sure that it had really happened.

There were four thick bamboo poles among the thinner rods. Four poles meant two coffins. He had buried a girl last night, next to Kousuke. Confirming this came as a relief.

What was going on next to the park, where he had pushed the girl into the car?

She had screamed. Had someone reported it? Had the buried girl's parents grown worried about their missing daughter and called the police? The police might've been able to use those two pieces of information to figure out that the girl had been kidnapped on the road next to the park.

Saeki put on his sandals and stepped down into the garden. He was hungry, but he wanted to chat with the girl a little before he ate. In unusual circumstances like this, he usually wasn't able to eat—but for some reason, he felt very hungry and alive.

He stood next to the bamboo poles. He didn't speak immediately but listened, trying to hear if any sounds were coming from belowground. There were none, so he said, "It's morning. Are you awake?"

The night before, she'd refused to answer him. He'd been worried she would keep that up this morning—but after a moment, he heard her voice again.

"I know it's morning. It's dark in here, but..."

The pole the voice was coming from shook slightly, despite the earth packed around it. She must have touched the end of it, which ran through the hole in the lid of the coffin.

"There's this pole sticking in next to my face. I was feeling around and found it. This is so I can breathe? I looked inside, and I could see white light on the far end—which means daylight?"

The poles were not fixed in place—they simply passed through holes in the lid. If Saeki wanted to remove them, he could do so easily. Likewise, if she grabbed the end inside the coffin and shook it, it would wave back and forth merrily.

"Let go of that. Those poles should never move. Someone might see and think it looks suspicious. If you move that again, I'll pull them out. And then you won't be able to breathe."

The pole stopped moving.

"What's your name?" the girl asked.

"Saeki. And you are Morino, yes?"

There was a long, thoughtful silence, and then the girl whispered, her voice full of disgust, "Saeki, I don't know why you've shut me in here, but this is evil. You should let me out—or the black bird of misfortune will settle on your shoulder."

Not only was this girl not afraid of him, she was casting some sort of curse on him. Did she fully understand her predicament? Saeki felt himself growing a little angry.

"What can you do down there? I could drown you at any moment."

"Drown...?"

He explained in as much detail as possible how he could kill her using a hose to pump water into the coffin, making it very clear that there was no hope of her surviving, trying to break her will.

The girl wasn't able to turn her eyes away from the black pit of despair before her. Or perhaps she was simply too tired to maintain her anger. Either way, her voice trembled. "I will end my own life before you have a chance to kill me. You didn't check my pockets—a fatal mistake. I'm sure you'll realize just how careless you were in time. I have a mechanical pencil in my pocket, and I'll stab that into my jugular."

"Perhaps you think committing suicide before I kill you would protect your pride, but that isn't true. It's all the same. Once you kill yourself, your body will rot away down there. No one will ever find it. You'll remain alone, isolated underground forever."

"No, I will not. I will not go undiscovered forever. The police aren't stupid, and they'll catch you one day. It may be a few days from now, or it may be a few years from now. And I know one thing for sure: I will not die alone."

"You won't?"

"My death will not be 'isolated'!"

"You mean someone will die with you? The boy you spoke of yesterday?"

"He won't let me die alone."

Was she crying in her grave? Her voice sounded a little moist, but there was still an absolute sense of conviction behind it.

Saeki had asked about her boyfriend, intending to scoff. They were high school kids, and it was only puppy love. But now he found himself getting nervous. There was a black cloud in his head, heavily laden with rain.

"I can't understand...how you can talk like that, in these circumstances. "Morino...you will die there and rot away underground, lonely...and alone. No other fate is possible," Saeki said, and then he left her.

When he heard her words, he'd remembered the question the young woman at work had asked him—if he would ever marry.

He was cut off from any deep bonds, the kind family and close friends shared.

He had to remain that way to survive. He could smile at other people and engage in shallow conversations, but his soul must never touch theirs. The girl's words had driven that home, unsettling him.

He decided to eat something and calm himself. He had lost his appetite, but if he ate, he would feel better.

He decided to eat out. He pulled his wallet out of his suit pocket and put on a jacket. Then, as he slipped on his shoes at the door, he noticed something odd.

Saeki had a work badge that he always kept on him. The ID

card was held in a brown leather case, and it was always in the same pocket as his wallet. He never went anywhere without it. But he hadn't seen it since the night before.

Saeki took off the one shoe he'd managed to get on and went back into the house, where his suit jacket was hanging. He reached into the pocket where his wallet had been. There was nothing inside, so he checked the other pockets. No sign of his badge. He looked around, making sure it wasn't on the floor somewhere. He picked up all the magazines on the table, even lifting up the futon covering his *kotatsu* to look for it. Nothing.

When had he last seen it? He knew he'd had it at work. Had he dropped it somewhere?

Saeki soon arrived at the answer, an answer that made him rather dizzy. The more he tried to dismiss the idea, the more certain he was.

If he had dropped the badge, it would've been when he'd fought with the girl...last night, next to the park, when the girl's scream had shattered the night, and the girl's elbow had struck him in the ribs—knocking the badge out of his pocket.

He could hear bird's wings flapping in the garden. The trees around his house drew a lot of birds. He could hear them singing in the morning, and when he walked through the garden, they would fly away in panic. But today the sound of their wings felt ominous, like a harbinger of destruction.

They had cleaned the leaves on that road yesterday. The badge hadn't been there when they cleaned, but if it were found today... then they'd know the owner of the badge had passed that way that morning or the evening before.

It would be easy to determine to whom the badge belonged. Saeki's name was written inside. He had no way of telling how many people would connect the fact that he had been there with the girl's scream and her disappearance, but it seemed like a good idea to go out and find the badge before anyone else did.

Saeki hurriedly put his shoes back on and went outside. He would run to the park—it was too close to bother driving.

Before he went out, Saeki decided to say something to the girl. He walked around from the entrance through the trees on the side of the house to reach the garden by the porch. As he neared the bamboo poles along the wall, he stopped dead in his tracks.

From the bamboo poles, he could hear the girl laughing like a broken record.

In all their conversations, the girl had never let herself get carried away. She had never screamed, instead speaking calmly to him, in firm control of her emotions.

But now she was laughing. The pain occasionally caused the laughter to give way to groans, but she couldn't stop herself from laughing anyway.

In the box underground, had her fear driven her to madness? She had been so quiet all this time that the laughter was all the more unsettling. In the end, Saeki went back the way he had come without daring to say a word.

iii

When he reached the road by the park, it was already noon. If it had been a clear day, the sun would've been high overhead, but today a layer of thick clouds covered it, and a cold wind was blowing.

The park was a cozy little number, nestled in the middle of a residential area.

There was a chain-link fence around it, to keep children from running out into the road. As Saeki walked along the sidewalk, he glanced through the fence into the park. There was a playground in a clearing.

Someone was sitting on a swing. He was facing the other side of the park, his back to Saeki, so all Saeki could make out were his black clothes.

Certain there was no one else around, Saeki relaxed. He had been worried that the police would already be there investigating, but apparently that was not the case. More than anything else, he'd been afraid that someone else would find the badge before he did.

Trees were placed at intervals along the sidewalk. There were no cars on the street; it was just the quiet, empty road.

With every breeze, dry leaves fell—not dancing on the breeze, but falling straight down, like dry rain. They'd just cleaned there the day before, but the sidewalk already was covered in leaves. There were fewer on the road, because the wind from passing cars kept that area relatively clear, but there were big piles against the curbs.

Saeki looked around the ground where he'd stopped his car the night before, where he'd grappled with the girl. But he didn't find his badge. There wasn't anything but leaves, which blanketed the ground. Perhaps the leaves had covered his badge, hiding it from the eyes of people passing by.

Saeki got down on his knees and began pushing around leaves. There was no need to search the entire sidewalk; he knew the badge would be where he had grappled with the girl. He was sure he would find it quickly.

As he gently turned over the fallen leaves, the wind caught them, carrying them away. Saeki watched them, thinking about the girl.

It was dark where she was, in that box. If she peered through the pole stuck into the lid, she could see the light of the world outside as a tiny dot, but that was the only light she had. In that tiny, dark space, she had no choice but to gaze directly on her own death. Yet still she claimed her boyfriend would not let her die alone.

Finding that out had shaken Saeki. He couldn't understand it, and that made him anxious. How could you believe in someone when you were trapped in a box underground, with the promise of eternal isolation hovering over you?

There had been a comfortable fog over his mind all night; as he'd thought about how powerless the girl he had buried was, it had given him ripples of pleasure, like honey on his tongue. But when he'd heard those words, it was like being dragged from his slumber by someone slapping his cheek.

He knew exactly what he had done to the girl now. He remembered every horrifying word he had said to her.

Feeling dizzy, Saeki fell to his knees in the leaves. His vision blurred, and the layers of leaves seemed to ripple like the surface of the sea. He could barely breathe, his lungs gasping for air.

When had he begun to relish such sadistic actions like he was eating candy?

Once, he had been a good citizen. He had worked hard, and he had been nice to those around him, greeting people he knew as he walked around, always stopping to chat.

Every time the notion of burying someone alive had floated into his mind, he'd struggled to banish the thought. He'd told himself that no one should ever do such a thing and that he should be satisfied with digging holes in his garden. He was a human being. He could never do anything as diabolical as enjoying burying someone alive…

But ever since he'd buried Kousuke and killed him, a vital gear inside him had gone out of whack. In a terrifying way, his feelings of superiority over the helpless girl in the ground had made him feel like he was finally alive… Could he still call himself human?

Despite his dizzy spell, Saeki never once stopped pushing the leaves around as he continued looking for his badge. Sweat rolled down his nose, falling onto the dry leaves.

No matter how hard he looked for it, there was no sign of his badge. He had even checked the leaves well away from where he had struggled with the girl, just in case, but it was nowhere to be found. Saeki was starting to panic.

A newspaper swept up against his legs, carried by the wind. When he stood up, kicking it away, he realized someone was standing against the fence, looking at him through it. He'd been so preoccupied with his search that he hadn't seen the figure approaching.

The swing was swaying empty in the distance. The person sitting there must have come over to him.

Standing on the other side of the fence was a boy who looked like a high school student. He wore a black uniform, and he stood staring at Saeki with both hands in his pockets. Saeki assumed today had been a half day at school, so the boy had come from school directly to the park.

Saeki met the boy's eye, and there was an awkward silence. The boy broke it first, bowing his head. "Sorry, I just...wondered what you were doing."

He must've been a sight to behold.

"Did you lose something?" the boy asked.

"Erm," Saeki stammered, not sure how to answer. He wanted the boy to go away, but it seemed too strange to come right out and say so. Perhaps he should leave himself, coming back to look some more when the boy was gone.

"You live around here?" the boy asked, when Saeki failed to respond.

"Yes, I do."

"May I ask your name?"

Without really thinking about it, he told the boy the truth.

"Saeki? Mind if I ask you a question? It might be a strange question, but..."

"A strange question?"

"I won't take up too much of your time. About the scream last night...do you know anything?"

Saeki felt like someone was pressing ice against his heart.

"Scream...? What scream...?"

"At around nine o'clock last night, someone was heard screaming near here. I know someone who lives in the area who told me about it; but it seems like your house was too far from here for you to have heard it," the boy concluded, after carefully observing Saeki's reaction.

Saeki was more than willing to go along with this, so he nodded.

"You see, one of my classmates never came home last night. Today was a half day, but my classmate didn't come to school."

Saeki could not stop himself from looking away. The boy was at least ten years younger than him, but his eyes terrified Saeki. He could feel himself sweating under his clothes. The boy was talking about that girl...

"My classmate walks this way to school every day, so I wondered if the scream last night was connected..."

It was her, the girl Saeki had buried alive. "You know her well?"

"I suppose," the boy said, indifferent. Was this the boy the girl had mentioned?

From the way he answered, no. He was very calm, and he spoke of her like she was a stranger. It was hard to believe they were close.

"So you came here worried about your missing classmate?"

"Oh, no. This is more like sightseeing."

"Sight—?"

"At the police station, they have a map of the city with red marks all over it."

"Places where fatal accidents have occurred?"

"Yes, you know it? I didn't think anyone had noticed but me. My hobby is going to each of those red marks and standing on the spots where people have died—standing over the spot where their lives ended, feeling the asphalt under my shoes... Coming here was simply an extension of that hobby. I like looking at places where horrible things have happened, and it also occurred to me that, if I were lucky, I might run into the perpetrator returning to the scene of the crime."

The boy removed his hands from his pockets and took hold of the chain-link fence. The fence shook, emitting the sound of grating metal. The boy was staring directly into Saeki's eyes.

The boy's words had almost made Saeki's heart stop. Was he saying this in full knowledge that the man he was talking to had kidnapped the girl in question? Saeki dismissed the idea. That was out of the question.

But his heart took no comfort from this, and he remained anxious.

He heard the sound of a bird flying overheard and looked up. A lone crow was flying under the cold sky, its black beak pointed right at Saeki.

Wait. Saeki had an idea.

Perhaps the boy had found the badge—had linked the badge to the girl's scream and had guessed that the culprit might come back here soon...

Now the boy was keeping the badge hidden, testing him. But was that really possible?

"So this missing classmate of mine...where do you think she is?" the boy asked. Once again, he appeared to be coldly observing Saeki's reaction.

Saeki wanted to run. The boy was on the other side of the fence and would have to run over to the park entrance before he could follow. But in that case...if he really had picked up the badge and he reported Saeki's suspicious behavior to the police...

"Do you know anything?"

"No, nothing."

"Oh? I thought you would somehow."

"Why...?"

"Perhaps I was overthinking it. You see, you said you hadn't heard the scream."

"So what...?"

"That doesn't make sense. I only mentioned a scream, but when I mentioned my missing classmate, you asked if I knew her. You used the word 'her.' But I never mentioned anything that could identify my classmate's gender. Saeki, how did you know my missing classmate was female?"

"Ah, I do have a reason for that. There's a high school girl I pass every morning here, but this morning I didn't see her. That's all. I just assumed you must've been talking about her."

The boy nodded. "A thin girl with long hair?"

"Yes—pale skin, with a mole under her left eye," Saeki said, remembering the photograph on her student ID. But how long would he be able to hold up his end of this conversation? The boy clearly suspected him. He was getting more and more uncomfortable, as if there was an arm slowly tightening around his neck.

"Are you okay? You look pale."

"I'm not feeling all that hot, no."

"Wait there—I'll be right over."

The boy left the fence, walking quickly toward the park entrance. On the way, he picked up his school bag, which he'd left next to the swings. Once out on the road, he came back toward Saeki, looking concerned.

Saeki wiped the tension-fueled sweat from his brow with one sleeve.

"Since yesterday... I've been feeling pretty sick."

"I do apologize for making you talk with me in such a condition. I said I wouldn't take up much of your time, but it seems I have... Perhaps we should find someplace where you can sit down?"

"Yes..." Saeki pretended to think about it for a moment, but he already knew what he would answer. "I suppose my house would be closest."

He planned to take a few steps and feign a dizzy spell, almost falling over. The boy would come running over, and he would take advantage of this, convincing the boy to help him home. Then Saeki would kill the boy, checking the boy's pockets at his leisure. But he didn't even need to do any acting.

"You don't look well—should I walk you home?" the boy frowned, not wanting to tax Saeki unduly. Convenient.

"Please. This way..."

They walked together, Saeki with his shoulders hunched and shivering occasionally. He did feel pretty terrible, so it wasn't hard for him to pretend he was sick.

As they walked, Saeki tried to figure out just who this boy was. He had apperared in front of him out of nowhere, and he was now walking with him. What should he do when they reached the house? How should he kill the boy?

Once again, Saeki felt himself getting dizzy. Before he even knew it, he had started thinking about killing the boy with the same methodical detachment he used when he thought about work.

There was a pure part of his heart begging him not to do anything else this horrific. But if the boy had picked up his badge and guessed at the connections between him and the girl, then Saeki had no choice—he had to kill him. Otherwise, the world would find out about the horrible things he had done.

What would people he worked with think when they found out the real Saeki was a terrifying monster? That the man who had brought flowers in from his garden to brighten up the office was really a killer, a creature not worth spitting on? Would this knowledge sadden them? Infuriate them? His ears echoing with their revulsion, Saeki would be so overcome with shame that he would only be able to stare at his own feet, the flames of shame burning all around him.

He could never let that happen. The boy had to die. He squeezed his eyes shut, telling himself this again, trying not to cry.

They were at his home in no time. He didn't remember what they had talked about on the way there, but he felt like they had both avoided anything significant.

"Nice house," the boy said, looking up at it.

"Yeah, but an old one. Come on in."

They went through the gate. It was always open so the car could get in and out. The boy stopped in the driveway, looking at the garage next to the house. The garage doors were open, and the front of a black car was facing them. Saeki had cleaned all trace of the girl from the back seat. There was no blood, no hair, nothing left. He had left the garage door open afterward.

"Is that your only car? Then you live alone, right?"

"Yes."

The boy looked at the garden.

"That's a lot of trees."

"My hobby. Like my own little forest."

After asking permission, the boy turned back into the garden. Saeki followed after him.

Under the cloudy sky, everything Saeki had grown looked as though it were dark green. The boy passed a row of evergreens, sounding impressed. "This is quite a big garden!"

Just past the evergreens, the garden opened up. This was the space on the south side of the house, between the porch and the wall. Several flower beds were framed by stones, but nothing grew there now. There was only the dry earth.

And over by the wall, there were several bamboo poles. Where the morning glories had been, there was scattered straw, and underneath that...

"No trees here?"

"Keeping the view from the porch."

...Underneath that was the girl and whatever remained of Kousuke.

The bamboo poles stood in a row along the wall, unmoving. The boy had not yet focused his attention on them, only perceiving them as part of the garden. But what if the girl in the ground grabbed the end of the pole and shook it? The boy would see it moving strangely and go to investigate.

Saeki had to end this before that happpened. He told the boy to sit on the porch.

"I'll get some tea," he said, stepping up onto the porch and heading inside.

"I wonder where Morino disappeared to...?" he heard the boy mutter. Saeki froze in his tracks, staring at the boy's back.

"I'm not quite sure how to explain this, but she gives off some sort of...pheromone that attracts strange people," the boy said, turning to look up at Saeki. It was obvious he had intended his muttered comment to be overheard. "Walking around in a cloud of those pheromones means those abnormal individuals often come after her."

"Wait a moment—I'll just get that tea," Saeki said, leaving the boy. He could not be sure if the boy had deliberately brought the subject up to distract him, but there had been something sinister lurking behind the boy's tone.

As he boiled water for the tea in the kitchen, Saeki took a kitchen knife out of the drawer. He could think of no other weapons to kill someone with.

The blue fire on his gas stove began heating the water in the kettle. He placed a cup and a teapot on a tray and the knife next to them. He gazed down at the metallic sheen of the blade, trying to imagine himself swinging it down to attack the boy on the porch from behind. The blade shimmered, reflecting the light of the burner. He was only making one cup of tea, so there wasn't a lot of water, and it began to boil quickly.

Saeki put his hand on the edge of the sink, steadying himself. Otherwise, he couldn't have remained upright. Nothing of the sweet sensation he had felt while burying the girl was left. Instead, he felt terrible, like he was living a nightmare. Everything he saw, everything he touched seemed to be giving off the stench of rot. But the ugliest thing of all was himself. He had killed Kousuke, he had buried that girl alive, and now he was about to stab this boy. Compared with the strength of the girl's belief in her boyfriend, his own heart seemed so pathetic. His nightmare had begun the moment he'd killed Kousuke.

Or perhaps he had been doomed to this nightmare the moment he had been born. The moment he had been granted life, his soul may well have been possessed by the unavoidable urge to murder.

The water boiled, steam pouring out of the mouth of the kettle. Saeki reached to turn off the flame and realized...

Kousuke...

Steam rose, the water in the kettle boiling furiously.

What had Kousuke looked like...?

Saeki could not remember the face of the young boy he had killed. Although he had gone with him to the park and they had played together any number of times, Saeki retained no memories of him, as if the boy had been disposable.

What was wrong with him? He no longer knew. Part of him was a good citizen who tried to be nice to people, but another part of him was a monster who buried people alive for fun. These two fought like multiple personalities, but they were not different people—they were connected, aligned, the same.

But in that case, who was he then? Who was the man he had thought he was? He could no longer believe in himself, so what could he believe in?

He picked the knife up off the tray, his hand trembling...

He turned off the stove and filled the pot. Then he headed toward the boy on the porch.

Saeki walked quietly. As he turned the corner, he was in sight of the porch, and he could see the boy's back. The boy was facing the garden, sitting on the porch.

In his hand was a cell phone, held to his ear. Was he calling the police? For a moment, Saeki was terrified.

He crept quietly forward.

Saeki could hear the boy talking on the phone. From his tone, he was not talking to the police, but to a friend.

As he stood behind the boy, the boards under Saeki's feet creaked.

The boy turned around, hanging up. "Saeki, that took ages!" the boy said. "And you look even sicker..."

Saeki put the tray down next to the boy. "Yes, well...I'm getting very dizzy..." He poured the tea into the cup.

He had to fight the terrifying beast that lurked within his heart. He held the cup out to the boy, silently making up his mind.

He had left the knife in the kitchen. When he realized he could not remember Kousuke's face, he felt like he had no choice. This seemed to be the only escape from the nightmare.

The boy took the cup. White steam rose from the pale green liquid, vanishing into the air. He watched it for a while, and then he put the cup down without drinking.

"Saeki, I have good news," the boy sighed, looking slightly relieved. "Morino did go missing yesterday, but apparently she just came home."

iv

When the clock on the wall reached midnight, Saeki was curled up in a ball in the corner of his room with the lights out, hugging his knees and breathing softly in the darkness. He couldn't stop shaking. He'd been like this since well before sunset, and he no longer knew if he was hot or cold, alive or dead.

The long hand of the clock moved forward another notch. As it did, it apparently moved into the perfect position to reflect the moonlight pouring through the window. It glittered white. The gleam caught the corner of his eye, and Saeki finally found his resolve. He stood up and went downstairs and to the garage. He picked up the trowel he kept there and a crowbar to pry the lid off the box, and then he went into the garden.

He had been waiting for the world to be submerged in darkness. He'd been afraid someone might look over the wall during the day and see what he was doing. But the longer he waited, the more his imagination had taken over, driving him half-insane. Overcome with terror, he had nearly passed out in the darkness, and before he knew it, he'd been curled up like that for more than six hours.

He passed the evergreens and came out in the clearing between the wall and the porch. Staring at the row of bamboo poles along the wall, he took another step forward. The back of his hand stung painfully, right where the girl's nail had broken the skin the night before.

Saeki stood in front of the chest-high dry bamboo poles, the poles that connected to the girl's coffin. His hand hurt so much he could have sworn it was bleeding.

First, he called out to the girl. She didn't respond. Hands trembling, Saeki yanked the pole out of the ground and dropped it to one side. He brushed the straw aside, uncovering the hole where the pole had been.

He stabbed the tip of his trowel into the ground and began to dig.

He worked without light, to avoid attracting attention. The

clouds that had covered the sky all day had been swept away by the wind. Like the night before, everything was bathed in the pale light of the moon. There were no sounds from the road beyond the wall, and he worked in almost total silence, the only sound coming from his trowel as it bit into the earth. He was still incredibly dizzy, his body weak like he was running a fever. As he dug, he remembered what the boy had said on the porch.

"It sounds like she had a pretty rough time of it, but she's safe and sound now. I just spoke to her on the phone. I'm headed over there now—thanks for taking the time to talk to me."

The boy had said all this before his tea was even cold, bowed his head, and then rose to leave.

Saeki had merely blinked at him, unable to parse the boy's meaning. There was no way the girl could be aboveground.

But the boy had picked up his bag and headed toward the gate without seeming to notice Saeki's confusion.

Saeki had stepped off the porch, slipped on his shoes, and followed after, through the trees.

"She's . . . she came home . . . ?"

That had to be a lie. But he couldn't stop himself from asking.

"Yes, she did. It sounded on the phone like she was still in a state of shock. But I wouldn't worry; she'll recover soon enough."

The boy went through the gate, turning toward the park. Saeki stopped just outside the gate. He put one hand on the gatepost, supporting himself, and watched as the uniformed boy walked away.

The boy had stopped at the intersection not far from the gate, and he'd waved down the cross street. Someone Saeki couldn't see must've been coming that way. Eventually, that person stepped onto the corner and stood next to the boy. It was a long-haired girl whom Saeki recognized at once.

He couldn't believe his eyes. He stared at the girl's face: even, beautiful features, pale skin. The girl he had buried alive. She was talking to the boy.

Was he dreaming? He was so dizzy that the houses and telephone poles were all bending. The road and walls were all moving like waves in a pond...

He'd glanced toward the bamboo poles where he'd buried the girl—and then he'd broken into a run. The moment he took his eyes off the duo at the corner, the boy had turned toward him. But all Saeki cared about was under those poles.

Saeki stood where he had buried the girl. He spoke to the poles that led into the coffin. There was no answer. No sound came from underground, and all he could see inside the poles was inky blackness, like dirty water.

The girl must have escaped.

No. Saeki dismissed the idea. The earth hadn't been disturbed. So then...what the hell had he buried...?

He called down the bamboo pole any number of times after the boy left, until it was dark. But she never once responded. No matter how hard he thought, Saeki couldn't figure it out. Eventually, he decided there was nothing he could do except wait for dark and open the coffin lid.

In the moonlight, it was silent save for the sound of earth turning over. Saeki poured all his attention into the work. The black walls of forest stared down at him from either side. The damp night air made the scent of the evergreens all the stronger.

There was a white mist drifting through the trees, covering the garden. The trees were breathing. Saeki felt like this white mist was the breath of the trees he had planted.

He could feel the trowel stabbing into the ground, could feel the weight of the earth as he lifted it and tossed it aside, but he felt like he was trapped inside a nightmare. The repetitive, simple task he was performing didn't help. He could no longer believe he really lived in the world; he was simply a human-shaped thing that had been trapped in the darkness for aeons, forced to turn over dirt for all eternity.

His hand hurt. He was sure the red scratches on the back of his hand harbored the girl's curse.

What was it that lay buried under him? The deeper the hole,

the less certain he was. Tears rolled down Saeki's cheeks. With each scoop of earth, he had to wipe his eyes with his shoulders just to see. He was terrified of what lay underground. The embodiment of the sin he had committed lay there. He was sure it would be like a mirror, reflecting his inhuman inner nature.

He felt like he had been working forever, but then he finished at last. The wooden box he'd made had gradually appeared in the hole at the edge of the garden, surrounded by white mist and the scent of the earth, and bathed in the pale moonlight. The lid was still nailed shut. It didn't appear as if it'd been opened. The thumb-sized holes in the lid were dark. The box terrified him. It was like some cold, otherworldly thing. Sobbing, Saeki pried open the lid with a crowbar.

The first thing that hit him was the smell of blood, so strong it nearly knocked him backward. Then he saw the uniform-clad girl in the box. She was lying on her back with her hands on her chest. Her face, the sides of the box, and the lid were all red. There was a deep pool of dark liquid in the bottom of the box.

It was blood, blood that had poured from the girl's throat. In her hands was a mechanical pencil. Just as she'd said she would, she'd stabbed the pencil into her neck.

The blood must have sprayed out of her, coating the inside of the box. Saeki slapped his hands to his mouth, backing away from the hole. He needed to get away from her. He stumbled along the wall, collapsed on his knees near the evergreens, and threw up. But he hadn't eaten a bite all day, and nothing came out but stomach acid.

"As you may have noticed, she was not Morino Yoru..."

As his shoulders shook with fear, Saeki heard a voice say those words. At first, he thought the voice came from inside his head, but it soon came again. It was the voice of the boy he'd met that day.

"Saeki, you only thought that she was Morino."

He heard footsteps near him. Saeki looked up, and a figure appeared out of the mist. It stood in the trees, backlit by the moon, staring down at Saeki. He couldn't see the figure's face, but he knew it must be the boy.

Farther away came a different set of footsteps. There was someone else beyond the mist, through the evergreens. They walked right past Saeki, over to the coffin he had excavated. It was a tall, sturdy male, bigger than either Saeki or the boy. He appeared to be about the same age as the boy. Saeki saw his face in the moonlight, but he didn't recognize him.

The man headed directly for the girl Saeki had buried but didn't recognize. What was going on? He couldn't understand. Was this real? Had he fallen asleep? He wasn't sure. Saeki looked up at the boy and shook his head, demonstrating his confusion. Tears flowed down his cheeks.

"He's another classmate. The girl you buried was his girlfriend. His name is—"

The boy said a name, a name Saeki knew.

"Oh...so that's him..."

He was the boyfriend the girl had spoken of.

He stepped down into the hole, bending down. All Saeki could see was his back.

He could hear him calling out and see his back shaking. He must've been shaking the girl's shoulders.

He was talking to the girl. At first, he spoke quietly, like he was making sure she was joking—but when the girl didn't respond, his voice grew louder and louder.

"Was there a mole on the face of the girl you just saw?" the boy asked. Saeki shook his head.

The bloodstained girl's face was puffed up where he had hit her, but there was no mole.

"The girl you always passed by but didn't see today...earlier today, you told me there was a mole under her left eye. That's why I suspected you. I knew then you had mistaken that girl for Morino."

"But there was a student ID in her bag..."

"Morino had lost it, and a girl who lived near her was taking it to her. Morino told me that today at school. That's why I knew you had seen the photo on her ID when you mentioned the mole.

At first, I thought you'd simply run over the girl. I thought her face had been crushed beyond recognition, and you'd only known what she looked like from the ID."

Saeki looked down at his hand. By the time he'd pushed her into the car, he'd already beaten her face badly. He'd been unable to look directly at her bruised features, quickly placing the coffin lid on—without ever looking at her. He had simply assumed the ID belonged to her.

Slowly, he began to understand the extent of his mistake. Earlier that day, she'd been laughing underground. He knew now she hadn't gone crazy. She'd been laughing because he'd addressed her by a different name. She had figured out Saeki's mistake, and that had made her laugh.

He looked at the hole again. The boyfriend was sitting next to the girl Saeki had buried. Saeki knew nothing about them, had no idea how deep their love had been. But during the brief conversation he'd had with the girl underground, the way she'd spoken her boyfriend's name suggested the weight of their relationship. In that small, dark, square space, she'd never allowed Saeki to conquer her. But her fear had been greater than he'd been able to imagine. The only hope she could see, the only one she could imagine saving her... was the name she'd mentioned.

He was sitting next to her now. He'd grown quiet, no longer speaking to her, simply staring silently down into the coffin.

"Saeki, I only knew you were hiding the girl somewhere in your home this afternoon when I was leaving and you stood at the gate. At the time, I had no idea where she was. But the moment you saw Morino alive and moving around, you went pale, looked at the garden, and ran back into it. So I imagined you had buried her somewhere in your garden."

The boy had called Morino Yoru on his cell phone, deliberately showing her to Saeki to provoke a reaction. And that reaction had led the boy to the garden, and to monitor his actions.

"You..."

Saeki stammered, staring up at the boy. Who was this boy? He could only imagine the boy had come to get revenge for his class-mate. But the way he spoke showed no sign of anger, no sign of contempt for Saeki's sins. It was a quiet, calm voice.

If he had not met this boy, his crime might never have been discovered. Why had he become involved with him?

Only then did Saeki remember his badge. He had gone out to find it and had met the boy in the process.

"My badge—what happened to it?" he asked. The boy looked puzzled.

"You didn't find it next to the park?" Saeki asked, and then explained his question.

The boy nodded. "That's what you were looking for?"

But he hadn't seen the badge.

"If you don't have it, then where...?"

"When did you last see it?"

"At work, it was in my jacket pocket..." Then maybe... Another idea sprang to mind.

"Would you check her body for me?" Saeki asked, pointing toward the girl. He couldn't go near the hole where the girl and her boyfriend were. "She might have it."

He had covered the girl with his jacket in the car, and she had woken before he had buried her...

The boy left Saeki, passing by the quiet boyfriend. He bent over and checked the girl's pockets.

"Here it is," he said, standing up, badge in hand. "And this would be her student ID. It was in her skirt pocket."

The boy took them both back to Saeki.

So the girl had his badge all along. She'd probably kept it to identify her captor if she saw a chance to escape. After she was nailed into the box, she'd probably hoped the badge would be found with her, leading to her killer's arrest. And her actions had been the albatross that brought Saeki's destruction.

The girl had defeated him from underground. The moment he had buried her, he was already caught in her trap.

"Saeki, you're..." the boy said, staring down at the badge.

He knew what the boy was thinking. On his hands and knees, Saeki hung his head.

"Yes, I am."

He had not wanted anyone to see that.

Saeki could not look at the boy. The boy's gaze pained him, and all he could do was stare at the ground. Shame washed over him like fire, and his body shook, convulsing.

What the boy had found and brought out into the moonlight was a police badge in a brown leather case. On the front was the prefectural police department's name in gold lettering; when you opened it, there was a picture of Saeki above his name and rank.

This never should have happened. Saeki had worked hard, and people trusted him. As he made his rounds, he would exchange friendly greetings with the shopkeepers. Kousuke's parents had trusted him with their young son. There had been a time when he never doubted he was the kind of person who should be working a job like his. But he had betrayed the law, his position, the grandmother who had called him gentle, and everything that made up his world.

"Please... I know... so please, don't say anything..." he pleaded. His knees on the ground, his face down, Saeki heard footsteps coming toward him.

"Raise your head," the boy said.

Hesitantly, he obeyed. The boy was holding out the badge, offering it to him.

Saeki bowed his head and took it. He could not bring himself to stand and was stuck sitting *seiza*.

"Saeki, there's still something I want to ask. When I learned you had mixed up Morino and that girl, my first thought was that there had been a traffic accident. That seemed the most likely explanation for why you hadn't known what she looked like."

Saeki listened, his hands clutching his police badge tightly.

"But there was no blood on the ground, and there were no marks on your car. And when I checked the girl just now, she had clearly been hit, having broken a bone, but her only fatal injury was the one to her neck, which looked more like suicide. You didn't bury her there to hide the fact that you'd killed her by accident."

Saeki nodded. The boy put his hands on his knees, leaning forward. "So why did you bury her?"

He was not chastising Saeki for having driven a girl to her death. He simply sounded like this was something he wanted to know. Saeki could think of no clear answer to the question; after a long silence, he simply shook his head. "I have no idea. I buried her because I wanted to."

He was being honest.

Why had he killed Kousuke? Why had he been possessed by the terrifying urge to bury people alive?

There was no reason. Saeki had buried the two of them as if he had been born to do so.

"I buried them because I wanted to," he said again, his chest aching. This was not the answer a human being could produce. His hands shook, and he dropped his police badge. "I…"

How was he supposed to go on living? He had found his true self at last, and it was horrifying. What was someone like him supposed to do?

Why had he been born with such a tainted heart? Why was he not like other people? The more his mind flooded with questions, the more his heart flooded with sadness.

He had wanted to live like an ordinary person, one unable to receive any pleasure from murder. He had never wanted to fantasize about burying people alive, to dig holes in the middle of the night to calm himself… He had simply wanted to live a life that caused no harm.

He hadn't wanted much. He would've been content with very little. He'd just wanted an ordinary, normal life—like his colleague with the pressed shirts or his boss with the pictures of his kids on his desk. How much better things would have been if he'd been that lucky.

Tears spilled quietly down Saeki's cheeks. He sat there on his knees, the tears disappearing into the earth beneath him. He had no idea what to do next. The world was covered in darkness, and Saeki felt trapped in an invisible coffin, barely able to breathe.

†

For a moment, he lost track of time. Before he knew it, Saeki was sitting on the porch. it was still dark out, but he could hear the birds singing and knew it was almost dawn.

The lights were on inside, and someone was walking around. He lacked the energy to go investigate. His hands were still shaking.

He turned his head, and at last the boy passed across the brightly lit entrance.

Their eyes met, and the boy asked if he was feeling better. Apparently, the boy had helped him to the porch.

"I'm missing a few memories."

"You cried the whole time."

Saeki touched his cheek and found it still damp.

"I assumed you wouldn't mind if I came in," the boy explained.

Saeki looked out at the garden again. There was no sign of the hole he had dug, and there were four poles. For a second, he felt like none of it had happened.

"Those bamboo poles were designed to pass through the coffin lids, allowing the occupant to breathe, right?" the boy asked as he stood next to Saeki. Apparently, the boy had filled the hole back in. But why had the boy not called the police immediately? Why had he filled in the hole?

There was no sign of the girl's boyfriend. Was he sleeping somewhere inside the house, shut down like Saeki had been?

The girl in the ground had believed he would find her and that he wouldn't leave her alone. Saeki could never pay for the sin of having shattered their love.

Saeki turned to look back into the house.

The boy had his cell phone out and was calling someone, a student contact book in his hand.

"I just found your ID on the street," the boy explained. Clearly, he was calling the real Morino Yoru.

She apparently hung up as soon as he'd finished the sentence, as the boy was staring down at his phone, muttering, "Right, it's awfully early." Apparently, Morino was never to know the profound effect of her lost ID on Saeki's life.

The sky was turning pale. Looking east from his porch, Saeki could see the row of evergreens. Beyond the black shadows of the trees, the sky was glowing red. The white mist was gone.

The boy came and sat on Saeki's left.

They stared at the bamboo poles for a while. The trowel he'd used to fill in the hole was lying on the ground next to the boy.

The morning sun rose beyond the trees, striking the pale cheeks of the boy next to Saeki. Saeki blinked, blinded by the sudden brilliance. The boy's profile glittered, the rest of his face lost in shadow, making his eyes all the more memorable.

The boy's eyes had no emotion. They were utterly blank. They were exactly like Saeki's own eyes had looked when he'd seen his own face in the rearview mirror while he was out searching for a victim. They were eyes that contained unfathomable darkness.

Saeki felt his emotions quieting. His tears had long since faded, and he was no longer dizzy.

"I . . ." Saeki said.

The boy turned toward him, listening closely, backlit by the rising sun.

"I think I should tell the police what I've done," he said, the words spilling over his lips. All the tension faded out of him. Tears began to flow again. But this time, they were not tears of despair. They glittered, pure as the morning light.

This would be the end of his life. Many people would hate him, their glares stabbing his body. But he wouldn't mind. He would confess his own sins and wait to be judged—his final choice as a human being.

"I'm glad...I'm glad I could make that choice."

How many times had he mourned his own lack of humanity? How many times had he cursed his own nature, one that led him to do and imagine such terrible things? But now his remaining humanity had scored a quiet victory.

"I don't think my sins will vanish, but I'm proud to have made that choice."

The boy opened his mouth. "I won't stop you from turning yourself in, Saeki—but will you wait another six months?"

When he asked why, the boy stood up.

"I'm going home now. Saeki, wait six months—or if not that, at least one month. If you are at all grateful, then please. And tell the police that you did everything yourself and that you decided to turn yourself in all on your own."

He made Saeki swear not to say anything about Morino Yoru or the boy.

"Remember, this is what he wanted. You need not feel guilty about it. Even if you try to rescue him, he will refuse. But you must tell the world that it was your doing. I have left no proof, so nobody will believe I was here, even if you claim I was."

The boy slipped on his shoes, stepping off the porch.

Saeki could not understand what he was saying. Before he could ask, the boy left the porch, heading for the gate in silence, without saying goodbye, without turning around. He simply vanished into the evergreens, leaving only the morning, the garden, and Saeki behind.

Then Saeki realized... If the boy was going home alone, then where was the boyfriend, who Saeki had assumed was lying down in the house somewhere?

He stood up.

He had a hunch.

Staggering, he crossed the garden, barefoot, his breath turning white in the cold morning air.

The bamboo poles at the end of the garden were standing

perfectly upright under the brightening sky. The coffin the boy had buried again was under these poles.

Saeki put his ear to the top of the nearest pole.

He could hear a voice inside, muffled as it echoed across the coffin walls. Inside the coffin, a male voice was calling the name of his lover over and over again. A quiet voice, choked with sobs, it echoed the girl's name again and again.

VI
VOICE

prologue

Recently, my sister had begun waking up, washing her face, and immediately taking the dog for a walk. It was the end of November and quite chilly out, so she always left the house looking cold.

That morning, she headed for the door, shivering as usual. I was eating breakfast at the table, scanning the obituaries.

There was a kerosene heater in the corner of the room, which my mother had just lit, so the room stank of oil. It was the smell of brain cells dying. I had just that moment found an article about a child dying of carbon monoxide poisoning from a heater.

I opened the window to air the room out, and a wave of cold morning air came in, sweeping away the stench. The windows were fogged up, and there were traces of mist in the garden.

My sister was standing outside the window, wrapped in a sweater and scarf.

When I opened the window, her eyes met mine, and she waved. The dog was next to her, a leash running from its collar to her hand.

"I can't get her to leave. Something in the yard has all her attention," she said, pointing at the dog. The dog was next to the wall between our yard and the house next door. It was sniffing the ground, pawing at the ground as if getting ready to dig.

"Come on! We don't have time for that," she said, yanking

the leash. She had to get ready for school after the walk. The dog seemed to understand her, and it followed her out of sight, their breath visible in the air.

My mother told me to close the window. I did as I was told, and then I went outside.

There was a large stone at the edge of the garden. I moved it to the spot where the dog had been trying to dig; that would stop it from trying again. I didn't want it digging there—a few more minutes, and my sister would've found the human hands I'd buried there earlier that year. When I got home, I'd have to move them somewhere safer. I had just caught another glimpse of my sister's strange ability to stumble upon the unusual.

I went back inside and finished reading the paper. My mother asked if there were any interesting stories, and I shook my head— once again, there was no new information about Kitazawa Hiroko.

Seven weeks earlier, Kitazawa Hiroko's body had been found in an abandoned building not far from where I lived, within the city limits. The abandoned building had once been a hospital. It was in a deserted area, away from the city center and toward the mountains, at the end of a gravel path leading from the road. The building was surrounded by rusty chain-link fences and had been left there without being demolished. All year long, there was nothing around it but dried grass, no other buildings at all.

Three elementary school children had been exploring the building when they'd found Kitazawa Hiroko's corpse. All three were now in counseling.

When the body had first been discovered, the case was all over the papers and the news. But now they were mentioning Kitazawa Hiroko less and less frequently.

There was no way to tell what was going on with the investigation.

The articles I had found about her contained nothing but the story of how her body was found, along with a photo of her. I had cut these out of the paper as I found them.

The photo had been taken while she was alive. She was smiling, flashing white teeth, and she had straight black hair down to her shoulders. No other photographs of her had been released.

Did the police have any idea who had killed her?

By the time classes ended that evening, it was already dark. The florescent lights were on, and the windows reflected the classroom like a mirror. When the last class ended, the other students surged out of the room. In the windows, I could see one immobile figure in the middle of this raucous flood. She had long black hair, and her skin was so pale it was like she was made of snow. Morino Yoru.

Only the two of us remained.

"You want to show me something?" I asked. She had whispered as much to me in the hall after lunch, telling me to stick around after classes.

"I have obtained a photo of a dead body."

Everyone goes through life in his or her own way. You take a hundred people, you get one hundred ways of life, and all of them find it hard to understand any way of life but their own.

Morino and I had a unique way of life that was well beyond the ordinary. Exchanging pictures of corpses was simply part of this.

She produced a letter-sized piece of paper from her bag. There was a glossy look to the page; it was specialty paper, designed for printing photographs.

Printed on it was a bare concrete room—but the first thing I noticed was how red everything was.

In the center of the photo was an oblong table, the surface of which was red—as was the floor around it, and the ceiling, and the walls...not bright red, but dark red, the kind that wells up in the dark corner of your room after you turn out the lights.

She was placed on top of the central table. "Kitazawa Hiroko?" I asked.

Morino raised her eyebrows marginally. It was easy to overlook, but this was how she expressed surprise.

"I'm impressed you could tell."

"You got this off the Internet?"

"Someone gave it to me. I was cutting out newspaper articles concerning her in the public library when someone passing by gave it to me. Apparently, it's a picture of her—but I never would've guessed."

Morino Yoru was a beautiful girl, so boys from other schools would occasionally try to strike up a conversation with her. Nobody in our school ever went near her, though; they were all well aware that she had absolutely no interest.

Apparently, someone had seen her gathering strange articles in an unusual place like the library and had used that as an excuse.

She took the printed photo from my hand, looked at it closely, and narrowed her eyes. "How could you know it was her at first glance like that?"

"The girl in the photo...is barely recognizable as human." Morino whispered this, and I explained that I had simply guessed. Kitazawa Hiroko's head was on the table in the picture. I had made an educated guess based on the hairstyle and profile.

"Oh," she said, nodding.

I asked about the person who had given her the photo, but Morino didn't answer.

I would search for it online when I got home.

I looked away, out the window. There was nothing out there but darkness—deep, never-ending darkness. The classroom was bathed in white light, and the reflected rows of desks floated in the air outside.

"There are two kinds of humans: those who kill and those who are killed."

"Abrupt. What do you mean?"

It was clear enough that some humans killed other people or wanted to kill people for no reason at all. I didn't know if they became that way as they grew up or if they were simply born that way. The problem was, these people hid their true nature and lived ordinary lives. They were hidden in the world, appearing no different from ordinary humans.

But one day, they would have no choice but to kill. They would have to leave their acceptable lives and go hunting.

I was one of these people.

I had looked into the eyes of a number of killers. Those eyes would, on occasion, look something other than human. It was a subtle difference, barely noticeable, but in the depths of their eyes lurked something alien.

For example, when normal humans spoke to me, they would believe I was human and treat me accordingly.

But the killers I had met were different. When I looked into their eyes, I felt like they saw me as just another object, not a living human.

"So..."

I looked over at Morino's reflection.

"You didn't kill her, did you...? The girl in the photo has her hair curled and dyed—she looks nothing like the photo in the papers, so how did you recognize her?"

As I listened to Morino, I thought to myself that she was very sharp today.

In her eyes, there was no sign of that alien tinge I had seen in those of the killers I had met. She viewed humans as humans. She would probably never kill anyone. She might have unusual interests compared with other humans, but she was still normal.

Morino and I had many things in common—but on this, we differed. This difference was a fundamental one, the difference between humanity...and otherwise.

She was human, the side that always got killed. I was not.

"There was another picture, after she'd had her hair done. It was used without the permission of her family, so it wasn't widely circulated. I recognized her from that one."

"I see," she said, accepting this.

I went home and turned on the computer in my bedroom. I searched all corners of the net, looking for pictures of Kitazawa Hiroko's corpse. The air in the room grew stale and stuffy. I found nothing.

I took out the knives I had hidden behind my bookcase. I looked at the reflection of my face in the blade. I could hear the sound of the wind outside, and it sounded like the screams of the people these knives had killed.

It was like the knives had a will of their own and were calling to me. Or perhaps something in the depths of my heart was simply reflected in the mirror of the blade. I looked out the window, at the lights of the city in the darkness mingled with the pale lights of the sky above.

I heard a sound from the knife in my hand that it couldn't possibly have made. I felt sure it was the sound of the knife growing parched.

I had lied to Morino. There had not been any photographs circulated of Kitazawa Hiroko's new hairstyle.

i

Every now and then, members of my family had temporarily left the house, such as when my father had gone on a business trip or my mother had gone traveling with a friend; each time, the house seemed strangely emptier than it did when all four of us were living there. When I was away on a field trip, my parents and older sister might well have felt the same way, as if there was something missing, as if I should have been there. When the missing family member returned home, everything would be back to normal, and the four of us could see one another again. The house was the size we were used to, comfortably cramped in a way that allowed me to trip over my sister's outstretched legs when I passed in front of the TV.

There had been four of us... but now my sister was never coming back, and when we sat at the table together, there would always be an extra chair.

Nobody knew why my sister had been murdered, but my older sister, Kitazawa Hiroko, had died seven weeks ago. Someone had killed her twelve hours after we'd last seen her, and the body had been found in an abandoned hospital on the edge of the city.

GOTH   185

I'd never actually been inside that hospital, but I had once looked at it from the outside, after my sister had been discovered. It was a cold place, nothing there but dry grass. The ground was gravel, and the wind turned my shoes white with sand. The hospital was a big, derelict concrete square, looming like a massive cast-off shell. All the glass in the windows was broken, and it was dark inside.

It hadn't been long after my sister had been found inside that I'd seen the place, so the entrance was sealed with tape, and there were police going in and out.

My sister had been found in there by some children. The police had not released any information, but the room where she'd been found had once been an operating chamber.

The body had been badly damaged, and it had not been easy to identify, but they contacted us when they found her bag nearby. My mother had answered the phone.

It was around noon, less than a day since we'd last seen my sister, and my mother had assumed the call was a prank.

But the body was definitely my sister's. This was not determined by having those of us who knew her—me, my parents, and my sister's boyfriend, Akagi—identify her. Instead, they used medical charts and several complicated forensics tests.

The police didn't release many details about her condition when she was found or how she had been killed. The world only knew that she had been strangled and cut up with a knife of some kind. That was horrible enough for the news to make a fuss about it, but the truth was far worse.

The police apparently decided that the truth about what had happened to her would have a detrimental effect on society, and so they kept everything secret. Even the kids who had found her were ordered to keep silent.

My parents had demanded that the police and doctors show them her body. The authorities were reluctant. It was impossible to make her presentable, and they had decided we were better off not seeing her.

I don't believe my parents had ever doted on my sister exces-
sively while she was alive. Their relationship with her had been
an ordinary one: chatting about TV commercials, arguing about
where the newspaper had wandered off to... We were that kind of
family. They had never bragged about her, and I had never known
how much they loved her until I saw their faces covered in tears
when they learned of her death.

"Let us see her!" my father begged, desperate. His face was bright
red, and he looked positively furious. When the doctors and police
realized that he wouldn't back down, they reluctantly allowed my
parents to enter the room where the body lay.

I watched them vanishing through the double doors from the
hall. I was too terrified; I couldn't understand how anyone could
be brave enough to look at her.

I could hear a doctor and a police detective talking. They didn't
know I was standing in the shadow of the stairs.

The detective said it had taken ages to pick up all the pieces.

My shoes squeaked on the floor, and he turned around and saw
me. He bit his lip, wincing at his mistake.

The pieces of my sister's body. I stood there, letting the meaning
of those words sink in.

When my parents came out of the morgue, I asked about her
body. But they were completely stunned. They'd been crying so
hard before, but after they went in that room, neither one of them
ever cried again. They stared silently at the floor, not making eye
contact with anybody. It was like they had left their emotions in
that room. Their faces looked oddly yellow, like unmoving masks.

The police would say nothing about the body, and everything
about it remained inside a black box as far as the world was concerned. Because of that, the initial flurry of news reports soon died
down. Seven weeks after she was murdered, both the police and
the press stopped coming to our house.

†

My sister was two years older than me, merely twenty when she died. It was just the two of us, so I spent my whole life looking up to her.

When I was in the fifth grade, my sister started junior high, wearing her new uniform. When I was in eighth grade, she was talking about the whole new world that had opened up for her in high school. I could always see the life that lay in store for me two years later in my sister. My sister was like a ship forging ahead of me through the dark ocean.

There were two years between us, but we were almost the same height, which meant people often told us we looked alike. One year when we were kids, we'd gone to relatives' homes for New Year's, and everyone we met said the same thing.

"We do not!" my sister had said, looking as baffled as I was.

As far as we were concerned, our faces were totally different. Where was the resemblance? It always puzzled me. Yet on that trip, when I'd been playing with some kids my age on the opposite side of the house from my sister, a passing aunt had looked surprised, saying she was sure she'd just seen me playing somewhere else.

When we were kids, my sister and I had gotten along well, and we'd always played together. She would take my hand and take me along with her to the homes of friends her age.

When had that changed? I couldn't even remember when I'd last chatted and laughed with my sister.

A few years earlier, a tiny rift had opened between us. It wasn't anything obvious enough for anyone around us to notice. It might not have even really been big enough to call a rift. But when my sister was talking to me, she often looked slightly annoyed.

One time, I was on the living room sofa, and I pointed at the magazine I was reading, talking about the interesting article I'd just read. That was all I did, but my sister glanced at the magazine, frowned, said something vague, and then left the room. I felt like she was irritated with me and was trying to hide it, but I couldn't be sure.

Perhaps I had done something that rubbed her the wrong way, or she'd been in the middle of something when I'd spoken up. In this manner, I tried to convince myself that her behavior didn't have any real reason behind it.

Her irritation that time may have been my imagination, but that wasn't the only time this kind of behavior had occurred.

For example, another day, when I'd come home from school, she was talking to a friend on the phone, laughing into the cordless receiver. I sat on the sofa, watching TV quietly so as not to disrupt her conversation.

When she finally hung up, the room was suddenly quiet. We were each sitting on different sofas, facing each other, watching TV in silence. I wanted to say something to her, but there was something about her expression that made me hesitate. She had been having so much fun a moment before on the phone, but now that she was alone with me, she was suddenly sullen. The warmth had vanished from her, and invisible walls had gone up between us.

If I approached her and tried to talk to her, she would shut me out, looking angry. Whenever we did speak, her answers were curt, as if she was deliberately trying to end the conversations quickly, far faster than she would conversations with our mother.

I had no idea what was behind this, which scared me. My skin sensed my sister's foul temper before she even said anything, and I could no longer bear to be around her. Eventually, just passing in front of her or being in the same room became stressful, and I was tense all the time.

"Natsumi, you shouldn't wear that anymore," she said abruptly one day six months ago, as I was on my way out the door to buy some study guides at the bookstore. She pointed at the white wool cardigan I often wore when I went out. I'd been wearing it for years—and looking closely at it, there were a number of balls on it. It *was* getting pretty ragged.

"But I like it," I said.

She scowled at me. "Fine," she said, like she didn't give a damn about me anyway, and then she turned her back on me. I stood there feeling like all the light in the world was suddenly fading away.

The two of us might've looked a lot alike like people said, but our interests and personalities were polar opposites.

My sister was outgoing, had a boyfriend, and was always smiling. Her friends adored her, and when the phone rang, it was always for her. She was active, involved in any number of things, and barely ever just sat quietly around the house. Even in my eyes, she sparkled.

On the other hand, I was studying for exams. I spent all my time at my desk, and it felt like I had heard nothing for ages but the sound of the tip of my pencil wearing away. When I did have some free time, I just read historical novels.

Once my sister had started junior high and began leaving the house, spending her time in places I had never been to, with people I had never met, I began spending more and more time alone at home, reading. I had only ever left the house when she'd dragged me, anyway. But that change was only natural, as far as I was concerned, and I still loved my beautiful, outgoing sister.

I often compared my sister dashing around outside with myself sitting in the house like a rock. I didn't have much of an inferiority complex, though; I was proud to have such a great sister.

However, as far as she was concerned, I may have been an embarrassment. Without my realizing it, the way I lived may have been an issue for her.

She was nice. She never expressed her disappointment in me openly, and I'm sure all her behavior was to avoid doing just that. She never once said she didn't like me, and she seemed to be trying to disguise her irritation. That might have been why it took me so long to figure it out.

Maybe my sister didn't love me the way I thought she had...

I had no way of telling if that thought was true, but this depressing explanation was the only one I could think of.

Why? That one word was all I had to ask, but it was too late now. Why had I not worked up the courage to ask her while she was still alive? I might have regretted the answer I'd gotten, but it would have been better than this.

But my sister had lost the chance to speak forever. I was stuck with my question, and it would be with me every time I thought of her.

With my sister gone, the house was quiet, like night waiting for a dawn that never came. It was so different that you could hardly believe it was the same place it had been two months before.

My parents talked less since they had seen my sister's body. Their faces lacked emotion, and they spent a lot of time watching TV in stony silence. Even if the screen was displaying a comedy, they wouldn't laugh, wouldn't even smile happily—they'd just watch quietly. My parents might be like this for the rest of their lives; I thought that every time I looked at them.

They had the faces of people struggling under a burden so great that they would never truly be able to enjoy anything, no matter what happened to them.

My mother still made dinner. She cooked out of habit, as part of her routine, working mechanically.

But when I saw the piles of dust in the corners, it made me want to cry. I felt so sorry for them. My mother had kept the house spick-and-span while my sister was here. But now everything was covered in dust. They never even noticed. They must have been too busy remembering how my sister smiled when she was a child, remembering when they'd first held her in their arms, felt her weight.

In that house of silence, my presence went unnoticed. If I spoke to my father, he would nod absently, meaninglessly. But to anyone else, I must have looked just like my parents. My friends told me I never smiled anymore either.

At night, I sometimes went into my sister's room, sat on her chair, and thought about things. Her room was next to mine. If I had gone in there without permission when she was alive, she would have been furious.

But now no one used the room, and it was going to seed fast. If I put my hand down on her desk, it came away covered in grime.

When she was alive and sitting here, what had she thought about? I sat on her chair, knees against my chest, looking around at the furniture, wondering. The curtains were open, and the darkness of the night lay beyond.

I could see my sister's face in the window. For a moment, I thought it was her, but then I realized it was just my reflection. We really must have looked alike if I was mistaking myself for her.

There was a mirror on the shelf. I reached for it to study my face, but I saw a little cylinder lying next to it that looked like lipstick; I picked that up instead of the mirror.

It was red, like blood. There were any number of lipsticks lying around in different shades of pink, but the bloodred one absorbed me.

I didn't need to look at the mirror. The very act of owning a lipstick like that defined the difference between us. I left the room, clutching the lipstick tightly.

I didn't know how I would live the rest of my life. And it was in that frame of mind that, one evening in late November, I heard my sister's voice again.

ii

It was November 30. On the way home from school, I'd stopped by a big bookstore in town, as I needed to buy a book of problems related to college entrance exams. I had no great desire to go to college now. There were loads of things I'd wanted to learn when my sister was alive, but not anymore. I simply kept on studying for lack of anything else to do, going on just as I had been before.

The shelf with the workbooks was at the back of the store. I stood in front of it, gazing up at the top shelf and reading the spines in order from the left. When I got to the right end of the shelf, I dropped my eyes a shelf, looking for one that seemed like what I needed.

I didn't see any good matches, though, so I bent down, searching the bottom shelf. I checked each spine in turn, gradually moving my eyes from left to right . . . until they rested on a pair of shoes at the edge of my vision.

They were black shoes, pointed at me, standing with me in front of them. When I looked up, the shoes quickly moved away, vanishing into the rows of shelves.

I felt like someone had been staring at me. Feeling suddenly nervous, I looked back at the shelf.

This time, I felt someone standing behind me. The fluorescent lights were casting my fuzzy shadow on the shelves in front of me, and that shadow had just grown larger.

I hadn't heard any footsteps, yet someone was standing right behind me, close enough to touch. I could hear him breathing.

I knew he was going to try to grope me. I had heard from some-one else that it had happened in this store before. But I couldn't scream. I couldn't run away either. My legs wouldn't move. I was too scared to even turn around. My body was petrified, turned to stone.

"Excuse me," someone said suddenly, on my right. It was a young man's voice. "You would be a groper then? I saw you in the mirror—see the one fixed near the ceiling? Most interesting. But I need to get through here, so do you mind moving to one side?"

Relief that someone else had come worked like magic, freeing my body. When I turned toward the voice, I saw a boy in a black uniform standing between the shelves.

The person behind me quickly ran away, moving away from the boy. I saw his back. He looked like an ordinary man in a suit jacket, and he looked so comically flustered as he ran that all my fear quickly melted away.

"Thank you," I said, turning back toward the boy.

He was taller than me, and thin. There was something about

him that made him look rather frail. I recognized the black uniform he wore; I knew a boy who went to that same school.

"No need. I wasn't actually trying to help you," he said flatly, his expression never changing.

"You mean you really just wanted to get past?"

"I wanted to speak to you, actually. You're Kitazawa Natsumi, aren't you? You look a lot like your sister. I recognized you immediately."

This was so out of the blue that I couldn't form a response. Before I could say anything, the boy was already talking again.

"I met Hiroko before she died. She told me about you."

"Wait a second... Who are you?" That was all I could manage.

The boy didn't answer me. Instead, he took something from his uniform pocket—a plain brown envelope, the kind you could find anywhere. There was a bulge in the corner, something inside.

"This is for you," he said, holding it out. Confused, I took the envelope. I opened the flap and looked inside. There was a cassette tape in a clear case.

"Sorry, but could you remove the contents and give the envelope back to me?" I did as he asked, removing the tape and handing the empty envelope back to the boy. He folded it up and put it back in his pocket.

It was an ordinary cassette tape, the kind you could buy at any convenience store. There was a sticker on it that read, "Voice 1: Kitazawa Hiroko." It wasn't handwritten but had been printed.

"What is this? Why does it have my sister's name on it?"

"You'll understand when you listen to it. Kitazawa Hiroko gave that to me when she was still alive. I wanted you to hear it, so I kept it. There are two other tapes. I'm saving those for another time. If you tell anyone about me, that time will never come to pass."

The boy turned to leave.

"Wait..." I said, and I tried to follow him. But I couldn't do it. My legs wouldn't move; they were frozen, like they'd been when that groper had been standing behind me. I didn't know why I was responding this way; the boy hadn't threatened me—in fact, he'd rescued me. But without being consciously aware of it, my whole body had tensed up. I was sweating all over.

A moment later, the boy had turned the corner and was out of sight. I was left standing alone, holding the tape.

On the train back home, I sat down in my seat, staring at the tape he'd passed to me. The sun had already set, and it was dark outside. The windows were pitch-black, as if charcoal had been rubbed all over them, and I could see almost nothing through them. It felt like the train wasn't moving. The sun had already moved on to its winter schedule. When my sister was killed, it had still been light out in the evenings.

Who was that boy? He'd been wearing a high school uniform, so he must be my age, or a year or two younger. He'd claimed to know my sister, but she'd never mentioned him to me.

If he'd first met her only shortly before she died, then it was more than likely she hadn't had time to mention him, though.

He said she'd given him the tape. Did he mean my sister wanted me to hear what was on the tape? What did "Voice 1: Kitazawa Hiroko" mean?

The train slowed, and my body moved out of habit. I stood up and got off the train.

There were a lot of people around the station, but once I stepped onto the residential side street, there was nothing more than the asphalt road, shrouded in darkness. Shivering in the cold wind, I walked toward home. The only light in the darkness came from the houses on either side of the street. There was a family in each of them, seated at the dinner table, going about their lives—a notion that suddenly struck me as amazing.

The windows of my house were dark. However, this didn't mean that no one was home. I opened the front door and went into the living room, calling out to let my parents know I had returned.

They were sitting on the sofa, watching TV, not talking, not bothering to turn on the lights. The light from the screen was the only light in the room. I flipped the switch, and they looked toward me, listlessly welcoming me home.

"You forgot to lock the front door again," I said. My mother nodded absently before returning her gaze to the TV. There was no life in her at all; it was as if she no longer cared about anything.

They were not actually watching TV. Nothing shown on that screen reached their eyes. I turned my eyes away from the wrinkled clothes on their backs and went upstairs to my room.

Without changing out of my uniform, I dropped the bag on my bed and put the tape into my stereo. It was a small stereo, and a slightly bluish silver. It was on the second shelf from the top. I stood in front of it and took a deep breath to calm myself.

I remembered my sister's face—not how she'd looked at me around the time just before she died, annoyed, but how she'd looked when we were younger and she'd grinned at me as we'd walked hand in hand.

I pressed Play. There was a whir as the motors began to move, and the tape began to play. I stared at the speakers.

The first few seconds were silent, and then came a hiss, like wind. My heart was beating quickly, betraying my nervousness.

What I had thought was the wind was not—it was someone breathing into the microphone.

Natsumi...

Suddenly, I heard my sister's voice. She sounded very weak, exhausted—but it was definitely her voice. It must have been her breathing. The boy had not been lying. My sister really had left the tape for me.

Natsumi, will you ever hear this? Right now I'm talking into a microphone in front me, but I have no way of knowing if this message will ever reach you.

Where and when had she recorded this? Her voice was so thin that it almost vanished. She spoke slowly, haltingly, as if she was suffering, as if in desperation, leaving long silences between her words. But that made it sound all the more genuine—this was no scripted speech but an attempt to put her thoughts into words.

Listen, I've been allowed to leave you a message... told to say any-thing I want into the microphone, anything at all... but I can only speak to one person.

I thought of you instantly—I realized I have so much I need to tell you. I know it seems strange that I need to speak to you and not Akagi...

He's holding the microphone out toward me... I can't talk about him—he won't let me. Sorry. He said he would deliver this message to you. He wants to enjoy seeing how you react to my words. I think that's a really nasty thing to take pleasure from, but if my voice reaches you, I don't really care...

I couldn't move. A horrible suspicion was welling up inside me. A voice echoed through my head, warning me not to listen to any more of this. Terror awaited, and if I listened to that, I could never go back. So certain of this was I that I could barely stand it, and my breath came out like sobs.

I was not going to stop the tape. I stood perfectly still, listening to my sister's voice.

Natsumi, I'm in a dark room. I can't move. Concrete all around... It's cold... I'm on a table.

I slapped my hands over my mouth, fighting back a scream. I knew exactly where my sister had been when she'd spoken into this microphone.

My sister was speaking through her tears now, sniffling.

This is... some sort of abandoned building...

There was a mournful echo as her quiet voice bounced off the cold, dark concrete walls around her. Her pain pierced my heart.

Without realizing it, I had reached out toward the tape deck speakers, touching the mesh that covered them with trembling fingers as if trying to capture my sister's voice.

I'm sorry, Natsumi.

Her words passed through my fingertips and vanished. My fingers sensed the slightest of vibrations, like I had snared a slight portion of her voice. The sound of my sister's breathing vanished, and all sound faded from the speakers. The recording was finished.

I turned the tape over and listened to the other side, but there was nothing recorded on it.

I was sure this tape had been recorded just before my sister died. I remembered receiving the tape from the boy in the bookshop: the tape had been inside an envelope, and he'd made me take it out and give the envelope back.

He hadn't touched the tape, not even once. The entire exchange had been designed to avoid his leaving fingerprints. Had he been holding the microphone? Had he killed my sister?

I should give this to the police; that was the right thing to do. But I had no intention of doing so. As the boy had left, he'd told me not to tell the police if I wanted to hear the other tapes.

There was more to the message. I wanted to hear the rest.

†

Shortly after I heard the tape, I skipped school and went to where I could see the gates of M**** High School.

M**** High School was a public high school, and only two stations from mine. The gates faced onto a busy road, but a tall, dark green hedge surrounded the school itself. The hedge was neatly trimmed, and it looked like a flat green wall. Above it, I could only make out the white roof of the school.

There was a convenience store across the street from the school entrance, and I stood at its magazine rack, watching the gates through the window. I spent about an hour pretending to stand and read, until classes had finally ended, and students began pouring out. The sun was already low in the sky.

As the students left through the gates, almost all of them crossed the street, passing in front of me. The station was on this side, and the sidewalk was much wider. I was able to check their faces, one by one.

Watching the flood of students pass in front of me, I remembered my sister's voice.

I had listened to the tape again and again, and it had hit me just as hard each time. I couldn't sleep. I lay in bed, staring at the ceiling, thinking, but my thoughts took me nowhere.

My whole body felt woozy—from lack of sleep? As I turned the pages of the magazine, I glanced at the clerk, worried that he might be angry with me for standing here this long. Perhaps he even thought I was suspicious. I was scared he would say something.

I looked out the window in front of me. A group of five boys were passing by, talking happily, laughing. One of them met my eye.

He stopped in his tracks, surprised, and then he said something to his friends. I couldn't hear him through the glass, but he was presumably telling them to go on without him. They moved on, leaving him behind.

I straightened up a little.

He came into the store and jogged over to me. "Kitazawa? What are you doing here?"

His name was Kamiyama Itsuki, and I'd known him in junior high. He'd been a member of the basketball team, and I'd been the manager. He had a bright, cheerful smile, an expression like that of a puppy. He was taller than me, but the way he ran up to me was more puppy than dog.

"What, don't tell me you forgot me?"

I was so relieved he'd come up to me that I'd almost started crying. I suddenly realized how scared I'd been.

"Don't be silly, of course I didn't. It's been a while, Itsuki…"

I remembered my sister's funeral. Surrounded by relatives and my sister's college friends, Itsuki had come running over to me, the two of us in our high school uniforms. He'd stayed with me the whole time. He hadn't tried to cheer me up; he'd simply stood next to me. And that had been enough.

I'd remembered the crest on his uniform. That's why I had known the boy who gave me the tape went to M**** High School. I didn't know the boy's name, so the school was the only way I had to find him.

"I'm surprised to see you here. Waiting for someone?"

I could hardly tell him I was watching the gates, waiting for someone who probably killed my sister, so I shook my head, not that. I don't know what I must have looked like, but he grew serious.

"Something happen?" he asked, sounding concerned. "Or is it still your sister...?" He knew about the friction between us. I'd told him all about it at the funeral.

The picture at the funeral had been taken just before she'd died, and that had made me want to talk about it with someone. It was a beautiful head shot of her, but it had been taken after we'd stopped being close.

"Not my sister."

"But something's bothering you? You said you wanted to talk to her again..."

"Yes, but...forget about it. I'm sorry about dumping that on you at the funeral."

Itsuki looked at me with pity in his eyes. "Do the police have any idea who killed her?"

I stared at him.

"You just seem different."

He had such good instincts. I shook my head. "The police still haven't..."

"Oh," he said, sighing.

As he sighed, the one I'd been waiting for appeared. The sun had started to set while I'd been talking to Itsuki, and it was getting dark out. But I could still see his face clearly through the store window as he crossed the street.

I was not certain the boy had killed my sister—but when I saw him out of the corner of my eye, I was instantly terrified, as if I'd been suddenly plunged into total darkness.

He was walking next to a female student, a beautiful girl with long hair. Both of them were equally expressionless.

They passed in profile across the glass beyond the magazine rack. Itsuki followed my gaze, wondering why I had suddenly fallen silent.

"Morino," he said.

"Is that that boy's name?"

"No, the girl's name—she's pretty famous. A teacher tried to molest her, but apparently she kicked his ass."

Like Itsuki, they were both second-year students.

"Do you know the boy's name?" I asked, a little too urgently. Itsuki looked taken aback. "Uh, yeah, he's—"

He said a name, and I chiseled it into my brain, making sure I never forgot.

I put the magazine down and left the store. Cold air and exhaust fumes enveloped me.

I stood in front of the store, staring after him. I could see their backs as they headed toward the station.

She must have felt me staring, because the girl, Morino, turned around and looked right at me. She looked me over, and then she turned back around.

The shop door opened, and Itsuki came over. "I was in his class last year."

"What's he like?"

Itsuki stared at me for a moment, and then he shrugged. "I dunno...normal?"

I hesitated. Should I chase after him? But Itsuki was with me. And Morino was with him. This didn't seem like the time to ask questions about the tape of my sister's voice. I abandoned the idea.

"Something wrong?"

I shook my head. The two of us began walking to the station, the same direction they had gone. They were already out of sight.

The shop signs and vending machines lined up along the road glowed, their lights shining brightly. As we walked, the sun set, and the cold winter darkness thickened, the vending machines' light the only thing that remained distinct.

As we walked, Itsuki and I chatted about recent events in our lives. All I talked about was entrance exams, which seemed like a safe enough subject, whereas he had all kinds of funny anecdotes about school, his friends, places he'd been...

They were nothing extraordinary, just the normal stories any high school boy would tell, but they went a long way toward helping me relax. Perhaps Itsuki had noticed my tension, and he was deliberately trying to cheer me up.

Cars sped past us, their headlamps on, the lights flickering over our faces. "Want to talk in there?" Itsuki asked, pointing at the family restaurant in front of the station. Through the windows, it looked brightly lit and warm.

Inside, it was filled with the hum of people's voices as they ate their dinners. The waitress led us to a booth at the back. The partitions and wall were covered in silver decorations, which glittered in the lights above.

"How are your parents?" Itsuki asked.

I shook my head. "Not good. They never leave the house."

I told him what it had been like since my sister died: the dust in the corners, the TV on but the lights off, how they always forgot to lock the door.

"So they still aren't over Hiroko's—?"

"Yes, especially since they both saw...her body."

He nodded. I'd mentioned at the funeral that her condition had been far worse than the news had reported.

"Will they ever be better?" I murmured, picturing their blank faces. I couldn't imagine them recovering from that. All I could see was their slumped shoulders, the spark of life forever gone.

"What about Akagi?"

"He came by a number of times after the funeral, but recently..."

Akagi, my sister's boyfriend...he was one of those left most devastated by her murder. He attended the same college as her; although I wasn't completely certain, I thought he'd probably met her there. She'd brought him home with her, and I'd spoken to him a number of times. He'd stayed with my parents at the funeral, supporting them.

"Maybe I'm the one who killed Hiroko," he'd said after the funeral. "We had a fight the day before she died, and she ran out of my room, and..."

The next day, she'd been found in the abandoned hospital. Akagi was the last person to see her alive.

If they hadn't fought, she never would've met the killer, and she never would've died—that's what Akagi told me as he covered his face with his hands.

"I'd better be going," Itsuki said. It was time for his train.

"I'm going to sit and think awhile."

"Okay, so . . ." He took a step away, and then he turned back. "If you have anything you need to talk about, please call me."

As I watched him leave, I thanked him silently. I sat alone, sipping coffee, watching the family across the aisle. I didn't want to be too obvious about it, so I watched them out of the corner of my eye.

They were here eating dinner, a young couple with their kids, infant daughters.

They reminded me of my own family. The younger sister was too young to speak, and she kept her fingers in her mouth, watching everything wide-eyed. As I glanced sideways at them, I met her eye.

I remembered my sister.

When we were children, the two of us had gone on a long walk together. It must've been a warm spring day. I had just started elementary school, and the guardrails and posts towered over me.

We climbed a long hill, passing house after house. At the top of the hill was a forest. We looked down at the city below from the shade—tiny little houses, as far as we could see.

There was a bird in the sky above, with long white wings. A big river ran through town, so I decided that it must've lived there.

It glided on the wind, drifting elegantly, its big white wings barely moving. I watched it for ages without ever growing bored.

My sister looked at me and smiled, flashing her teeth. Her canines always jutted out, even after she got her big teeth in, and we often played vampires. But I hadn't seen my sister smile—hadn't seen her canines—for an awfully long time.

When she'd dyed her hair, I wondered aloud if I should do the same.

"Don't, it would look awful on you," she'd said. I couldn't take this as kind advice. There was an edge to her voice; she'd snapped at me.

Every time she did something like that, I felt like she didn't want me around. Why had she died? I couldn't believe anyone had hated her enough to kill her. And what was it she'd wanted to talk to me about before she died?

A shadow fell on my table. I looked up, and a boy in a black uniform was looking down at me. It was the boy who had passed in front of the store, walking with the girl named Morino.

"Kitazawa, you were waiting for me to leave school."

I was not terribly surprised. I felt it was only natural he would suddenly appear like this. I didn't stand up; I just looked up at him and asked, "Did you kill my sister?"

For a moment, he said nothing. At last, his lips parted quietly, and words emerged: "Yes, I killed her."

His quiet voice faded from my ears, fading into the soft hum of the restaurant.

iii

The boy sat down across from me, where Itsuki had been sitting. I couldn't move—it was like I was paralyzed. I just stared at him. But even if I had been able to move, I wouldn't have stopped him from sitting, I wouldn't have stood up and screamed.

"I killed her." The boy's words echoed through my mind. I had known it was possible, but my mind couldn't deal with the words as easily as my ears had. It was like too much water had been poured into a potted plant: his voice got stuck between my skull and my brain, the bulk of it sitting there unabsorbed.

He looked at me and cocked his head. Then he leaned forward slightly, his mouth moving. It seemed he was asking if I was okay. I could see his lips mouthing the words. He reached across the table and tried to touch my shoulder. My voice finally broke free just before he touched my clothes.

"Don't!"

I pulled back against the booth, getting as far from him as I could, pressing myself against the wall. This was not a conscious movement but an instinctive one.

Abruptly, all the light and noise of the restaurant turned back on. No, they didn't turn on—the music playing and the customers' voices had never stopped in the first place. They simply hadn't reached my eyes and ears. But to me, it felt like time had stopped and then started moving again.

Apparently, I had spoken loudly enough that the family across the aisle heard me. Both parents were frowning in my direction. When I met their gaze, they looked away awkwardly, returning to their conversation.

"Are you okay, Natsumi?" the boy asked, taking his arm away and sitting back on his seat. I resumed my original position and shook my head.

"No." My chest hurt. I wasn't crying, but there were tears in my voice. "Nothing's okay..."

My head was overheating. I couldn't figure out if I should be afraid of him or furious with him, but I was sure that the boy sitting across from me was more than I could handle.

As rattled and flustered as I was, he remained utterly calm, as though he were observing me scientifically, like I wasn't a human but an insect under his magnifying glass.

"Natsumi, I don't want you to scream," he said without the slightest flicker of emotion in his voice, like he had no heart at all. I knew the thing across the table from me was very frightening indeed.

"Why did you kill her...?"

This boy would never laugh like Itsuki or be surprised if someone unexpectedly dumped her problems on him. He was like a tree stripped of branches and leaves, reduced to the simple essence. A strange way of putting it, but that was how he felt to me.

"I don't know why I killed Hiroko, not really," he said slowly. "But it had nothing to do with her. All reasons for her death lay with me."

"With you?"

He said nothing for a moment, apparently lost in thought—but he never took his eyes off me. Finally, without saying a word, he jerked his chin at the family across the aisle.

"You were looking at them a moment ago?" The infant girls were laughing at each other.

"You were remembering the past, thinking about how much those girls are like you and Hiroko were? It brought back fun memories of your own childhood, and you stared at them the way you would a precious treasure."

"Stop it…"

I wanted to clap my hands over my ears to stop from hearing his voice. It was like he was climbing into my mind without even taking off his shoes.

"I have a sister myself. A dozen years ago, we must've gone out to dinner, much like that family. I don't remember it, but we must have done so. Does that surprise you?"

With each word he spoke, my heartbeat grew faster. It was like I was rumbling down a slope into an abyss, going faster and faster.

"Look at that little girl—carefully, though, so she doesn't see you looking," the boy said softly.

I took my eyes off him, glancing sidelong at the little girl in the seat across from me. She was sitting in the booth, her innocent eyes staring into the distance, her little fingers clinging tightly to her mother's clothes. I didn't know the girl, didn't know her name, but I found her lovable anyway.

"Natsumi, do you think that girl will kill someone, ten years from now?"

My heart froze. I turned back toward him to protest, but before I could say anything, he continued.

"She might kill her parents, or her sister. It isn't impossible. She may already be planning to do so. Perhaps she's only pretending to be childish. Perhaps she really wants to grab the knife off that hamburger plate and stab it into her mother's throat."

"Please...stop it. You're insane." I lowered my head, closing my ears tightly, fighting his words. Each word turned to pain as it reached me, like the words were slapping my cheeks.

"Natsumi, look at me... I'm kidding. That child most likely won't ever kill anybody. Everything I just said...described me."

I looked up and stared at him. He shimmered—there were tears in my eyes.

"That's the way I was born. When I was as small as that girl, I didn't understand that, but by the time I started elementary school, I knew I was different from other people."

"What are you talking about?" I stammered.

He explained, not looking the least bit annoyed. "About how I was destined to kill. That's the only way I can look at it. Just as a vampire has no choice but to drink human blood, I have no choice but to kill people. My fate was already decided the moment I was born. I wasn't abused by my parents and scarred mentally. I have no ancestors that were murderers. I was raised in a very ordinary household. But whereas ordinary children play alone with imaginary friends and pets, I spent my time staring at imaginary corpses."

"What are you?" I could no longer see him as human. He was something much more horrible, much more horrifying.

For a moment, he was quiet. Then he shook his head. "I don't know. I've thought about why I have to kill people, but I've found no answers. And I've had to keep it secret, pretending that I'm normal. I've been very careful not to let anybody see inside my heart."

"Not even your family?"

He nodded. "My family believes I'm an ordinary, normal boy. I've been extremely careful to carve that position out for myself."

"Your...whole life...is a lie?"

"Meaning that I could only believe that everything else was a lie." I didn't understand this.

He explained further, "I couldn't believe that the conversations my family had or the friendly attitudes of the people I knew were genuine. I was certain there had to be a script somewhere—and once, when I was very young, I searched the house for it. I wanted to read the same words everyone else was saying. But there was no script. The only thing that ever felt real to me was death."

"That's why I long...for human death." I saw him mouth those words.

"That's why my sister...?"

"That night, I was out walking, and I saw her sitting in front of a vending machine. She'd been crying, so I asked if she was all right, and she flashed her canines and thanked me."

He killed her because he'd liked those canines, he said. He claimed it was a twisted kind of love.

As I listened to him, I felt like I was tied to the restaurant booth. I looked at his hands where they lay on the table: white hands protruding from his black uniform sleeves, thin fingers, neatly trimmed nails. Those hands were clearly human hands. But seven weeks ago, those same hands had killed my sister.

"Because you liked her canines?"

He nodded, and then he took something out of the bag next to him: a small rectangle, small enough to fit in the palm of his hand.

"I set them in resin. I thought you might like to see."

He set the thing down on the table. It was a clear block. Inside were twenty little white things in a row. Two curved rows, one on top of the other, were suspended in the block.

"They were all over the room, and it took a while to find them all."

Teeth, fixed in resin so that they looked like they were floating in the clear block—like the dentures of an invisible man, each tooth in exactly the right place.

I recognized those jutting canines.

I heard children laughing. The shiny decorations glittered in the shop lights.

Next to my sister's teeth, the families peacefully eating dinner around us seemed like something out of a dream.

Weirdly, I wasn't scared, only sad. Nobody had told me she was missing all her teeth.

He put the block back in his bag and took out a notebook. "But all that is beside the point. Here's the second tape."

He opened the envelope, turning it upside down. The cassette tape fell out onto the table.

"Voice 2: Kitazawa Hiroko," said the printed label on the front.

"There's one more tape."

"Let me hear it."

He stood up and turned his back on me.

"Think about that when you finish the second tape."

After he left, I couldn't stand up for a good long time. I left the tape sitting on the table, remembering my sister's teeth in that clear block.

I took a sip of my coffee, which was cold. The girl at the table across the aisle was looking at me. There was ketchup on her mouth. She was staring at my hands with her pretty little eyes. The rattling noise the cup made in my shaking hand must have confused her.

On the train heading home from the restaurant, I sat curled up on the seat. I must've looked terrible; the middle-aged man across from me kept looking at me. I was afraid he was sneering at me. I was scared the other passengers or the conductor knew about the tape in my pocket, about my conversation with that terrifying boy, and that they were going to have words with me about it.

When I left the train, I ran down the dark residential streets. When I reached my house, the lights were on inside. These days, there was no telling if my parents would actually notice that the sun had set and respond by turning on the lights.

Just as I was about to open the door, it opened from the inside and someone stepped out. It was Akagi. He saw me standing outside the door and jumped.

"Oh, Natsumi," he said, mustering a feeble smile.

"Nice to see you here."

"I'm heading home now, but I was worried, so..."

Apparently, he'd stopped by after classes. I chatted with him awhile outside the house. He was a tall man; if I looked directly ahead from this distance, the top of his face—everything from the glasses up—was out of sight. I had to look up the whole time, which made my neck tired.

He knew a lot about books, and the floor on the second story of his home was creaking under the weight of them. We always had a lot to talk about. But today, I wasn't in the mood, and all we did was express concern for each other's well-being. I thanked him for thinking of my sister.

All the time we spoke, I was thinking about the tape. I knew I should let him hear her voice, and yet I said nothing.

"Well then, Natsumi...bye."

Akagi waved his long hand and left. I watched him go in silence, surprised by my own transformation.

Before, when I'd spoken to Akagi, I couldn't ever stay calm. My heart would bounce this way and that, never at rest. Every time he'd glanced at my sister, I'd feel dejected.

There was a lot I admired about him, but now my heart was silent, like a cold stone.

I rubbed the back of my neck, realizing that I hadn't even said goodbye. Before, I would've waved enthusiastically, shouting "See you again soon!" despite my neck pain.

The link between us was fading. With my sister's death, he was becoming a stranger again. I would've never known him if it wasn't for my sister, so perhaps that was only natural.

I doubted it was Akagi who was reluctant to maintain that relationship, though; if that were the case, he never would've come here.

I went inside, entering the freezing living room. My parents were sitting under the kotatsu. I told them I'd run into Akagi at the door, but they barely answered. I could feel my mood dropping like a heavy stone.

I went upstairs and into my room, closing the door. I took the tape out of my pocket and put it in the stereo, removing the original tape and putting it on top of my desk.

I pushed Play. I could hear the whir as the tape started. I sat down on the chair, staring at the stereo.

I found myself remembering the past, when we were both in elementary school and we were taking turns recording our voices. We'd been baffled by how strange our voices sounded on tape. Then our parents had come in, and we'd all sung a song together, recording it. It was a very childish song but one we'd loved to sing. My father often played that tape when were out driving as a family—even after my sister had entered junior high, and she'd start shrieking every time he put it on. My mother always laughed really hard at that.

It was so much fun.

Natsumi...

Tell Mom and Dad, and Akagi...thank you for everything. I'm sorry for all the trouble I've caused...

Or are they all listening to this tape with you? I don't know anything, anymore...

He...he's going to kill me after this. I thought he was joking at first...

Natsumi...I was left alone in the dark, blindfolded and gagged, until a minute ago.

Crying and screaming is pointless...and when I figured that out, I suddenly felt...regret.

I need to apologize... That's why I'm leaving you this message. I hate that it took something like this to make me realize.

You know how I sometimes said things to hurt you or to confuse you? You always looked so anxious when I did.

I'm sorry...none of that was your fault. I was just angry all on my own. You'll be disgusted when you hear why.

But if I die without saying anything, you'll never know the truth... I have to say it.

The tape went silent.

And then…not my sister's voice, but a familiar boy's voice…

Kitazawa Natsumi. At 11 p.m. on December 3. Come alone to the abandoned hospital where Hiroko died. You know the place, right? Come to the room where they found the body. I'll give you the last tape there.

His voice was the last thing on the tape.

†

December 3 came two days after I heard the second tape. In that time, I hadn't gone to the police. Instead, I'd gone about my life as I always did—going to school, studying for exams.

In the hall after class, a friend stopped me in the hall. "Natsumi, we should go somewhere this Sunday."

She seemed to be worried that I didn't smile much since my sister had died. She often tried to cheer me up.

"Okay…but if I end up not being able to, I'm sorry."

"You have plans?" she asked, puzzled.

I did not—but there was no guarantee I would come home alive that night. I planned to follow the instructions the boy had left on the tape. I'd made that decision the moment I first heard his message.

If I went to the abandoned hospital, I might get to hear the rest of my sister's message. In exchange, I might not come home alive. I didn't know why he had summoned me, but it might well be to kill me.

"No plans, but…" I said, suddenly wanting to throw my arms around her. What kind of life would she lead? Until a few days before, we'd both been utterly ordinary people. We'd gone to school yawning and then spent the day copying everything from the blackboard into our notebooks. Every day was the same. These were ordinary, happy lives.

But now I didn't believe that life lay before me. I'd spent too much time with death to lead a peaceful life. My friend still had a future, though, and when I thought about how I might never see her again...I loved her very much indeed.

"See you tomorrow," I said, waving.

I left the school, feeling the cold December wind against my cheeks. The sun was not yet setting, but there were gray clouds covering the sky, and it was pretty dark out. I held my coat tightly closed, watching my feet as I walked.

My phone rang near the school gates. It was Itsuki.

"Now? School just finished. I'm just going through the gates."

I stopped next to the gates as I talked to him. There were cars rushing by, and it was hard to hear him between the traffic and the wind.

"What did you say? I can't hear," I said, louder. "Oh, yeah, thanks again for... No, I'm fine..."

This might well be the last time I ever spoke to him. The thought made me want to sob into my phone loud enough to be heard over the roar of the wind and traffic. I'd known Itsuki since junior high, and he was like a little brother.

"Can you talk louder?" I closed my eyes, trying to pick his voice out of the din. "I said I'm fine... I didn't mean to make you worry. Hmm? No, I'm not crying..." Our conversation ended a moment later.

I checked my watch on the train home. It was already five. The sun had begun to set on the road to the station, and it was dark outside. I had six hours until I would meet that boy.

I didn't know why, but I wasn't shaking with fear. My heart was calm, and I sat with my eyes closed, feeling the movement of the train. My senses were already shut down in the face of the danger to come. My sister's teeth in the restaurant had been the anesthetic. Everything felt numb, nothing felt real.

I had never even considered trying to fight the boy. I would go to the hospital without any weapons, without telling anybody. All I cared about was hearing my sister's voice. I needed nothing else—even if that boy planned to harm me.

My parents had forgotten to lock the door again. I went inside and told them I was home.

My mother was in the tatami room, folding laundry. She smiled faintly when I spoke to her, but she looked like she would topple over if I nudged her.

My father was in the living room, slumped over the kotatsu. I couldn't see his face. When we were kids, my sister and I would hang from his arms. His tiny back reminded me just how long ago that had been.

"I'm home, Dad," I said, kneeling down next to him. He didn't respond. Thinking he was asleep, I rose to leave.

"Natsumi," he said. "I'm sorry... we're making you worry."

"What are you talking about?" I had said the same thing to my friends today.

"People always told us you looked like Hiroko, but I never realized how much you do. I never noticed while Hiroko was alive, but now that there's only you... they're right."

My father raised his head and looked at me. He said he sometimes mistook me for my dead sister. His eyes were half-kind, half-sad.

"But, Natsumi... did you just come home from school?" I nodded. He looked puzzled.

"I thought I heard someone going upstairs..."

"Not Mom?"

"She was in here."

The footsteps had come in without the doorbell ringing first, so they'd assumed it was me.

I went upstairs to my room. The tapes were gone.

That boy must have snuck in and taken them away. I could imagine him doing that easily.

If I hadn't come home that night, the police would've found the tapes in my room, and they would find out about him. He'd taken them to prevent that scenario from occurring.

That meant he didn't plan to let me come home.

I felt like all the strength was flowing out of me. I sat down heavily on the chair.

For two days now, I had guessed I would be murdered. And now I knew for certain.

If I followed the instructions on the tape and went to the hospital, I would die.

What was death? That boy had said death was the only thing that really existed.

He had to experience people's deaths the way a vampire had to drink blood.

For a long time, I sat on my chair, not moving at all. Silence surrounded me. I tried to imagine him killing my sister. Soon, my own face replaced my sister's. But it was not as big a shock as I had expected.

Once, I had seen a firm divide between life and death. I was alive. My sister, my parents, everyone was alive. That had been obvious. Now that divide had become very fuzzy, like white and black had mixed together and formed gray where I stood. My parents had been the same since they saw her body: one foot in the world of the dead, frozen there.

But my sister...my sister was definitely dead. To me, the recording of her voice was alive, though. She existed on those tapes; she was still breathing, still thinking, still trying to speak—and waiting for me.

I could no longer understand what separated life from death. But I knew I was standing right on top of it.

"Natsumi," my mother called from downstairs. "Dinner!"

I stood up and tried to say, "Coming!" If I didn't go, it would be just the two of them. They would be too exposed.

We were all a mess since my sister's death, but we'd been careful to eat together as much as possible. Although the extra chair kept us from saying much of anything, meals were the last thing that kept us feeling like a family.

Today, however, I started to stand, and then I stopped halfway.

"Natsumi?" my mother called again, surprised that I hadn't responded. Remembering how my father had looked at me, I felt like I wouldn't be able to go to the hospital if I ate with them. If

I didn't come home, how would they survive? Love—or perhaps pity—would be a chain, keeping me here.

"Dinner?" she called again.

My eyes found a cylinder on my desk. I stared at it, unable to take my eyes off it.

It was the bloodred lipstick I'd taken from my sister's room.

I closed my eyes and made up my mind. I sat back in the chair. "I'm not hungry," I said.

The door was closed, and I couldn't see my mother, but I could sense her presence: she stood at the bottom of the stairs staring up at my door for a long time.

Guilt pierced my heart, and I clutched my chest. When my mother knew her daughter was not coming down, her shoulders slumped, and she moved away from the stairs. I could almost see her.

I sat on the chair, apologizing to my parents again and again. But no matter what, I would not change my decision. I was a terrible child. I was going to that hospital, and I was leaving them alone.

iv

Late that night, I got up and put on my coat.

I picked up a toy rabbit from my shelf. I had loved this toy when I was little. I brushed its head, feeling how soft it was. It had been in my room since I was very young. Now I said goodbye to it. I placed it back on the shelf, and I put my sister's lipstick in my coat pocket; I was bringing it with me so I wouldn't lose my resolve.

I also took a flashlight, and then I left the house quietly, making sure my parents didn't notice. If they had called out, I would never have been able to leave. But no voices came.

The abandoned hospital where my sister's body was found was twenty minutes away by bicycle. I rode along a small road with no streetlights. It was dark all around, the light on my red bike the only break in the darkness.

My sister and I had shared this bike. One of us had crashed into something, and the basket was bent. I didn't remember crashing, so it had probably been her fault. It was a red bike, which reminded me of Little Red Riding Hood. It was like I was that little girl—only I was going to my grandmother's house knowing full well there was a wolf waiting for me there.

The sky was brighter than my surroundings. I could see the divide between the sky and the earth distinctly. The asphalt road was headed toward the mountains, and it soon gave way to gravel. I got off the bike there. As I walked, I found a fence with a sign that read, NO TRESPASSING.

The hospital was beyond that fence, but too far away for my flashlight to reach.

The light vanished, swallowed by the darkness. There were no houses or shops around, no little points of light in the distance—nothing but dry grass. Without wind to shake that grass, it was utterly quiet.

I parked my bike and made my way toward the fence, carrying only the flashlight. Gravel crunched underfoot. My breath produced white clouds, which faded quickly. There was a gate in the fence across the road, which opened easily when I pushed it. I stepped through.

The night my sister died, how had she arrived here? Had she walked in through the gate like I just had? Maybe the boy had held a knife to her and forced her to. Or had she been unconscious? Carried here, helplessly? The road to this hospital had been a one-way street for her, leading to her final destination.

Had this been a parking lot once? It was big enough. The long beam of my flashlight stretched across dry earth and gravel. In the distance was a massive white lump of concrete—two stories, hulking against the night sky. The building had once been a hospital, but now only the frame remained—like a dinosaur fossil, reduced to bones alone.

I stepped in through the entrance. Once there had been glass doors here, but now there was just an empty square mouth. I ran my flashlight around the lobby. I could barely recognize the benches, and there were lumps of concrete everywhere. The round beam picked walls out of the darkness, tracing the shapes scrawled there in spray paint.

My breathing had grown very shallow, and I felt out of breath. The ceiling above me went on forever, and it seemed to be pressing down on me from above. There were traces of the light fixtures here and there, with broken florescent lights underneath. I didn't notice until I stepped on one and heard the glass shatter underfoot.

The hallway went on into the darkness. I moved forward, headed for the room where my sister had died. I had a general idea where it was: on the first floor, in the back.

It had been the operating chamber. I followed signs pointing to that location. My footsteps echoed off the walls, shaking the cold winter air.

I finally found the room at the end of the hall. The doors were gone, replaced by a square hole that opened onto darkness. I stepped through, and there was another empty doorway immediately behind it. Beyond that was empty space.

I ran the flashlight beam around the room. It was cold and lonely enough to freeze one's very heart. It was so quiet that even the sound of a pebble rolling echoed. I felt like I could almost hear an isolated soul crying softly in the darkness.

There were long, thin sinks along the side of the room, for washing hands. And there were several doors leading to smaller rooms along the wall. Beyond those were the operating chambers— smaller rooms, three in all. I checked them each with the light.

There was no one here. The smaller rooms were only about fifteen feet wide. The first two were completely empty, but when I opened the third door, the farthest one, I froze in my tracks, sensing something sinister.

It was darker than the other room—much darker. The walls and ceiling and floor were all black, as if there'd been a fire.

I stepped into the room, making sure there was no one there.

The door was constructed to swing shut on its own if you didn't hold it, so it closed behind me as I stepped in. There was a row of cylinders along the wall, chained in place to keep them upright. In the center was a rusty metal bed: an operating table.

It was then I realized that the walls and ceiling hadn't been burned. That black stain started from the central table, spread out to the floor under my feet, covered the floor of the room, and reached out under the door.

Before I knew it, I had my back to the wall, my free hand over my mouth, and I was trying not to scream. That black stain was the blood that had flowed out of my sister two months before.

In the darkness, I had almost seen her, the pieces of what had once been my sister, the ones the police had been forced to clean up.

Natsumi...

Will you ever hear this?

Suddenly, I heard my sister's voice, right next to me. They were the first words from the first tape. I turned my flashlight toward the door of the room. In the round beam, I saw the door closing, as if someone had just stepped through it.

"Kitazawa Natsumi." The boy's voice came from the other side of the operating table, from the far wall. The entire area suddenly lit up, blinding me.

Against the light stood the boy—not in his uniform, but still dressed head to foot in black. The light in his hand was much more powerful than my flashlight. His other hand held a tape player, a tiny little thing. My sister's voice was coming out of that.

He said he would deliver this message to you. He wants to enjoy seeing how you react to my words.

My sister's voice played on, very loudly. Her ragged breathing echoed a little off the concrete walls, filling the bloodstained room. I looked at the operating table in the center of the room, where the bloodstains were darkest. It was a dark shadow across the otherwise empty room.

"Hiroko recorded this tape while lying on this table."

The boy put the light and tape player down in the corner and moved over to the table. He stroked the black stain with his hand, lovingly.

"Why did you make me come here?" I asked, my voice trembling.

The operating table had been covered with black leather, but now it was splitting, and only part of it was left. Part of it had been cut away entirely, exposing the metal frame. The black stain covered everything, and the boy's fingers ran softly across it. I could almost hear the faint sound of his fingers stroking the bloodstain. It gave me goose bumps, as if it was me he was touching.

"Like Hiroko just said, I was curious to see how you would react when you heard the tape."

Staring at me, the boy tapped the operating table twice with one hand—quietly, wordlessly. His eyes made it clear what he wanted me to do.

My back against the wall, I slowly shook my head. If I moved toward him, I would die. I would be killed like my sister. But it was not fear that made me refuse.

Standing quietly next to the operating table, the light made him look like he was floating in the darkness. His profile was lit so brightly that he seemed almost divine. I felt less fear than awe, like of some higher being dealing out death that was meaningless, indiscriminate, and absurd.

You know how I sometimes said things to hurt you or to confuse you?

"Natsumi, come here," the boy said.

He was telling me to climb onto the operating table. He was only three steps away.

If he moved quickly, he could easily grab me, could easily overpower me. But he didn't move. He simply waited for me to come over to him.

My legs almost did as he wanted. Deep down inside me, I felt a strange certainty that I had to do as he asked. When I realized that, it startled me.

Why would I go to him of my own accord? I kept my back against the wall, staring at him, confused.

Logically, he explained, "Narsumi, you already know."

"What?" I asked, puzzled.

"That I'm going to kill you. And you've already decided to let me."

My sister's trembling voice, her breath ragged, washed over us. The boy stared at me, barely even blinking, his gaze so penetrative it was like he was looking right into my head.

"You are attracted to death...and you came here all on your own."

"That's not true," I insisted.

The boy narrowed his eyes. "I believe that death means 'loss,'" he said quietly. "At the moment of death, all connections dying people have with the world around them are severed. Everything that bound them to those they loved, those they cared about, vanishes. They will never again see the sun, feel the wind, sense darkness or silence. Joy, grief, happiness, despair—they lose all connection to those things. Natsumi, I know exactly what you went through when you decided to come here."

I had my head in my hands. The flashlight I'd been holding was rolling across the floor. I remembered my parents, Itsuki, my classmates, Akagi.

"It must have been hard to come here—but you made up your mind. You know how much your parents will grieve if you don't come back home, yet you came anyway. You severed all connections, said your silent goodbyes, and came to hear a dead person's voice."

The boy's words stabbed right into the place that shook me the most. A voiceless something escaped my lips, something between a scream and a groan. My hands on my head, I forced it back.

Natsumi, the reason I made things hard for you really was of no significance. It was about Akagi.

What I had done was abandon my parents, even though they were already damaged by the loss of their eldest daughter. Guilt raged through me like a wildfire.

"You had two days after I gave you the second tape. During

that time, you said goodbye to everyone you met—and as you bid farewell to everyone and everything connected to your life, you moved steadily toward your death."

Finally, I realized it: Everything I had done since I met the boy was a slow-motion suicide. When I'd left the house without telling my parents, I'd left behind my last chance to turn back. I had chosen to sever the heaviest chains binding me to this world... and to come here.

I never told you how I met Akagi, did I?

"I..."

I lowered my hands and looked around me. The cold concrete room was filled with empty darkness. There was nothing in it but the bloodstained operating table and the boy—a very lonely place.

My feet moved. My back left the wall, and I stepped toward the operating table.

I had abandoned everything in my life of my own free will. Nothing mattered but my sister's voice. Could I even be considered alive, right at this moment? My flesh was still functioning, but I was halfway into the land of the dead already.

He came up to me on the street. I only found out we went to the same college later.

I was standing across the table from the boy now. He never once moved a muscle, merely prying all hesitation out of me with words alone.

The boy stared at me, so close to me now, looking down at me slightly, as he was taller.

"I first found out that you existed when Hiroko made this tape. Ever since, I've been wanting to meet you," he whispered. "You really do look like her."

My sister's voice echoed through the room, vanishing into the silent building. "I know why you gave me the tape, why you had to bring me here," I said.

He looked intrigued.

"You aren't doing this for fun, are you? Not for cheap thrills. You said so yourself, in the restaurant. Everything other people say seems like it's scripted—everything seems fake...and only death seems real."

After we started going out, Akagi said that he'd often seen me in the bookstore, and that's when he first got interested. I was always in a white wool jacket, standing in front of the historical fiction shelf, he said...

This boy had killed people. And he felt absolutely no guilt about it. I knew I shouldn't feel any sympathy for him, but even so...I did feel a little sorry for him.

"You wanted to see if I would try to recover my relationship with her, even if that meant accepting death. Trying to understand that which you cannot."

For a long moment, he stared at me without expression. There were no words, only my sister's voice echoing through the room. There was no way for me to tell what he was feeling.

You see? Akagi saw you first.

At long last, he placed his hands on the operating table. "Sit here, Natsumi."

Feeling no fear, I sat down on the table stained with my sister's blood, my back to the boy. I could feel him standing behind me.

The table was cold, and the chill passed right through the fabric of my jeans. I was about to die, but I felt peaceful, like a calm sea.

My hands gripped the edges of the table, feeling my sister's dried blood. I couldn't move. Or I felt no desire to move, so it felt like I couldn't move. Everything felt cold and stiff, down to my fingers.

The light was behind me. I could see our shadows on the wall in front of me. The boy's shadow half covered my own, standing slightly to one side.

We always dressed the same, and people always told us we looked alike... Akagi had called out to me by accident, thinking I was you.

The boy's shadow moved. He raised his arm, his shadow rising over mine.

His arm came across my field of vision, and I could no longer see anything. I was trapped in darkness, embraced from behind, with one arm around my neck, the other covering my face. If he squeezed, my neck would break with a snap. My breath brushed against his arm. I could feel the heat of my own breath. The boy's chest was against my back. I could feel his warmth through my clothes.

"Please...let me hear the rest of her message."

I could hear her voice, even with the boy's arms over my ears. I had never heard this about Akagi. It was like a thread unraveling, explaining everything about my sister's strange behavior.

The joints of the arm around my throat contracted and expanded, as if testing the bones inside. The arm over my face was ready to break my neck, moving my head back and forth, like an athlete warming up for a short-distance run.

My neck felt like the stem of a delicate flower. It would snap so easily if someone went to pick that flower.

Even after I knew the truth, there were no problems between us. That had merely marked the start, and real love had bloomed between the two of us. It was me he loved, what lay inside of me...

But I was nervous.

My chest hurt, listening to her quiet voice.

"You might be right," the boy whispered softly. His voice came from right next to me, his arms around my head. I could feel his chest vibrate as it pressed against my back. My heart beat faster.

"I had two candidates for my second victim...one was Kitazawa Natsumi, and the other was a girl at my school."

"Morino? I saw you walking with her..."

My voice sounded muffled, blocked by his arm. My heart was beating faster and faster, and blood was racing through my veins. Gentle pressure on my throat, my veins pulsing—my head grew hot.

"Kamiyama Itsuki told you her name, right? In the end, I chose you as my next victim, and that might have been for the reason you mentioned."

The voice at my ear seemed less like he was telling me and more like he was asking himself. Perhaps he didn't clearly understand the workings of his own mind. The thought, strangely enough, made me feel like we were friends.

I never told Akagi, either... that he had seen you, not me. I couldn't tell him.

I had been so blind. I had known nothing about my sister. Wrapped in the boy's arms, listening to her monologue, I was overcome with shame.

I had been so sure she was filled with confidence I didn't have. I thought she'd been bright, outgoing—a strong girl whom everyone loved. But the truth had been so very different...

I couldn't even look at you... We're so very much alike. I directed all my irritation at you, changing my hair and clothes so I would be less like you... because I knew how you felt about Akagi.

My sister had actually been locked in a constant struggle with her own fears and anxieties. Unable to tell me about Akagi, she'd clutched that secret to her heart. The lipstick in my pocket... she had used that to hide her own fears from the world around her.

I wished I'd noticed while she was alive. If I'd only known, I could've put my arms around her and assured her there was nothing to be nervous about.

His arms tightened. He was done warming up. He began to embrace my head tightly. My head was squeezed inside his arms. In the darkness, I felt less like I was about to die and more like I was wrapped in a loving embrace.

When my sister's voice ended, my neck would be forcibly twisted. The arm tightening around my throat and twisting my head would put too much pressure on the bones in my neck, and they would snap. Somehow, I was sure he would time my death to that moment.

Even as I record my last words like this, I wish... I wish I'd told you all of this, months ago.

With his arm as my blindfold, I could heart my heartbeat getting louder. I could hear it pumping blood through my body as clearly as I could hear my sister's voice.

I could feel his heartbeat too—feel it where his chest pressed against my back.

I felt a tightness in my chest, like I wanted to cry. I felt no hatred or anger toward him; he felt like something as inevitable as death itself.

My sister's confession was almost over. I could tell from the tension in his arms and the strain in her voice.

I was glad I'd heard the tape.

"You knew you were going to kill me...that's why you came to my house to get the tapes, so the police wouldn't find them when I didn't come home," I said, careful not to talk over my sister. She had left me these words as the last thing before dying. It was my duty to hear every last word of it.

But I can't turn back time. Natsumi...I did love you.

"Natsumi," the boy said, the arm around my neck loosening. The tension in his muscles slackened, weakened. I hadn't expected this, and I was confused. "I've never been in your house."

I couldn't understand him at first. He hadn't taken the tapes? Before I could ask, there was a sound at the entrance of the operating chamber.

Someone had stepped into the room.

His arms might have loosened, but they were still wrapped around my face, and I could see nothing. I couldn't see the third person in the room. His arms were tight enough that I couldn't move, either—all I could do was listen to this new set of footfalls.

"Who...?" I gasped.

The footsteps came through the door, past the operating table where the boy and I were. I could hear them on the dusty linoleum floor.

The boy slowly unwrapped his arms from my head. I was free. I could see again—there were now three shadows on the wall in front of me.

I said a lot of things that made you sad...but none of it was your fault.

Not me, not the boy, but the third shadow bent over. I heard him press Stop. My sister's voice vanished. The room was quiet again.

Still seated on the table, I turned my head. The boy was behind me, his back to me, looking at the back of the room. Beyond him, next to the wall, stood Itsuki.

Itsuki was just taking his finger off the tape deck's button. "I took the tapes, Natsumi."

I had assumed I would never hear his voice again. Why was he here? Was I imagining this? No, he was definitely real: The light was casting his shadow on the wall. He was no illusion.

"The hospital is so large that I had trouble finding you. If I hadn't heard Hiroko's voice, I might never have known where you two were."

I remembered him calling that evening. I'd told him I was outside my school because he'd asked where I was. He'd been making sure I wouldn't come home while he was in my room.

In the restaurant, I'd told him how my parents always forgot to lock the door.

That was how he'd gotten in so easily. And he'd found the cassette tapes with the sinister names. That explained what he was doing here. The end of the second tape had given the time and place.

"Kamiyama. Haven't seen you in a while," the boy behind me said, putting his hand on my left shoulder. His palm was very hot. Then he stepped away from the operating cable, facing Itsuki. The hand on my shoulder went with him. I couldn't move the whole time. I just sat frozen, staring at Itsuki.

"Hello," Itsuki said, addressing the boy by name, never once taking his eyes off him. From his profile, you would think he had forgotten I was even there.

They faced each other silently, standing on opposite sides of the room. The operating chamber filled with soundless tension. It was so quiet that my ears hurt.

I longed for my sister's voice. Sitting on the table, I looked down at Itsuki's feet.

The tape was still in the player.

I sent a signal to the fingers gripping the cold edge of the table, telling them to move. They seemed to be paralyzed, and they wouldn't budge.

"You came here to save her?" the boy asked. His voice broke the silence, but it only seemed to add to the pressure, the overbearing tension in the air.

I told my muscles to move again, but my fingers, my legs— nothing responded to my will. My heart was beating quickly, but it was like the rest of me had been drugged.

I closed my eyes, took a deep breath, and prayed.

Please move. Let me walk to that tape player... My fingers shuddered, shaking.

"Was I interrupting something?" Itsuki's voice.

Now that my fingers were moving, they set off a chain reaction, and my arms and legs woke up as well. But my muscles were very tense. They were moving, but I couldn't put any strength into them. Even so, I managed to fall over the bloodstained edge of the operating table onto the floor below. As I moved away from the table where my sister had died, I felt vaguely like I was alive.

My legs were shaking too much to stand. I crawled across the linoleum, all my weight on my arms, my legs dragging after me. All the dust on the floor ended up on me. Around the operating table, toward the tape deck next to Itsuki's feet... Itsuki and the boy were still talking, but I could no longer hear any of it. Scrabbling like an insect across the floor, I thought of nothing but the tape.

A jagged fragment of concrete stabbed my arm as I put my weight on it, but I didn't care.

The boy had described death as loss. He said I'd abandoned everything, choosing to die.

But I wasn't dead yet. I hadn't yet abandoned life. I had come to this abandoned building to get something back, to overcome that loss.

As I drew near the tape deck, I thought hard about my sister.

The light next to the tape deck blinded me. Itsuki's feet moved, crossing in front of the light. His shadow passed over me, moving out of sight. I didn't turn my head to follow him.

At last, I was close enough that I could reach out and touch the tape deck. I stretched myself out, my fingers brushing against it. I dragged it quickly to my breast and pressed Play, fingers trembling.

There was a whirr as it came to life again. My sister's voice emerged from the wire mesh over the speaker. Not shaking the air—the vibrations of her voice went directly into my arms as they clutched the tape deck.

Natsumi, I was always worried about you. Every time I said something mean, I regretted it... I'm sorry I ever upset you.

These last few years, we had never been friendly. We had lived like strangers in the same house. I had thought she hated me.

Perhaps leaving a message like this just makes things worse... I'm sure it does. I would be a mess listening to it. But I'm glad I could apologize, before... I mean, I would hate it if you could never smile when you thought about me.

I curled up on the floor, clutching the tape deck to me, listening to the voice of my beloved sister. In my arms was the same sister I had been so close to.

I'm lying here remembering everything we did together when we were kids.

I closed my eyes, listening.

There was a big forest at the top of the hill...

I remembered what we had seen when we were little.

The darkness, the cold concrete walls... it all faded away, and I was standing on the asphalt road, bathed in sunlight.

The guardrail, the posts—they were all so big. I was wearing tiny children's shoes, and the hill looked so steep. Houses on one side and nothing but the guardrail on the other, a great view of the town beyond it...

You remember walking up it, hand in hand?

I turned around, hearing a familiar child's voice. My sister was standing there.

She wasn't much taller than me, and everyone we met said we looked alike.

My sister took my hand in hers. She pointed to the top of the hill, suggesting we climb up there.

I was excited. I ran after her, pulled along by her hand. Warm sunlight left little shadows racing after us, our sneakers squeaking on the concrete as we headed for the tall trees at the top of the hill.

At the top of the hill we stepped into the forest, our sweat drying in the cool air. We walked between trees until we found a cliff with a beautiful view of the town below. We stood looking down, holding hands.

I felt her tiny, warm hand in mine. Standing next to me, she looked at me and smiled, her canines flashing from the corners of her mouth.

There was a bird flying high above the town...

A white bird, its wings stretched all the way open. I had decided that bird must be living in the big river that flowed through town. Its wings never seemed to move at all, just drifting on the wind through the endless blue sky.

Natsumi, I'm going to die here, but you're still alive. You'll live on. Promise me you'll smile—I won't forgive you if you don't. Goodbye, Natsumi...

Her voice faded away, to be heard no more. The sound of her breathing and the hiss of the tape vanished, as well. The speakers went silent—her confession was done. Through the clear plastic door, I could see the tape spinning in silence. A clear drop fell on it, a tear dripping off my cheek.

Silently, I whispered, "I'm so sorry...but thank you."

It was so dark and quiet. I was in the empty hospital. But a moment ago, I had been with her, on that hill.

How long had I been lying there crying?

I was alone now, nothing around but the table and the light. No sign of either boy.

The light shone across the floor, illuminating only that area. I blinked, and I realized part of the floor was wet. There was a big puddle of blood on the floor—fresh blood, not dried. I prayed it didn't belong to Itsuki.

I tried to stand, still clutching the tape deck. At first, my legs were too weak. I took my time and managed to stagger to my feet.

I left the room, walking unsteadily. I called Itsuki's name. My voice echoed off the walls, vanishing into the depths of the darkness.

I waited for him at the hospital entrance. The quiet, cold air went right through my clothes, and I shivered, hunching my shoulders, crouching low in the darkness. When the sun finally rose, I was half-asleep. There was no sign of either Itsuki or the boy.

epilogue

"Oh, it's not a big deal. I was playing with the dog and fell over," I explained as Morino and I walked down the stairs, my bag in one hand.

It was December 4, after school, and we'd left the classroom together talking. As we passed the landing, Morino had pointed to the red line on my neck, asking about it.

"Oh? It was obviously trying to kill you."

"The dog?"

"I'm sure of it," she nodded with conviction.

It was, in fact, an injury I'd obtained the night before at the abandoned hospital.

I'd also acquired a number of bruises, but these were hidden beneath my uniform.

"By the way, I was gathering information for a scrapbook about Kitazawa Hiroko's murder yesterday..."

Morino had received a fair amount of information from the person she'd met in the library. I'd asked who this person was, but she didn't want to tell me. I'd considered following her and discovering who it was myself, but it no longer seemed to matter.

"You finish it?"

"Almost. All I'd need now is an interview with the killer to make it perfect."

As we left the building and headed toward the school gates, Morino told me about how the case was a lot more grotesque than the police had announced. The sun was already setting, and a cold wind was blowing. Between the school and the gates was a wide road lined with trees. There were only a few students walking here. A white plastic bag drifted past us on the wind.

We left the gates, stepping out onto the street. Kitazawa Natsumi was standing in the convenience store across the street. She was standing at the magazine rack, and her eyes met mine.

I stopped in front of the store. Morino stopped with me.

In the shop, Kitazawa Natsumi put down the book she was holding, never once taking her eyes off me. She headed for the entrance and came outside.

There was a parking lot in front of the store, just large enough to hold a few cars.

She faced me across the parking lot, the pale florescent light from the store shining down on both of us.

I had killed someone the night before, while she lay clutching a tape recorder.

There had been a dull sound as the knife slid home, and then he'd been dead.

But I'd gone home without Kitazawa Natsumi, not feeling up to dealing with her. She hadn't noticed the struggling going on around her, and it didn't appear that she'd known which of us the blood belonged to until she'd seen me come out of the school gates.

Before I could say anything to her, Morino spoke up. She had been staring fixedly at Kitazawa Natsumi's face.

"Are you...Kitazawa Natsumi?"

"Yes, I am."

"I thought so. You look just like the pictures of your sister in the newspapers."

"The picture from before she changed her hair, right?"

"Yes. My hobby is investigating cases. I was looking into your sister's. I couldn't find any pictures of you, though. When I saw you standing here a few days ago, I'd thought you looked like her, but I hadn't been sure then."

"You were investigating her?" Kitazawa Natsumi asked, surprised. She looked at me for help.

"She seems to have found a source. She won't tell me who..." I explained. Kitazawa Natsumi didn't appear to know what to make of this.

Morino looked at me. She was as expressionless as ever, but it was clear from her voice that she was greatly interested. "So how do you know Kitazawa?"

Without answering, I took some change out of my pocket and put it in Morino's hand. She stared at the coins for a moment, and then she asked what they were for. I explained that there was a vending machine a half mile down the road, and I asked politely if she would go buy us something to drink.

"I know there's a convenience store right in front of us, but I would very much like to drink something from that vending machine in the distance. Of course, this is not an underhanded method of driving you away so you can't hear us talk."

Morino looked at me and then at Kitazawa Natsumi, hesitating. But eventually she turned her back on us and began walking toward the vending machine.

"She doesn't know, does she? That the killer was targeting her?" Kitazawa murmured.

I nodded.

For a moment, we both watched her walking slowly away from us. Her black clothes almost vanished into the darkness around her; her small shadow whipped around her each time a car zipped past, headlines glaring.

"She showed me a picture of Hiroko's body the other day."

"Of her body?"

"Yes. Someone had given her a photo that never would have circulated publicly. It was definitely Hiroko's face. The same hairstyle as the picture at her funeral..."

"Then, when you saw that ... ?"

"I knew there was a chance the killer had taken it. I didn't quite believe it ... but if it was true, then that meant the person who'd killed Hiroko was also getting close to her, and she might've been his next target."

"You were half-right, but he ultimately chose me instead of her."

"When I saw you standing here, I knew he hadn't yet made his move. You were acting strange, so I wondered if he'd approached you."

"Yes ... yes, he had. So that's why you snuck into my room ... looking for proof of that."

"You never would've told me the truth."

The light from the shop sent our shadows across the dry asphalt of the parking lot, like shadow puppets. She stared down at them, nodding.

"But, Itsuki, I never thought you had so little sense."

"About as little as you."

"I was worried last night ... you just vanished. I called in the morning, but the call didn't go through."

"He broke my phone."

I had once been in the same class as the boy who killed Kitazawa Hiroko. I hadn't known him well, but if I'd spent a little more time with him, would I have noticed how unusual he was?

"What ... what did you do, after?"

I had buried his body deep in the grass behind the hospital. All his cruelty had been sucked out of him by the silver flash of my blade—or at least, that's how I chose to see it. When the knife had sunk deep into him and he'd groaned, blood spilling out of his mouth, the hand gripping the knife had felt like its thirst was sated.

"He ran away. I chased him, but I couldn't catch up ..."

He had looked down at the pool of his blood as if it made sense to him, as if this was simply another possible outcome. He had fallen to his knees, accepting his own death as easily as he had taken Kitazawa Hiroko's. He had looked up at me, praised the quality of the knife, and stopped moving.

"Oh. Do you suppose we should call the police?"

"If you want. But I don't want any trouble, so if you could avoid mentioning me? I did break into your house, after all."

I looked back up the road. There was a tiny speck in the distance, visible as it passed under a streetlight but fading into the darkness beyond. A moment later, it appeared again under the next light. It was Morino, coming back.

"My dad was furious when I got home this morning," Kitazawa Natsumi said, kicking the parking bumper. She was smiling. She had ridden her bicycle home. When she'd arrived home, her parents had already realized she wasn't in her room, and they were in a panic. When she'd come in the door, looking exhausted, they'd yelled at her and hugged her tight.

"My mother burst into tears the moment she saw me—only natural, after what happened to my sister. It really drove home that I was still alive, and so were my parents. We've decided to move early next year, somewhere far away."

She looked up, down the road, her profile gleaming white in the light of the convenience store.

"I won't see you again."

Drinks in hand, Morino stopped a fair distance away, leaning against a telephone pole, watching us, her hair dancing in the wind of a passing car. She looked like a little match girl somehow.

"You done?" she called. Just a little longer, I said, and she muttered something listlessly, turning her back on us. We were too far away for me to hear; all I could do was stare at her narrow shoulders.

"Is Morino..." Kitazawa Natsumi said, looking at me and trailing off.

"What?"

"No, never mind... but she might have the wrong idea about us. You don't plan to tell her what happened?"

"Not unless I have to. I never have."

"Then she doesn't know that you protected her. Itsuki, did you come there to save me? Or just to stomp out the flames before they could reach her?" She looked me right in the eye. "I'm right, aren't I? Are you in love with her?"

This was not love…merely obsession. I chose not to say this out loud.

Kitazawa Natsumi looked away, staring into the distance. She placed her right hand on her left shoulder.

"Did you hurt your shoulder?"

She smiled faintly, shaking her head.

"He put his hand here, as he turned away."

"He?"

"Never mind. How long are you going to make Morino wait?"

She was still leaning against the telephone pole. I called out, letting her know we were done.

Morino came silently over to us. She was only holding one can of citrus soda. I pointed out that there were three of us and she should have bought three drinks; she, in turn, pointed out that I had kept her waiting so long that she'd drunk two of them. Furthermore, she no longer had any intention of handing the final drink off to anyone else. You could never have guessed how foul a mood she was in by looking at her, though.

The three of us walked to the station. Kitazawa Natsumi and I walked together, chatting. We talked about moving, studying for college exams, nothing particularly interesting—but I was used to playing my part. She seemed to be happy, and she smiled often.

Morino followed a few steps behind us. I glanced back at her every now and then. She had her bag in one hand; in the other, she held the soda can, like she wasn't sure what to do with it. She was staring at her toes. Her long hair fell forward, hiding her face.

She said nothing, making no attempt to participate in our conversation. Even as I glanced back at her, I pretended not to notice anything, carrying on like normal.

When we finally reached the clearing in front of the station, it was already dark out—but there were so many stores there, with brightly lit signs and windows, that it wasn't actually very dark.

Schools were out, and most offices had closed as well. The station was packed with people heading home. The first floor of the massive station was carved into a square sort of tunnel—the station entrance. People flowed in and out like the building was breathing them.

I said goodbye to Kitazawa Natsumi at the station entrance. She waved and walked away, heading for the ticket machines. She slid through the crowd like a spaceship moving through the enemy fleet in a sci-fi film. There was a long line at the ticket machines, and she took up a place at the back of it.

Morino and I stood against the wall so as not to obstruct traffic. Neither of us really cared for loud, crowded places. Staying here long would give us each a headache.

The wall was a smooth white stone, probably marble. At regular intervals were large posters, advertisements for makeup with female models. Morino leaned against one of them.

"Surprised at how much Kitazawa Natsumi looks like her sister?" I asked.

"More important, doesn't it wear you out, changing the way you speak depending on whom you're talking to?" Morino folded her arms. I could see the end of the soda can in her right hand sticking out from under her left arm. I was sure her body heat had warmed it by now.

Morino looked across to where Kitazawa Natsumi stood in line. "I can't understand how either of you can smile so naturally."

"I'm not smiling because I'm amused."

No matter what the conversation, I took no pleasure from it. I always felt like I was standing at the bottom of a dark hole. But I carried on an unconscious performance, making sure no one ever noticed anything wrong.

"And she hasn't smiled much. She smiled a bit talking to me, but she hasn't always been like that recently."

Morino frowned. "She doesn't usually smile? She seemed pretty cheery to me."

I explained a simplified version of the friction between Kitazawa

Natsumi and her sister: two sisters that looked alike, in an awkward sort of relationship for a long time. She'd been convinced she was hated and had been unable to smile.

Morino listened in silence, interjecting nothing.

"I went to Kitazawa Hiroko's funeral, for the usual reasons. She told me about it there. But the other day, she found a tape recording of Hiroko's voice..."

A chance encounter with her sister, whom she had thought she would never meet again.

I didn't mention the killer or the events of the night before; it would just complicate things. But I briefly outlined the contents of the tape and the transformation it had presumably brought about within Kitazawa Natsumi.

I remembered how she had curled up on the floor, clutching the tape recorder.

I had stood there, knife in hand, wiping the blood off on his clothes. From the description on the tape, I could easily imagine how they had played together as children.

When I'd finished describing those memories, Morino remained leaning against the wall, arms folded. Her eyes turned downward in thoughtful silence. Her eyelids were half-closed, her eyes hidden beneath the shadows her eyelashes cast in the harsh overhead light.

"None of that was in my scrapbook," she said, so softly that I almost didn't hear her. She slowly lifted her head, looking toward Kitazawa Natsumi in line at the ticket machine.

The line had moved forward, and Kitazawa Natsumi was putting coins into the machine. She pressed a button and bought a ticket for a nearby station. Then she headed into the crowd, occasionally visible among the flood of people.

Morino unfolded her arms and looked down at the can of soda in her hand. Her back pulled away from the wall. A moment later, her long hair followed. She began walking like still river water that had begun to silently flow again.

It was such a quiet motion that it took me a moment to realize she was moving at all. Not sure what she was up to, I just watched her go. I didn't begin to follow until she'd vanished into the crowd.

Her gaze was fixed on Kitazawa Natsumi, who had purchased her ticket and was headed for the platform gates. Morino Yoru headed after her, drifting as absently as a sleepwalker. She didn't appear to be any good at walking in crowds, and she bumped into one person after another. She seemed to be trying to avoid this, but crashed into suit-clad businessmen and young women with unerring regularity. Each time, she bounced backward, clutching her nose, and then forged forward again. I had never seen anyone have this much trouble with crowds before. It was very easy to keep up with her.

Meanwhile, Kitazawa Natsumi passed through the congested gates. There were only a few gates serving a vast number of people, and a crowd had formed, waiting their turn. Their heads and backs blocked our view, and we could no longer see Kitazawa Natsumi. She had moved into the station without noticing Morino's approach.

Morino slammed into someone again, a large middle-aged man; it was like seeing a tricycle crashing into a dump truck. She bounced away, staggered, and almost fell backward into me. As it was, her head slammed into my jaw. This was the single greatest damage I had taken over the last few months, despite everything that had happened. She didn't appear to notice, all her attention focused on the direction in which Kitazawa Natsumi had vanished. She straightened up, gulped hesitantly, squared her shoulders, and called out, "Natsumi!"

I had never heard her voice that loud. It was like there was an amplifier hidden somewhere in her slender frame. All the noise and bustle of the crowd was instantly silenced. A lot of people stopped walking and talking, all turning to stare at her.

Morino began walking again, directly toward the gates through which Kitazawa Natsumi had vanished. Everyone who had heard her shout stepped out of the way, letting her pass. I followed.

Noise returned to the station, and everyone started moving

again. Morino was already at the gates. She didn't ride the train to school every day and so had neither ticket nor train pass, which prevented her from passing through the automated gates. They closed in front of her, and she stopped.

"Morino?"

It was Kitazawa Natsumi's voice. She stepped out of the flood of humanity, appearing on the other side of the gates. She must've heard Morino's shout and come back. She jogged over to us, looking surprised, and stopped with the closed gate between her and Morino. With Morino blocking one of the gates, the congestion around us had increased dramatically. Morino didn't seem to care.

"Natsumi, this is for you," she said, holding out the can of soda.

"Th-thanks," Kitazawa Natsumi said, hesitantly taking it.

"I apologize for my bad temper earlier. I should've talked with you longer. I hear you were able to make things right with your sister."

A lot of people were glaring at us, unable to get through the gate. Station attendants had noticed the commotion and were pushing toward us. I tugged Morino's arm, trying to drag her away, but she resisted, refusing to move.

"I was also fighting with my sister, when... well, the circumstances weren't exactly... I wanted to congratulate you, that's all."

And with that, she allowed me to pull her away from the gate. She was really light, like she was weightless. A flood of people passed around us. Kitazawa Natsumi was instantly swallowed by the crowd; but just before she vanished, I saw her smile, thanking Morino.

Morino followed my lead listlessly, as if exhausted. She'd lost her bag somewhere.

I looked around and found it sitting against the wall where we'd been standing earlier.

I pulled her hand until we were standing in front of the picture of a foreign lady again. It was hard work pulling her through the crowd. I had to keep a firm grip on her to keep us from being separated. She stared at the ground, never looking where she was going. Her lips were moving, muttering something, but I couldn't make it out over the noise of the crowd—not until we left the crowd and had reached the spot where she'd left her bag.

"I think you're my opposite, Kamiyama," she was whispering, over and over. She was going to have to get home alone from here. I had to take the train, so she would have to walk by herself. But it seemed highly dubious that she could manage that in her current condition.

"At first, I thought you were like me. You reminded me of my sister. But you aren't. We're nothing alike."

Morino's bag was a simple black one. I picked it up and put it in her hand. It fell to the ground a second later.

I picked it up again, putting her fingers around the handle, but it was useless: She was too out of it to hold on. Her fingers couldn't stand up to the weight of the bag, and it slid right out of her hand.

"Sometimes I think you're smiling with nothing inside you at all, Kamiyama. I'm sorry if you take that personally, but that's what I always think when I see you acting happy around everyone else. And sometimes, I feel really sorry for you."

She said all this without looking up at me. Her voice was trembling, like a child about to burst into tears.

"But I'm the reverse."

She looked up now, looked me right in the eye. I was taller than her, and from this distance, she had to look up at me. Her expression was as blank as ever, but her eyes were a little red, and they seemed damp.

"I know," I said.

For a long moment, she stood in unmoving silence. Finally, she lowered her head and nodded. "Okay then. I'm sorry I babbled on like that."

I held out her bag, and she took it like nothing had happened. This time, she held it firmly and didn't drop it.

She looked at the crowd passing by, people heading to our left and to our right. I didn't know exactly what she was looking at, but there was nothing in front of us but the crowd.

She opened her mouth and said quietly, "I'm genuinely glad for Natsumi. And I envy her."

Morino was herself again, no longer needing my guidance. We moved in opposite directions, without even saying goodbye.

AFTERWORD 1:
FROM *YORU NO SHO*

Hello, I'm the author. This is the Bunko edition of a book I wrote called *GOTH*. For reasons I don't quite follow, it was divided into two volumes for this release. My editor, A-san, said, "Write an afterword—something interesting and easy to read." I get requests like this because I used to enthusiastically write funny and interesting afterwords. I'm starting to get fed up with it.

†

Anyway. I wrote *GOTH* the year after I graduated from college; I believe I was twenty-three at the time. I wrote the short story called "Goth," collected in *Yoru no Sho*, and my editor really liked the characters; suddenly, I found myself creating other stories with them. The short stories that resulted from this all have the main characters getting involved with gruesome murders. Together, they formed the work known as *GOTH* collected here. Killer after killer appears, secretly taking lives—and the more I wrote, the more worried I become that these events just seemed terribly unrealistic. In the real world, it's absolutely unthinkable that so many crazy people could live in the same town.

I was trying to write a dark fantasy, like the series *Youma Yakou*, published by Kadokawa Sneaker Bunko. In that series, each story involves a unique *youkai* causing trouble, and I was trying to write my own version of that without the consent or permission of Group SNE (the company that created the series). I do apologize, SNE-san! So the killers that appear in *GOTH* are not human, but youkai. And the male protagonist is also a youkai, with the same power as the enemies, whereas the female lead has a powerful psychic gift that attracts youkai. As I didn't use any items or jargon to suggest that this was not our world, people tend to believe the book is set in reality; but in my mind, it absolutely is not.

Because I wanted to write about killers as if they were monsters, I wasted no time talking about their reasons for killing or traumatic pasts. If I wrote about their motives, I would be writing about humans, and that seemed to be rather missing the point. Writing about what led them to the desire to kill sounds inherently fascinating, but that seemed like something I should do in some other work. This was a battle between monsters. Clash of the youkai. Add a little romance, and you get the rather slapdash work known as *GOTH*.

I named the book *GOTH* for the entirely arbitrary reason that the lead female seemed to be sort of Goth-y. When I was a teenager, I had Goth friends, and we often loaned each other that kind of book, so Goth culture was as familiar as air (to me). But at the same time, it wasn't well-known (among the general public), and any number of people asked me to explain it. I nearly panicked when I saw someone post on a friend's home page, asking if I had made up the word. Of course not! And if I gave the impression that I had, I must sincerely apologize to everyone who loves Goth culture.

It was not a well-considered title. As you will understand once you read the book, there is little to no description of Goth culture in the work itself. As a result, I have created a connection between Goths and murders. Paying no attention to the soul of Goth culture, I've simply added a superficial aspect of the fashion as a selling point for my book. I knew I would have to write something apologizing for that eventually, as I've received a letter telling me off for it. Everything written in that letter was absolutely true, and I found myself bowing apologetically as I read it. I wanted to write back, but there was no return address, so I've been forced to use this space to offer my apology. I am extremely sorry for having taken advantage of Goth culture.

There is one other thing I must not forget to mention: This book was awarded the Honkaku Mystery Award. I never imagined that a book like this would win an award, and I didn't even know that the Honkaku Mystery Award existed. I received a letter informing me that my book had been selected for the final round but had been so convinced I wasn't the type to win awards that I completely forgot about the letter, and I never even mentioned it to my editor.

That bears further explanation. *GOTH* was originally written as a "light novel." Defining the term "light novel" is fraught with danger, but the point is that, at the time I wrote it, there were no prizes for which light novels would even be considered. In other words, the possibility that *GOTH* would win an award was absolutely out of the question. All light novelists are writing under the assumption that their work will never win any prizes, and I was just one of those.

So I may be forgiven for completely forgetting the date on which the prize was announced and going to see a play with a friend of mine. It was completely impossible, after all. The judges were all die-hard mystery fans and would never vote for a light novel. Yes, it was published as a nice hardcover with no manga-style illustrations, or any illustrations at all—but the stories "Goth" and "Wrist-Cut" (collected in the other [Bunko paperback] volume) were originally published in a light novel magazine, so it seemed like everyone would assume the work was a light novel.

I went to see a play with the writer Y-san. I have only just remembered, but the play we went to see that day starred Yukiko Motoya-san. I've spoken to Motoya-san four times since then, and her conversation speed is frighteningly fast; for someone like me, who rarely speaks, it's rather like being caught in a tornado. At the time, however, I hadn't met her, nor even seen her on stage, and she hadn't yet become a radio personality, nor had I ever heard her on the radio.

At any rate, I was headed to the spot where I'd agreed to meet Y-san. On the way, my cell phone rang. "You appear to have won the Honkaku Mystery Award," my editor said, sounding quite perplexed. My editor had been unaware the book was even up for the prize until she was informed that it had won, so she was naturally quite unprepared. "Get over here, now." I was forced to abandon plans to see a play and hurried directly to where the prize was being awarded. All kinds of astonishing events awaited me there—but what, exactly? You'll have to read the afterword in the other [second paperback] volume of *GOTH* to find out.

—Otsuichi
June 2005

AFTERWORD 2:
FROM *BOKU NO SHO*

Hello, I'm the author. I've been forced to write an afterword for the second half of the Bunko edition of *GOTH*. The deadline is tomorrow, and I haven't written a thing. Instead, I've spent the day returning DVDs to Tsutaya, eating a *natto* set at Sukiya, putting away my kotatsu, and generally procrastinating—much like the astonishing amount of cleaning one does before exams. Like I mentioned in the afterword for the first half, I was asked to write something interesting and funny. This is my own fault for once actively trying to write that kind of afterword. I have no idea how to stop.

The book known as *GOTH* was awarded the Honkaku Mystery Award. This afterword will begin by talking about that prize.

†

I know little about the publishing industry and had no idea what kind of prizes actually existed in Japan. So when *GOTH* won the Honkaku Mystery Award, the first thing that went through my head was surprise that such a prize existed in the first place. The Honkaku Mystery Award was created by the Honkaku Mystery Writer's Club and is given to the best Honkaku Mystery novel published that year.

"Honkaku Mystery? What's that?" many of you are probably thinking. Everyone I knew in college certainly did. Honkaku Mystery is a subgenre of mystery focusing on deductions, tricks, and the surprising moment in which the truth is revealed. *Kindaichi Case Files* or *Case Closed* probably qualify (the actual definition seems to vary from person to person, so I'm not really sure about this...).

GOTH does have a few tricks and deductions. I believe it was these elements that allowed a light novel to receive the Honkaku Mystery Award. When I wrote *GOTH*, I was making a deliberate effort to incorporate elements of Honkaku Mysteries in it. I even believed I was trying to write a Honkaku Mystery (but only at first). I decided to do so because I wanted light novel readers to understand what was so interesting about mysteries.

When I was a teenager, a friend of mine, K-san, brought a book called *Slayers* to my house. That was when I began reading voraciously. Before that time, I had read fewer than ten novels a year; but after *Slayers*, I read every light novel I could get my hands on. I won't attempt to define the term "light novel" here, but they tend to have manga-style covers and illustrations as a big selling point. I'm not at all sure that the term had been created at the time, but *Slayers* is what we would call a light novel. I also read *Zanyaruma no Kensi*, *Sword World*, and *Tamago no Ouji: Kairuroddo no Kunan*. I would go to the store almost every day and pour over Sneaker Bunko's green spines or Fujimi Fantasy Bunko's yellow or blue spines. For five years at technical school, I had no friends, but there was a classmate with whom I could talk about light novels once every three days or so, which was one of the few saving graces.

Then one day I was reading a gaming magazine, and I found a column saying, basically, that light novels weren't considered proper books, but trashy things that only a child would read. Oh. I'd had no idea, but the world of publishing frowned on light novels. This came as quite a shock. I was sixteen, though, and no matter how furious I was at the lack of respect given to light novels, there was nothing I could do to change that. And it made little difference to my life what the world thought of them. Shortly after that, I fell in love with mysteries and read a bunch of mystery novels. Light novels and mystery novels are the two pillars of my reading experience.

One day, I looked at the word processor in my room and had an idea. "I should practice typing while I still have time. But if I'm doing that, I might as well write words that mean something...like a novel. It would be nice if I could make a living writing novels or manga. If I write constantly, I might be able to write something good by the time I'm thirty." And a few twists and turns later, I was a published writer. Once I began writing professionally, something unexpected happened: I was constantly running up against the problem of how light novels were looked down upon, something I had assumed would never actually affect my life. If I were to describe all the light novel discrimination I've been a victim of, this would become an extremely brutal essay, so I shall not.

Anyway. As I read both light novels and mysteries in college for some reason, I joined the sci-fi club. There I made my first friends in five years. When we talked about books, I discovered that they all read nothing but light novels. I was somewhat horrified to discover that even though they were remarkably intelligent, well educated, articulate, and confident of their passion for books, they only read light novels. But they were a future I might have been part of. There must be plenty of people in Japan who are surrounded by people like them, who read only light novels and never realize there are many other kinds of books in the store.

Right! I would write a mystery light novel! Then people who had read only light novels would be exposed to the joys of mysteries and break out of their reading niche! With that in mind, I began writing *GOTH*.

†

Then, that fateful day…

"A phone call arrived at the editorial desk informing us that you have won the Honkaku Mystery Award… Does that ring a bell?" asked my editor, A-san. Her voice, emerging from my cell phone, sounded rather perplexed. Of course. She had gone to work like always and was doing her job as usual, when suddenly the phone rang and she'd been informed that a book she'd edited had won an award; most people would assume it was a practical joke.

At the time, I was in Shibuya Station. "Oh…now that you mention it, I did get a letter about that."

"They appear to be looking for you. Come to Kadokawa Shoten at once."

As I later learned, what I did that day was rather an unusual course of action for a prize candidate to take on the day the winner was announced. Most people apparently sit around with their editors, swallowing nervously and jumping every time the phone rings, thinking, "The results are in!" only to have it be a wrong number and find themselves asked to deliver tendon and soba.

I went to Kadokawa Shoten, up to the floor that housed the anime and manga division, which oversees Sneaker Bunko, and all the editors bowed to me, congratulating me on my award. Award? Uh…huh? While I was still reeling, I was thrown into a taxi and driven away.

We got out of the taxi in front of a strange building and rode the elevator up, and a huge crowd of people turned toward me at once. I wanted to run away. I was led along helplessly to a sort of conference room packed with people and TV cameras, and I was forced to stand in front of them. A microphone was placed before me, and someone asked me how I felt.

Award? Uh…huh? My head was still spinning, but I was convinced that if Tokyo people knew they had me rattled, I would be forced to put my stamp on a number of dubious documents, be introduced to dubious friends, and be promised profits that were unlikely to materialize, so I pretended to be calm and answered.

There were loads of people with cameras pointed at me, with flashes going off like strobe lights, and I felt like a criminal being dragged out of a patrol car. I wanted to bow my head, tears in my eyes, apologize, and promise not to do it again. Nevertheless, I managed to survive the post-award interview and was able to calm down enough to look around me—but the more I looked, the more famous mystery novelists I saw in the crowd. Yikes! Time to go! But before I could run, people started handing me business cards, and I had to make polite conversations. One of the cards handed to me said Hideo Uyama, which terrified me.

"Th-this is *the* Uyama-san . . . !"

I stared in awe at the man who'd handed me the card, but before I managed to recover enough to speak, I was swallowed up by the crowd again. Eventually I escaped, went home, and lay in bed trembling, still in a state of shock.

And that is basically all I have to say about the day *GOTH* won the Honkaku Mystery Award; however, I think Uyama-san deserves a little more explanation. Uyama-san is the famous Kodansha editor who created the Shin Honkaku Mystery boom, and without him, there would have been far fewer Honkaku mysteries, I never would have read any mysteries of quality, and *GOTH* never would have been written. There are few opportunities in life to meet with people who have changed history, which is why I was so terrified when he gave me his card.

†

Several years have passed since that chaotic day. During that time, I've been rewriting a half-written novel, throwing it all away and rethinking it from the beginning—and in between, writing the occasional short story. I've also been to Turkey, played Dragon Quest 8, made a movie, gone to Okinawa with a few other writers, had stories turned into movies, written a new short story called "My Intelligent Underwear," been given hand cream as a present because my hands were in poor condition, spilled beer and been handed a pen that removes stains, and all kinds of other things.

Probably the biggest change has been the money I now have due to the success of *GOTH*. Because of that, I'm able to work less and spend more time enjoying myself.

I spent my teenage years writing stories and attending class, and I almost never did anything for fun. I've almost never been able to do things simply because I wanted to. And what I want to do involves making movies and games. I became a novelist despite wanting to do those things instead.

So I went and bought a video camera, and I've begun making movies. I'd helped with a friend's film in college, but I thought it was time I directed my own. I've made two films now, but the results were much too horrible to show anyone else. I have a new-found respect for people who are good at this. I've been asked to write several screenplays. If asked which I like better, novels or movies, the answer is clearly movies, so of course I accepted immediately with all the passion of a drooling dog. I would be perfectly happy to change careers and focus entirely on movies, but I don't know if that's possible.

When I tell people I'm making movies, people often seem to think I would be able to get funding from somewhere. Good heavens, no. Certainly I've heard offers, but "funding" essentially means borrowing money from people to make a movie, and that is far too much responsibility. The movies I make cost only a few hundred thousand yen, so I can readily afford them without wasting anyone else's money. They usually involve me, the camera, and the two actors, with no lighting or sound, and are absolutely unprofessional.

So, at the moment, I'm learning how to direct and continuing to write. If I were to spend ten or twenty years to make twenty-odd movies, would I be able to make something satisfactory? This is not the sort of luxurious challenge most of us are afforded. Everyone I know who's over thirty and calls himself a director is always working horrible day jobs while filming and dreaming of someday working for a major studio. I have no need to work a horrible day job. And that is because of my publishers and readers. And I owe a debt of gratitude to *GOTH* for allowing me to begin making my own movies. Thank you very much. I began writing stories during the summer when I was sixteen. This year I am twenty-six, so we have been together ten years.

—Otsuichi
June 2005

MORINO'S SOUVENIR PHOTO

OTSUICHI

TRANSLATED BY

JOCELYNE ALLEN

BONUS:
MORINO'S SOUVENIR PHOTO

0

The prohibition of graven images in the Old Testament is more accurately a prohibition against the worship of idols. To avoid this criticism, those who champion the use of icons draw a line between "worship" and "veneration."

Icon venerators declare that icons are not used with the intent to worship the image itself, but rather to call to mind that which the image expresses. The thinking is this: Though the image is to be treated with respect, this respect does not make it the object of worship. In discussion, proponents frequently liken the icon to the image of a loved one. A drawing or a photo of a loved one is not the actual loved one, but the person enduring a separation from their beloved cherishes the image. The assertion is that the sacred icon similarly causes the bearer to recall the existence of God or the saint—or the vestiges thereof—through the image.

1

When I look at photographs for work, I analyze the various bits of information shown in them. I think about composition, shadows, the lens, the way in which these elements are combined, the chemical reaction that occurs, and the deeper impression the photo makes on the viewer. I can't help but be conscious of the idea of the "symbol."

The act of taking a photo is one of positioning a symbol into a square frame or one of finding it there. The person with the camera may press the shutter with some vague intention, but in most cases, what they capture is nothing more than a scene of high entropy. Given all the information scattered about in the image, viewers don't know where to rest their eyes. Thus, the photographer makes sure to control the many disparate elements. They make the illumination brighter or the shadows darker, or they fiddle with the lens and the aperture to blur the background, in line with their own style. Cutting out and framing a piece of the natural world in this way creates all sorts of symbols, symbols which helpfully and clearly tell the viewer what kind of photo they are looking at.

I imagine that words are symbols. As long as a person is alive, they have no choice but to use words to infer the intentions of others. And when a person is producing some kind of work, they have no choice but to rely on these same words.

There is something that must not be forgotten: the fact that the symbol itself has no intrinsic meaning. It is not the circle or the square that moves people. These objects are only symbols and have no greater meaning in and of themselves. To have faith in the object is the same as worshipping the image.

In many religions, the worship of images is forbidden. People likely learned this from years of experience. God cannot be drawn or sculpted. The moment it is drawn, it is no longer God; the moment it is sculpted, God becomes a fake. The moment it is expressed, its divinity peels away and recedes from its true nature. Which is why all personages drawn in pictures are a compromise between God and human, like Christ or Mary—you rarely see God, the father of Christ himself, depicted in icons. The sole reason for this is that the expressive possibility for Christ and Mary is as symbols indicating that they themselves are in the presence of God.

A symbol is a fixed concept. However, its true weight is in the context hidden in the gap between symbol and object, the world on the other side of the symbol. Emotion, the ability to move someone, is not a part of the symbol itself. Which is why when I take photos, I do everything I can to eliminate symbolic elements. But there are limits to what I can control, and nothing ever goes the way I expect. What troubles me most is the subject of the photo.

On December 6, I killed a girl.

> *Hark, the glad sound! the Savior comes,*
> *the Savior promised long;*
> *let every heart prepare a throne,*
> *and every voice a song.*

> *He comes the prisoners to release,*
> *in Satan's bondage held;*
> *the gates of brass before him burst,*
> *the iron fetters yield.*

A hymn, the saintly voices of boys and girls, was playing in the convenience store. Today's background music appeared to be Christmas songs. I bought some hot coffee and a bottle of water and went back to the car. After starting the engine, I looked out the windshield. Rows of apartment buildings stood in a line, separated by small patches of green. Although it was the middle of the day, there wasn't a soul around. The steam of the coffee and the breath coming out of my own mouth clouded the glass.

I pulled out of the parking lot. The houses dotting the sides of the road grew gradually sparser as I drove out toward the suburbs. When I crossed the river, the outline of the mountains in the distance ahead of me snapped into focus. I turned onto the mountain path, and the road narrowed and began to snake. Weeds tangled themselves around rust-covered guardrails. The car shuddered, and I heard the clatter of the camera, tripod, and other things

I had packed into the trunk. Any time I traveled any distance, I made sure to bring all the equipment I needed to take photos, just in case. I also had photographic chemicals in the glove box.

I had been on a break recently. I was struggling with whether I should keep going the way I had been or if it was time for me to stop for good. I would look at the photos I had taken and try to remember how fresh and genuine it had all felt at the time, but a whole day would go by without the urge arising in me. What point was there in continuing with it? I could have a richer, perfectly tranquil life if I wanted it. But I had unfinished business. Which was why I was on my way to the suburbs today.

Along the way, the road intersected with some railway tracks. Lately, whenever I looked up the name of this place online, I got a lot of hits for ghost stories. At some point, this mountain road had become haunted.

People believed it. They believed these stories about the ghost of a female high school student murdered seven years ago. They wrote firsthand accounts about their experiences with ghosts on online forums, and the town hall got call after call from people looking for information about the incident. The neighborhood elementary school had a staff meeting about how these stories were scaring the children.

All this had nothing to do with me.

No, it didn't have quite *nothing* to do with me.

It was 2:30 p.m. Before I knew it, I was very near the pass. There was also a bus stop up here, although I couldn't imagine what a person would have to have in mind to get off in a place like this.

I stopped the car in a clearing. I got out of the driver's seat, pulling my head in at the chill of the wind. The area was mostly deciduous forest. At a certain point in winter, the trees scattered their leaves and revealed their twisted, almost entangled, branches. The fallen dry leaves covered the ground, where they would eventually turn to mulch.

A space of about a meter interrupted the thick growth of dead trees along the road, a path that went deeper into the deciduous forest. Given that the ground there was left to nature, the path was impossible to traverse by car. A nostalgic fondness welled up inside me. One point, however, was different from the vision of the place in my memory. Barbed wire had been strung across the entrance to the path, with a sign that read PLANNED SITE FOR WASTE DISPOSAL FACILITY dangling from it.

But the barbed wire was only strung across the entrance, so it was simply ornamental. From the road, I slipped through the dead trees to make my way onto the path. I walked deeper into the forest. If it had been warmer, the area would have made for a perfect hike. But in the cold, it felt savage. The thin branches, which threatened to snap with the lightest of touches, overlapped like the brushstrokes in the shadows of a pen-and-ink drawing, covering the area above my head on all sides.

Finally, I came out into a clearing about as large as the playing field at an elementary school. Dead grass covered the field. There was nothing special here. It was simply a wasteland, soon to be home to waste disposal. This was my destination.

But I had no plans to meet anyone here.

I stopped, wary. A human form stood in the midst of the sea of dry grass. I might have to run. It depended on who it was. Anyone who would come here on this particular day was probably with the police. Or a relative of the girl who had died seven years ago.

Sensing my presence, the figure turned. Long hair, school uniform, coat over that, everything black. A bag hung from her right hand, while the left was shoved into the pocket of her coat. The outline of the person standing there held a physical pressure, carving itself into my brain.

Our eyes met. And locked for what felt like hours, despite the fact that it could only have been a moment at most. I became flustered. The girl approached me; there was no fear in her posture. She pulled her left hand out of her coat pocket, clutching a small digital camera.

"Would you take a picture for me?"

This request would have made all the sense in the world if this place had, for instance, been a tourist destination and if she had had a smile on her face. But this was a dreary empty clearing with nothing in particular to recommend it.

"A picture?"

The girl stopped a few steps away from me. "I'm taking some photos as souvenirs."

Now that she was quite close to me, any sense of her reality grew even more distant. She had that kind of look.

"Photos? Here?"

She nodded silently.

"Do you know what this place is?"

She nodded again and turned her back to me. This place, surrounded by a deciduous forest, held only dead trees and dry grass; nothing lived here. White breath expelled from the gap in the girl's lips and melted into the air. I was surprised. She knew. She knew that this was the spot where the corpse had been left.

The body of a high school girl had been discovered here seven years earlier in December. A middle-aged couple came to illegally dump their own garbage and found her. If they hadn't, it likely would have been spring by the time anyone else did. The girl was identified from her belongings. She had gone missing the night of December 6, a week before the body was discovered.

An autopsy found that it was not suicide, but murder. The cause of death was heart failure due to an injection of highly concentrated potassium chloride. She was found in her school uniform; there were no signs of a struggle, or violation, found. She had apparently just been lying in the shade of a tree, as though she were simply resting. A fact that drew further attention was that marks—a group of three indentations in the ground—were found next to her body, as if a tripod had been set up there. Fortunately, this cluster of depressions was found in several other places as well. From the depth of and the distance between the three points, they were judged to indeed have been made by a camera tripod, and the assumption was that the murderer had photographed the girl's body.

"Umm, you..."

"Morino," the girl said, and held out the camera. Still bewildered, I took it from her.

"Why would you want a commemorative photo here?"

Without replying, Morino started walking toward the lone tree in the empty clearing to stand beside it. "Right around here, please," she said, in a melancholic tone that brought to mind returning home from a wake. She was standing right next to the place where the girl's body had lain seven years earlier. She had apparently done her homework.

Was this real? Was someone trying to catch me in a trap? I turned the camera on her. Rather than flashing her fingers in a peace sign or smiling, the girl Morino simply stood stiffly, expressionless. I pressed the shutter. The picture was displayed in the LCD. I was surprised. It was like a photo of a ghost. Her mien combined with and was augmented by the dead trees in the background, making the rigid girl standing there almost a sharply defined phantom. *Should I retake it?* I thought.

"I see. It looks good," Morino said as she checked out the photo I had taken. Apparently, she was somehow happy with it. "It's a good souvenir." This was in a monotone, as if she had prepared the line in advance.

"While you're here, could I ask you to take a few more?" she said, and lied down on the roots of the tree. Her hair fanned out on the ground, and her coat opened up.

"What are you doing?"

"I'm being a corpse."

I waited a few seconds, but there was no further explanation. My imagination took over, and I finally understood. Morino wanted to pretend to be the girl killed seven years ago and have me take pictures of it?

While I stood there bewildered, the girl lying at my feet turned toward the tiny lens of the digital camera.

"A little more to the left," I instructed her. The girl Morino slid her body a bit to the left. Perfect. She was lying on the exact spot where the girl seven years ago had lain.

2

I had photographed three subjects up to that point. The first was the girl seven years ago. I left her where I had photographed her, which is why she drew such attention. After that, I was careful to hide my second and third subjects and strike the set, as it were. And so, even now, there are still no signs that they've been found. You could look up the places where those second and third subjects were buried, but you wouldn't find any news about the discovery of unidentified bodies or rumors about ghosts haunting the area. I had no doubt that the girls had been filed away as missing persons and forgotten by everyone other than their families and friends.

I had a certain talent: I knew when someone was lying to me. Nothing beyond human understanding like a superpower or anything like that—my powers of observation were simply sharper than most. Looking at the way a person's eyes moved, the state of the muscles in their face, the position of their hands, and the curve of their body, among other things, I could determine with a fair degree of accuracy whether or not they were telling me the truth. I won game after game when I played cards with friends. And it was very obvious who hated me and who liked me.

In my photography courses at university, I ran into problems when we had to photograph other people. The broad smiles and composed faces of my subjects simply looked fake. The so-called expression of the subject was comprised of a pack of lies. I tried talking to them to make them look natural, but that never went very well. What was strange about all this, however, was that the photos I produced of these people got me excellent marks. Perhaps this was the result of my efforts to eliminate the lie of the subject. At any rate, when my work was viewed through other eyes, they apparently saw something true to life. I began working as a photographer specializing in portraits and got a fair bit of good press. But with each photo I took, the despair inside me grew.

When a lens is turned on a person, that person will try to perform themselves. There's no way around this. You could perhaps call it a defensive instinct. The party taking the picture and the party having it taken are closely related to the party pointing a gun and the party with a gun pointed at them. There isn't a person alive who could sit and do nothing faced with the dark barrel of a gun. In the case of the photo, this manifests in the form of performing the self. The subject is defensive because their very emotions are quite clearly being transcribed onto the image. The subject's self-awareness and the sensation of being watched make them this way. Just having the camera lens before them causes the subject to unconsciously fabricate an expression. The facial expression and physical mannerisms the subject creates in this situation are symbolic. It is a performance planned to make me—the photographer—and the viewers of the photo accept them.

A symbol has no value beyond that. It exists to call to mind the essential nature of that which is depicted. This "summoning," the fact that those who come into contact with the work will call to mind the object depicted, is the truly critical part of a work of art. There must be an empty space from which to evoke the thought itself. However, when the awareness of the subject begins to perform the self before the lens, the photo becomes less natural and grows faded. The symbols that should be there to spur the recollection are bloated and crushed into the empty space. This act means that the symbol of the cross is praised, and God is ignored.

When taking photos, I had to fight back against the self-awareness of the subject. I would find a crack in the wall of that self-awareness and then snap the shutter like I was firing a gun. But despite this, I was never once satisfied with the photo I captured.

How could I get the photo I wanted? People were my subjects, but the performance of these subjects was an obstacle to taking the photo I desired.

The answer was suggested to me by a picture I happened to find online.

It showed a lone girl.

A subject without self-awareness, not performing even though the lens was turned on her.

The empty space to stir the imagination.

And then I realized.

I could make one myself.

A subject just like this one.

†

Another girl was lying in the spot where I had laid the body down seven years earlier. This girl, who called herself Morino, seemed unconcerned that she was getting dirt in her hair and on her clothes. I readied the tiny digital camera I'd been handed and moved within the range of her sight. The surfaces of her eyes reflected my shadow, but her pupils, turned up to the sky, didn't so much as flicker. Her gaze did not follow the camera lens. I pressed the shutter down over and over. The girl's skin was so pale that the blue of her veins was clear underneath. She had a small mole under her left eye, almost like a mark from a tear that had flowed there once. She had scars on her wrists from a history of cutting, it seemed. A red ribbon was tied around the collar of her black sailor-style school uniform with its embroidered school crest. I peered at her eyes; her pupils were tightly constricted. Proof she was alive. That said, she didn't shake or blink or pull her face back even when I brought my own face in closer to look into those eyes. This girl's mind was fascinating.

Once I had taken ten or so of the "souvenir photos" she had insisted on, the session ended. The girl got up and silently brushed away the bits of dead leaves stuck in her hair. I felt a sense of regret. I had only taken the warm-up shots. An interest in this subject rose up in me. I wanted to capture her on film. And not with a little digital camera. I wanted to shoot her with the equipment in my car. I wanted to take a photo of the dead face of this beautiful girl and carry it around with me. How incredible it would be to stare at that photo while drinking coffee at Starbucks.

"These are pretty good." Morino nodded crisply as she checked the pictures I had taken on the digital camera LCD. No light lived in her eyes in the photos; they were simply dark holes. I had captured a corpse. She seemed to like that.

The girl tucked the digital camera away in her bag. Something red flashed in the corner of my eye. She had scratched the back of her right hand, and a red welt sat there now. Looking carefully at the place where she had been lying, I saw that it was scattered with pointed rocks. Blood began to ooze out from the cut before my eyes.

"Are you okay?"

No answer. She stared at the back of her hand, expressionless. I imagined that she would remain expressionless even at the moment a knife was slid into her stomach. She pulled a gauze bandage out of her bag. I was surprised she would always keep something like that in there. She began to wind it around her wound awkwardly with one hand.

"Can I help?"

No answer. Her right hand was now covered in white, but the bandage looked as though it would pull off quite easily. Even allowing for the fact that she had done it with one hand, she could hardly be said to have done a good job.

"So kids these days walk around with bandages now?"

"I like wrapping bandages around things."

Then you should be able to do it better than that. You were pretty awkward there.

The girl Morino took her bag in her left hand and shoved her thickly bandaged right into the pocket of her coat. Her hair hung down her back, flowing past slender shoulders. Without looking at me, she shifted her gaze toward the place where she had lain. For a short while, I too stared at the place silently.

"Well then, I'll be on my way." Leaving a puff of white breath hanging in the air, Morino turned around and started walking toward the small path that led to the road.

My feet automatically started moving as well. "How are you getting home from here?"

"I'll take the bus."

So here was someone who used that bus stop. I still thought it was strange, though, that anyone would get off the bus on a mountain pass.

We stepped onto the path, her in front and me following behind. The path was too narrow to allow us to walk side by side. With every step, I heard the crunching of the dead leaves. The roots of trees erupted here and there out of the unpaved surface, but they were hard to see, hidden as they were by the fallen leaves. I worried that she might catch a small black shoe on one and fall.

The sun was setting, and the hue of the cold December sky gradually shifted to that of evening. Morino glanced back at me out of the corner of one eye. The fair-skinned, well-formed bridge of her nose was fascinating, like looking at a rib in an X-ray.

"Now that I'm thinking of it, it's quite the coincidence you came along when you did."

"What?"

"Well, that is a dead end, after all." She seemed to have jumped to the conclusion that I had just happened to pass by.

"It's more than a coincidence."

"So then why *did* you come along?"

"Preliminary inspection of the building site." I hated lies, but I lied. The girl nodded, as if accepting it.

The announcement that a waste disposal plant would be built on the empty land had come six months earlier. Within a few months at most, the clearing encircled by dead trees would be dug up, and concrete would be poured; the scene would change completely. Many people were against the planned facility. Perhaps the opposition had deliberately circulated the rumors about the ghost that had made this area a recent topic of conversation. A sort of pushback: You'll be cursed if you build a thing like that where a dead body was discovered. Naturally, I had no proof to support this theory.

"That reminds me—today's the anniversary. The last anniversary before the place where the body was found is irrevocably changed forever."

Seven years ago today, on December 6, a girl had died. In my arms. Why had Morino visited that place on today of all days? Why had I gone there myself on today of all days? Assuming there was a reason, it had to have been that today was December 6.

"The photos before, they were like Rosalia Lombardo," I said, and the girl Morino glanced back at me as she walked. What kinds of thoughts were happening inside that well-formed skull? The answer came from her lips.

"You have a similar air about you as a friend of mine. Maybe that's why it's easy to talk to you."

I had no recollection of the conversation getting that involved, but apparently today was a chatty day for her.

"How am I like this friend of yours?"

"You know Rosalia."

Rosalia. When I murmured that name in my heart, I grew serious, an emotion similar to what I experienced when I came into contact with true art. She was not a work of art, however. She was a corpse.

The path ended, and we exited onto the road, avoiding the barbed wire. The paved asphalt surface cut across in front of us. I suddenly had the strong sensation that we had come back out into the world of the living. From where we stood in front of the PLANNED SITE FOR WASTE DISPOSAL FACILITY sign, you could see my vehicle parked in the empty space on the side of the road.

"Thank you for taking the photos." Morino started to walk off. It was a simple, easy farewell. But she stopped as if she had remembered some forgotten thing and looked back at me. "You know, you weren't surprised when you saw me there."

"What?"

"Several cars passed me while I was coming here from the bus stop, and the drivers all turned pale when they saw me."

I almost laughed. "Maybe they all thought you were a ghost."

Now that she mentioned it, the girl did look exactly like the rumored ghost. Long black hair, black sailor-style uniform.

"*You* weren't surprised when you saw me."

"I'm an atheist."

"That means there's no God, right?"

"Right. There's not."

The girl Morino took her eyes off me and stared at her shoes for about five seconds. I couldn't quite understand what this gesture meant. Turning her back to me, she pulled her cell phone out of her bag and started to make a call, walking in the direction of the bus stop as she did.

I opened the trunk of my car and checked that all my photography equipment was there. Camera, tripod, reflectors, knife, rope, handcuffs. I got into the driver's seat and opened the glove box. Small bottle of potassium chloride, prescription sleeping pills, syringes.

I started the engine. The car began moving and reached the rust-covered bus stop after about three hundred meters. The black outline of the girl stood there, bag hanging from her hand. I stopped the car in front of her and opened the driver's side window. "How long do you have to wait until the next bus?"

She glanced at me. "Ninety minutes."

"Well, do you want a ride?"

Morino shook her head. Her eyes were wary.

"The sun's setting soon; this area will be pitch-black. There are no streetlamps."

"I'm okay with the dark." A note of displeasure crept into her voice. She appeared to have misinterpreted my goal in talking to her. She thought I wanted to pick her up. All I really wanted to do was kill her and take her picture.

"But there might be bears."

"There aren't."

"You'll get bitten by bugs."

"I won't."

"A murderer could be hiding over there."

"That would be a remarkable coincidence."

She was no longer looking at me. Negotiations were over. Her whole body radiated annoyance. She hated me. I couldn't come up with anything other than forcing her into the car. I would have to be careful not to hurt her and damage her face. If that happened, it would spoil my photos. Moving to put this plan into action, I opened the driver's side door.

At that moment, I heard a dog barking somewhere off in the distance.

"Maybe a stray," I muttered, looking far back. You didn't see them too much in the city these days, but apparently they were still living out here.

I heard the sound of the back door opening.

Morino wordlessly got in and closed the door.

Okay, please go then. She sent me the signal with her eyes in the rearview mirror.

3

Some people feel pleasure at killing another person. I am most definitely not of that persuasion. I'm not like those deviants. If I could, I'd never kill anyone. I would even go so far as to say it's repulsive to me. But the fact is, I need a subject who will not put on some contrived expression when the lens is turned on her.

The sixth of December, seven years ago. I started talking to a young woman on a street corner. At first, I thought she was in university; she had an adult face, she was tall, and she was in street clothes. But she was an eighteen-year-old high school student. She had changed out of her uniform after school so she could hang out in town. I asked what she had done with her uniform and learned she had stuffed it into her bag. We hung out at the video arcade and then had dinner once she had shed her reserve. I crushed up a prescription sleeping pill, dissolved it in an alcoholic beverage, and gave it to her to drink. She fell asleep in the car while listening to a boring story I crafted. I pulled over onto the shoulder of the road and got the syringe and bottle of potassium chloride from the glove box. I stabbed the needle into the girl's vein and shot the liquid into her. She woke up then, tried to fight back. But she was intoxicated by the pill, her brain was cloudy; she didn't fight for long. It was a lucky thing, however, that the needle of the syringe didn't break. I held her body close. Her heart soon stopped.

I set her down in the empty field circled by the dead trees of winter and changed the clothing my subject was wearing. Blood from my nosebleed had gotten onto her street clothes. Opening her bag, I saw her uniform packed in there, just as she had said when she was alive.

After the incident came to light, I checked the news and learned that the police knew everything—the fact that I had taken pictures, that I had changed her clothing and taken her street clothes away, everything. I had left footprints at the scene, and they had a witness testifying that a car had been parked very near the scene of the crime late one night. I braced myself to be arrested at some point in the days that followed. I don't know what sort of good luck was at work on my behalf, but I was not arrested, and so I was able to photograph the second and third subjects.

I always kept the photos of the girls with me, no matter where I went; I would pass the time at my workplace or in the park or on some street corner staring at them. Whenever I was abruptly overcome by loneliness and almost unable to breathe because of it, I had only to look at the photos to feel at ease again. And when the tears welled up and I wanted to cower in a corner in the dark, then too the photos of the girls saved me. The developed images of their dead faces evoked the unfathomable universe on the other side. They were myth itself; they were love itself. Cheeks devoid of all color shone with a saintly glow, and eyes that could see nothing somehow seemed to see everything.

I always saw the lies and deceit on people's faces. I knew instantly if the person before me was putting on an act. I could see the secrets in their hearts, no matter how they snuggled up to me with doe eyes and warm smiles. People performed themselves. Lies ran rampant among parents, friends, lovers, no matter how great the love for each other might be. They were a plague, eating into the space around them, only to pass on by with an innocent look. They were inescapable. I myself lied. I gave voice to things I didn't believe so as not to be hated. Fearing that someone would pull away from me, I smiled ingratiatingly. I was scared of being disconnected from society, and so I became a deceiver myself.

In general, people didn't look back on every interaction to pick out each of these little distortions. For some reason, it seemed that I alone, my eyes alone, reacted to all these performances on the faces of other people. My mind was given no chance to rest. Each time I read a lie on the face of a loved one, my heart sank. The lone beings I could count on in a world like this. The ones who would face me honestly. The ones who would accept my gaze when I turned it upon them without putting up those walls. The ones who made me think it would be okay to give myself over and lean on them. That was precisely what these girls were to me, on the other side of my square frame, their faces devoid of pretense.

†

I snaked my way down the mountain road, turning the steering wheel back and forth. The sun was approaching the ground in the west, the sky dyed red. It was a clear red, as though the sky itself was radiating the color. As I went around a bend, the light pouring into the car changed, flowed like water. The shadows cast on the face of the girl in the backseat also shifted like a soft-bodied sea creature. In contrast with the burning sky, darkness began to permeate the withered trees. The spindly branches were a woman's hair standing on end, painted in a shadow so black it was hard to make out the details. FM radio played inside the car. I couldn't

decide whether to put a CD on, and so I just left the radio mur-
muring its songs. I turned on my headlights to banish the gloom
before the car.

I could see her in the rearview mirror. The girl with the name
Morino took a sip of bottled water, put the cap back on, and
turned her eyes wordlessly out the window. It was the water I had
bought along the way. I had handed it to her when I started the
car, with the remark that she was probably thirsty. After carefully
checking there was no sign of it having been opened, she brought
the lip of the bottle to her own lips. If there had been a vending
machine on the mountain pass and thus another way for her to
replenish her water levels, she likely wouldn't have touched my
offering.

I was unable to relax, imagining her face in death. My heart
pounded like a schoolgirl in the presence of her first crush. Once
I excised this girl from the land of the living and the heat of her
body faded, leaving nothing but a soulless shell, a beautiful blank
space—too beautiful for mere words to capture—would suddenly
appear before me.

The girl had at some point started fiddling with her cell phone,
her profile colored by the sunset. She was typing out an email with
her unbandaged hand.

"You emailing a friend? Family?" I asked. Morino stayed silent.
"A boyfriend then?"

"It's a friend." Her response came with a startled look.

"You have a lot of friends?"

"Only him."

Her words contained no lie. Now that I was thinking of it, I still
hadn't gotten the feeling she was presenting lies or any sort of performance to me—talking to this girl had not made me unhappy.
She did seem to be on guard, but she wasn't doing those things
that made me sick, like putting a hand to her mouth and laughing
even though nothing was funny. Perhaps she was the type who
didn't hang out with friends simply to hang out or to keep the harmony in her relationships. I imagined she lived alone and didn't

talk with anyone in class. And she was very good at acting like a corpse. Maybe with her, I could find love. No, that was ridiculous. Rather than give myself up to love and its ilk, I had to capture her in a photo to live on forever. If I were going to make her my lover, it would be as a corpse.

At any rate, she had referred to the person she was emailing as "him." The friend was a boy. Maybe someone in her grade? Or someone older, a university student? The two of us weren't dating, but an interest rose up in me nonetheless at her relationship with this "friend."

"Is this the same person you called before?"

No answer. Morino pinched her lips shut tightly and looked outside. Apparently, she wasn't interested in continuing this conversation. I supposed I had pressed her too hard and made her angry. I knew it wasn't good to ask too many questions. But once she was dead, she wouldn't be able to give me any more answers. I simply had to ask now while I could.

The flowing silhouettes of the trees intermittently interrupted the mass of boiling blood that was the sunset and flickered inside the car where we sat. The road was a gentle downhill slope. Perhaps because of this, it seemed as though the car was diving into the darkness.

The Christmas song special on the radio continued with "Silent Night."

"When I saw a picture of Rosalia Lombardo…" I began, and the girl cocked her head in the rearview mirror, turning her dark eyes on me. "You know those bisque dolls? I guess you'd call them ball-jointed dolls. I had the thought that maybe all those dolls are modeled after Rosalia."

The most adorable corpse in the world. That was Rosalia Lombardo. She breathed her last a mere two years after she had breathed her first. Her grieving father asked a doctor to do something to preserve the girl's body. For a long time, no one knew just what this doctor had actually done. Because he kept his methods to himself, right up to the end.

At a glance, you can see there is a strangeness to Rosalia's corpse. Vibrant and fresh, it has not decayed. People are surprised and frightened by this. Perhaps they feel there might be an air of magic to it. Or the hand of God. Even now, more than ninety years after her death, the girl sleeps peacefully. She was enshrined by the Order of Capuchin Friars Minor in Italy, and a great number of people go there to see her. A modern investigation revealed that the reason she does not decay is because her body has, in fact, turned to grave wax. However, knowing the scientific principle behind it doesn't change the solemn feeling that comes from seeing her restful face. The glossy hair tied with a ribbon. The cheek nestled into the blanket wrapping her body, as though she were testing its softness. She makes you imagine she might open her eyes even now and peek out with a sweet look. You expect her to perhaps open those tiny lips and start speaking the words she's only just learned. Rosalia is alive. She is alive as a corpse.

"When I look at her sleeping face, I get the feeling I can almost see the dream she's having."

I waited a little, but Morino gave me no response. It seemed she wasn't interested in talking, after all. The girl in the rearview mirror dropped her gaze to the cell phone in her hand. Maybe the answer to her email had arrived.

I was at the point where I wanted to hurry up and shoot her veins full of potassium chloride. However, before I got my needle out, I would have to give her the other medication to intoxicate her, just like always. Weakened like that, she wouldn't fight back, and she wouldn't be scared, either. If I was lucky, she might go to sleep for me. I had prescription sleeping pills in the car's glove compartment. All I had to do was crush them up and put them into that bottle of water. Given that she had opened it herself, I was certain she would continue to drink from it unguardedly.

The bottle was sitting to the left of her in the backseat. I had to get the drugs in there without her noticing. It was a difficult task.

"You really are alike," the girl said.

"What's that?"

"Your eyes are like my friend's."

"My eyes?"

Morino dipped her head in the rearview mirror.

"Hmm. Well, anyway, I'm glad you're in a better mood now."

"Mood?" Morino cocked her head to the side.

"You weren't mad before?"

"Not really. I was fine."

"When I started talking to you, you didn't answer, so…"

"It takes time for me to think of what to say. And by the time I thought of something, the moment had passed, so I just stayed quiet."

Her face was almost entirely expressionless, but she didn't appear to be lying. In fact, she seemed relieved she'd been able to say that much without stumbling at the length of it. The look that had seemed discouraging was not one of anger; rather, it was, apparently, her official uniform.

"Do our faces really look that much alike? Mine and your friend's?"

"Your faces don't look alike, but you have the same air about you."

"What's his name?"

"My friend's?"

"Yes."

"His name…"

The girl shifted her gaze onto the passing trees. I took in her profile in the mirror. A change in emotion appeared on her face, like water rippling. Sadness, a smile, and other feelings overlapped momentarily, and even now, I think she might have been about to cry. Or maybe her expression didn't actually change that much at all, maybe I simply perceived it like that.

Ahead, I could see the train tracks and the crossing. The gates were just coming down. Warning bells clanged as red lights flashed. I stepped on the brakes to bring the car to a halt. There was no sign yet of the coming train.

"I'm going to get out and make a phone call," Morino said, and with her cell phone in one hand, she opened the door and stepped out of the car. She probably didn't want me to hear the conversation. I didn't stop her. This was the chance I had been hoping for. In the backseat was her bag and the open bottle of water.

I checked on her in the rearview mirror. From where she was standing, she wouldn't be able to see what I was doing even if she did turn around. The evening sun had sunk almost entirely out of sight. The interior of the car was dark, colored intermittently red with the flashing of the crossing lights.

I took the sleeping pills out of the glove compartment, dumped them out onto a landscape photo that was as good as garbage, and smashed them up with the pill bottle. I reached an arm back into the rear seat and grabbed the plastic water bottle. I took the cap off and dumped the pills in.

A train with few cars came clattering along on the tracks, about as loud as a bus passing before us. I put the water bottle back in the rear seat and turned to face forward again. The clanging of the bells stopped, and the area returned to its earlier dusk. The sky was no longer the least bit red. Rather, it was a blue as dark as the depths of the ocean.

I waited for Morino to get into the car. And I waited for her to put the water bottle to her lips.

But she didn't come back.

I got out to look for her, but I could find no sign of that beautiful silhouette. The sun had already set. I used a flashlight from the trunk to shine a light on the area. Something white flashed in the bushes a little ways off on the side of the road. I parted them and turned the lamp that way, and the outline of light caught a bandage stuck on a branch at about chest height. The sparkling-white, brand-new bandage danced in the darkness. Evening ended, night began, and she was gone.

4

Hark, the glad sound! the Savior comes,
the Savior promised long;
let every heart prepare a throne,
and every voice a song.

He comes the prisoners to release,
in Satan's bondage held;
the gates of brass before him burst,
the iron fetters yield.

I could hear the voices in song leaking out from the open driver's side door. It was the Christmas music special on the radio. The saintly voices of boys and girls spoke to me as I gripped my flashlight.

The awaited savior has returned.

So let's give him a big welcome.

I was fairly certain that's what the lyrics meant. I felt a chill. Now that the sun had gone down, the temperature was dropping. Maybe I should go back to the car. I could look all I wanted to, but I wasn't likely to find the girl. The trunks and branches of dead trees jumped to life in the illumination of the flashlight, gray like rocks. The car headlights shone into the space dead ahead. I should move the car to the shoulder of the road before another vehicle came along.

I regretted letting my subject get away. The girl had seen through to my real intentions, and so she had disappeared into the deciduous tree forest. She had run off, not paying any notice when the bandage she had so awkwardly wound around her hand got caught on a branch and was pulled off. The words I had spoken perhaps contained something to heighten her awareness of the danger I presented. Maybe it was the talk about Rosalia? At any rate, I had definitely failed somehow.

But I realized there was no need to be so defeatist. For two reasons. The first was that her bag was still there in the backseat. I opened the rear door and picked it up. An utterly ordinary black school bag. There might be something inside to tell me who she was. I checked the interior with excitement. There was almost nothing in it. A single paperback of *Night on the Galactic Railroad*. Perhaps right from the start, she had left the bag as camouflage. A little tool to make me think she wasn't going to run off or any-thing—she had left her bag, she'd come back once the train passed. As proof of this hypothesis, I couldn't find any sign of the digital camera that would have been tucked in there. It was clear she had taken the important items from the bag.

But that was fine. There was one more good reason not to lose heart. The black sailor-style uniform she wore. I had a clear memory of the school crest embroidered on it. I would find out what school she went to. As long as Morino wasn't a fake name, finding her would be easy. And even if it was a fake name, if I knew the school she attended at least, I'd be able to find her someday.

This wasn't the end yet. My tie with this girl Morino hadn't been completely severed. I wanted the look on her face when she was dead. I didn't need anything else. What experience could be more incredible than turning the lens on her deceased face and pressing the shutter? I would love this subject body and soul. My thirst had returned. A thirst that could only be quenched by a face in death, just like seven years earlier. A longing for water in the burning desert. Surprisingly, this feeling was not unpleasant.

I returned the girl's bag to the backseat and went to slide into the driver's seat. At that moment, I heard the vibration of a cell phone from somewhere. It wasn't my phone. I pricked up my ears and sought out the origin of the sound. In the woods, not that far from the car. I found it soon enough when I went to look. Morino's cell phone had fallen atop the dried leaves. A light-emitting diode flashed as the device vibrated.

Had she dropped it? I picked it up and peered at the LCD screen. A message indicating an incoming call. The caller was apparently set not to display, however; no name was shown. Someone was calling Morino. Maybe her family? Or that friend?

Phone in hand, I waited for the caller to hang up. But the vibration showed no sign of stopping.

I went back to the side of the car, leaned against it, and took several deep breaths. I felt like the temperature had dropped radically. I focused on moving my finger, sluggish because of the cold, and pressed the Accept Call button. I held my breath and put the cell phone to my ear.

"Hello?" A boy's voice came through the receiver to me. It wasn't as low as an adult's, but it wasn't high like a child either. Most likely, he was also in high school, like Morino.

"Who are you?"

"A friend of Morino's." His voice was calm. It didn't waver at all, even when he heard my voice coming through the connection instead of the girl's. The hand I gripped the phone with started to sweat.

"Morino? I just found this phone. I guess Morino would be its owner then?"

"Yes, that's right. Earlier, I advised Morino to run away."

"Run away?" My heart beat faster.

"I was the one who suggested she leave her cell phone."

"Why?"

"I wanted to speak with you."

I felt as though the breath expelled by the boy was hitting my ear through the phone. Disturbed, I hung up.

I got into the driver's seat and closed the door. Turning off the radio left only the sound of the engine. Darkness hung around the car, a gloom so black that one could be forgiven for wondering if someone had simply pasted drawing paper colored completely with black crayon over the windows. I was desperately thirsty. My mouth was sticky with thick saliva as though I had just woken up. I was assaulted by the absurd sensation that I was being swallowed up by some unknown something. My body was frozen from venturing out into the cold night.

I fiddled with Morino's cell phone, opening up any number of menus. She might have information about the boy in her phone. Before I learned more about Morino, I first wanted to know about this boy. To get rid of this unfamiliar eeriness that had been planted in me when I spoke with him. I didn't believe Morino had had enough time when she ran off to delete her messages. I poked around and there was the email, just as I expected.

> Sent 16:20, December 6
> I ended up getting a ride from that person before! (^_^;)

The time was immediately before sunset. This had to be the email she had written in the car. So she used emoji. Unexpected. The emoji was about a hundred times more emotionally expressive than her face.

Email received three minutes later: When the car stops, get out and call me. When you run, go in the direction of the setting sun. I checked a map. There should be houses that way.

That had probably been sent by the boy. The sender's name and email were displayed. And these were the only email exchanges today. I checked her email from other days as well, but they were all one line, business-y. This one boy was the only person she emailed. The received call history was nothing but private numbers. Supposing that these originated from the boy's cell phone, then this phone in my hand was essentially a completely private communication line for one individual.

Why had the boy told the girl to run? I tossed the cell phone into the passenger seat, leaned forward so that my body was up against the steering wheel, and glared out ahead of the car. The railroad tracks cut through the space illuminated by the headlights. The warning bells were silent; there was no sign of a train. I adjusted the heater temperature to warm the inside of the car. My fingers were still cold, but sensation was returning to the tips. My respiration rate and my pulse had also returned to normal.

The cell phone rang. The display said PRIVATE NUMBER. I braced myself and accepted the call. I heard the voice of the boy.

"Hello?"

"Why did you tell her to run?" I asked, omitting the usual courtesies.

"Just in case. You could be a deviant, a bloodthirsty murderer."

"Me? Don't be stupid!" I had committed several murders, but I was no deviant.

"That's good then. My worry was unnecessary."

"Why were you so worried?"

"Because she's been in danger before. Maybe she was born under an unlucky star. Anyway, did you take the pictures of the corpse?"

"What are you talking about?"

"Strange. On the phone, Morino said that she pretended to be a corpse and took souvenir photos."

Although the word "strange" did come out of his mouth, the boy didn't seem troubled in the least. That said, he didn't seem to be toying with me either, even as I hesitated and mumbled. He was simply speaking dispassionately. His voice was even—were I to describe it in one word, that word would be "empty." Was this cell phone in my hand connected to a dark hole? Maybe this voice wasn't something originating from a human being, but echoing up from a deep, pitch-black hole.

"Who exactly are you?"

But the boy did not respond to my question. "Is it all right if I ask for your license plate number?"

"There's no reason I'd tell you that."

"Then I'll say the number myself. Please confirm." Having said that, the boy recited several digits. It was indeed my license plate number.

"That's not it."

"You're lying, hm?"

"Don't ask then."

"When I told you to confirm, I wanted to confirm with you that I know your license plate number."

"When did you find that out?"

"Earlier, on the phone with Morino."

"I was going to drive her to the station. The way she up and disappeared like that puts me in a bit of a bind, doesn't it? What if she gets lost and gets in some kind of trouble?"

"Please don't go anywhere for a while."

"Let me guess. You've got the wrong idea. You think I'm the murderer from the case seven years ago."

"If that's the stance you'd like to take, we can set aside the question of whether or not you're the criminal."

"That's not enough for me. You suspect me. I want to hear why."

"But telling you wouldn't be any fun." The boy sighed. Apparently, talking to me was bothersome. As before, I found him unsettling, but this sigh meant he did have an actual body. In this instant, the owner of the voice turned into a silhouette in my mind, and I breathed a sigh of relief.

"This isn't about fun. I want to know why you suspect me."

"Please don't be disappointed now that you've asked. I warned Morino to run from you because I received a phone call."

A phone call?

"Just as I mentioned before, she called me, so I told her to run from you."

I didn't understand what he was talking about.

"Today, December 6, is the anniversary of the death of the girl killed seven years ago."

That was correct.

"For the last six months or maybe even longer, Morino has been planning to go to the site where the body was discovered. Since they announced the plan for the waste disposal plant. She said that in that case, she was going to go and take a souvenir photo on the anniversary."

I had gone there for the same reason, that feeling that I had to make sure to go now before I lost that place.

"I was planning to go too, but something came up, and she ended up going by herself. So I gave Morino instructions."

Call if you meet someone who's not surprised to see you.
Because that person is not normal.

"Why?" I asked into the cell phone.

"They say that the ghost of the murdered high school girl appears there," the boy calmly explained.

"You're talking about those rumors?"

"Morino always goes out in her school uniform. Although there is the occasional exception, she said she was going to slip out of school at lunch and take the bus there, so I knew she had to be in her uniform today. Incidentally, the rumored ghost also wears a black sailor-style uniform."

I recalled my conversation with Morino.

Several cars passed me while I was coming here from the bus stop, and the drivers all turned pale when they saw me.

Maybe they all thought you were a ghost.

You *weren't surprised when you saw me.*

I had known right away that Morino wasn't a ghost. To begin with, I didn't believe in ghosts. I even scorned the people who were misled by them. If they had looked into the incident seven years ago, they would've soon learned the name of the high school the victim attended. And that school's uniform was not a black sailor-style outfit. I remember that uniform well because I dressed her corpse seven years ago. It was a plaid skirt with a navy blue blazer that she had put in her bag that evening.

If they had been able to take a look at the weekly magazines of the time, they would have also known the victim's hairstyle. In articles about the case back then, they had printed a photo of the girl's face taken when she was still alive. Instead of being long and black, her hair was shoulder length and a color close to blonde. And to go even further, the girl was in street clothes when I killed her. If the ghost had been in street clothes splattered with droplets of blood from my nose, I would have joined the world in being afraid of these stories. But the truth was that the ghost and the girl who became my subject looked nothing like the so-called ghost.

The boy had perhaps realized this. That the criminal would

have faced Morino squarely, without being influenced by rumors of a ghost.

"So from a random thing like that, you decide that I'm the one who killed that girl seven years ago."

"I don't know whether you did it or not."

"But that's what you're implying."

"Given Morino's poor luck, it wouldn't be at all strange for her to run into a murderer."

The girl was apparently famous for her bad luck. I became curious about the experiences she'd had thus far. Since I knew that I myself was a murderer, I could sense the truth of his words. However, at that moment, I would only say, "Could your reasoning be more ridiculous?"

A criminal feigning innocence is an ugly sight.

"I don't care if you're the one who did it seven years ago, if you're a homicidal murderer, if you're a serial killer."

"Is there a difference?"

"I warned Morino. Not to get close to you. I don't know who you really are, but if she had never gotten close to you, then this whole thing would have ended without incident. It should have. But then after she called me, she got into your car. It's beyond my understanding. I don't know what kind of tricks you used to get the Morino I know to obediently hop into your car."

I could have asked him the same question.

"At any rate, how about making a deal with me?"

"A deal?"

"Something simple. As long as you don't try to have anything to do with Morino or myself, we won't concern ourselves with you."

I stared silently at the railroad crossing on the other side of the windshield. The tracks led into darkness. I ruminated on the boy's words. Ridiculous. What kind of validity would a deal like this have? What the boy was saying, in effect, was "How about we have nothing to do with each other?" What was in it for me? I would ignore his request. I would find Morino and make her my subject.

No, I couldn't. The boy knew my license plate number. That

changed the situation. And this girl Morino knew what I looked like, as well as the make of my car. I thought again about the boy's deal. Now, I could hear another meaning to his words: "If you try to lay a hand on us, I'll report your license plate number to the police." The police would be able to find out who I was from that and possibly search my home. In which case, I wouldn't be able to talk my way out of it.

I didn't seem to be in a position to promptly reject this deal. I even got the impression that I was the one at a disadvantage. I had already broken the law, after all. It didn't matter if the boy called the police right after this phone call. The issue if he did wouldn't be whether or not he had proof that I was the murderer. All the police would have to do was take an interest in what the boy said and focus their attention on me. Eventually, I would be destroyed.

What was the best option? Find and kill the boy before he could call the police, and then find the girl Morino and make her my subject? If I was going to do that, it would be best to do it tonight. But maybe that was impossible? And even if it was possible, there were serious risks involved. I also couldn't say I would be completely happy once I'd succeeded. I didn't like killing people. I thought it was repulsive. Would I actually carry out the ugly deed of killing a normal human being, someone who would never be my subject, in the name of self-preservation?

How could I bring the situation back to normal with the least fuss?

Make the deal with the boy. Keep the agreement; don't break it. Live without interfering with each other; don't try to remove the other. Tolerate the existence of the other; live life without taking any hostile action. I would lose my subject Morino. There was no way around it. But I would avoid having my life destroyed.

How much could I trust this boy and his deal?

Human beings are liars. I knew that. Which is why I sought the face in death. The face with no forced smile, no performance, no deliberately composed expression. I had never thought about it before, but had I ever truly trusted anyone from the heart? At some point, I had started to feel that it was obvious that the look on a person's face was contrived and in no way reflected their actual feelings. I had lived my life, giving up on people, fully expecting them to betray me one day. When a person proposed something to me, I didn't even think about trusting them. But now, what was required in this situation was faith. In a person.

"Why did you choose December 6 seven years ago?" the boy asked.

"I didn't do it, so I don't know."

"Why do you suppose the person who did it chose today seven years ago?"

"I could make a guess. Maybe—"

"It's the day Rosalia Lombardo died?"

Was Rosalia Lombardo special to the boy like she was for me?

"Right. She died on December 6, 1920. She passed away when she was two and still looks the same now as she did then. The expression on her face is so lively you could almost believe she's asleep."

"You know quite a bit about her." I could almost hear a *trust me* in the boy's stream of words. I had to trust him. Otherwise, we'd both be at a disadvantage. I knew this in my head. But in my heart, I was afraid. I was overcome with paranoia. Suspicion that he would betray me and break our agreement, while I naïvely felt secure in my trust. Wasn't that how it would turn out in the end? Those who trusted the words of others never got ahead in this world; the deceivers were life's winners. I had witnessed it myself. I had seen people trick and exploit others for their own gain.

My fear was actually the cause of my inability to trust people. Fear of being deceived. Fear of being lied to. My fear of people was stealing from me the freedom of thought.

Could I live my whole life like this? Or would something change if I could trust the boy right here and now? As I cradled my head in the driver's seat and curled into myself, I heard the boy's voice almost in a whisper.

"I know Rosalia too." His voice was very gentle. "The most

adorable corpse in history." There was even an intimacy to it, as though he was speaking to family.

How far can I trust you?

I knew what I had to say. I had to trust a living person.

I'll make this deal with you, so let's not have anything to do with each other.

I just had to say it.

But.

"I've always wanted to trust people. But I'm scared. I can't help it." I didn't really know what I was saying. But I wanted to confess, like I was seeking salvation from him.

The boy had a response. "That's fine, no need to change. You don't have to trust these creatures, these people. They only lie—it's smarter not to trust them. So then, let's do this. You can just think of me as not being a person. I'm not human, so you don't need to be afraid of trusting me."

"Absurd."

"I warned Morino and had her leave her cell phone there so we could make this deal. So that you wouldn't come after her anymore."

When I hung up, the only sound inside the car was the vibration of the engine. No train crossed the tracks before me. No other cars came along to pass me. It was simply dark outside the car. The deeply suffocating, cavernous darkness of night. I imagined that eventually this darkness would smash through the front windshield and even compress me to the size of a milk bottle, just like the water pressure of the deep ocean crushed everything. What exactly was this boy? Morino said that he and I had the same air. I peeked in the rearview mirror and stared at my own face, but I couldn't see it. Soon, I became afraid that the amorphous, concentrated darkness outside the car was perhaps the boy himself, and I suddenly wanted to hear a human voice. I turned the radio back on.

Before I started the car, I remembered something. Opening the driver's side door, I shone my flashlight on the darkness. I collected the snowy-white bandage from the branch where it was still caught and stared at it. The tiniest bit of blood had soaked into it. I held it to my chest and wept.

I started driving and soon entered the town in the foothills. I slid through the flat band of fields and came out into an area with plenty of oncoming traffic. I passed by several signs for 24-hour convenience stores. The sound of the radio didn't make it into my brain. As I drove, I remembered the exchange with the boy.

†

"Right from the start, I didn't believe in the rumors. The ghost didn't even remotely look like the victim reported seven years ago, or her clothes. I knew that. That's why I wasn't surprised when I saw that girl Morino." Right until I hung up, I denied having committed the act.

"If that's true, then I must apologize for keeping you so long on the phone with me." The voice betrayed no information.

"I'm more annoyed by everyone else."

"What do you mean?"

"If they hadn't all believed in these ghost stories, you wouldn't be suspecting me right now."

Seven years earlier, the body of a high school girl had been discovered on the mountain pass. Now, a ghost appears in that spot. The ghost wears a black sailor-style uniform and has long hair.

"All of them neglected to check the facts. The people of the world, the person who started the rumor. It's so obvious that someone who doesn't want that waste disposal facility to go up planted the rumor." They had no doubt been trying to tap human emotion—which logic can't touch—to stoke the desire to fight the government.

"Oh no, that's not it." The boy curtly rejected my suppositions.

"How would you know?"

"I'm the one who started the rumor. I started posting it online, regularly, about six months ago. I made up all the stories about seeing a ghost. I was preparing for when Morino and I went to the place where the body was discovered. I was supposed to go too. I thought I might get lucky and see the person who did it, maybe."

I needed time to digest what I had just heard. Did this mean that the boy had circulated false information and set a trap to find the murderer? Even the fact that the rumored ghost looked exactly like the girl Morino was part of the boy's plan?

"I don't know about lucky. But why would you want to see the murderer?"

"The same mentality that makes us go to the zoo to see the lions."

"How much did that Morino girl know about this? Did she know that you were the one who started the rumors about the ghost?"

"She knows nothing."

"Nothing?"

"She probably thinks you just happened by and were trying to pick her up."

"So she knew nothing, but still called you and ran away when you told her to?"

"Exactly. Because we're friends."

Friends. The instant I heard the word, a shiver went up my spine, and I broke out in goose bumps. Because the boy's voice held no emotion at all. He spoke as though he didn't recognize the existence of even the concept of friendship. So why try to protect that girl then? Maybe he had romantic feelings for her?

"And, for the sake of argument, had I been the murderer and had I killed Morino and taken her picture, what would you do?"

"I would find you."

"You'd get revenge?"

"No, I'd probably ask you to show me the photos."

"And after that?"

"Nothing."

I couldn't see a shred of this thing human beings define as love in this boy. I remembered the look I saw on Morino's face in the car. That sad air—there was something quite human about it—in contrast with the way this boy talked.

I hung up the phone and didn't talk to the boy again.

†

Giving up on the girl Morino broke my heart. But if I went to look for her, I would end up meeting the boy somewhere along the way. I got the impression that nothing good would come of tangling with him. The more time passed from the moment I hung up the phone, the more this vague feeling turned into a certainty. I would have to give up on that mysterious girl, reminiscent of a wood at night just as the characters that made up her name suggested. But the longing for her face in death was as strong in me as it had been before, perhaps stronger now, seeking the ineffable feeling that Rosalia Lombardo provoked in me. The deal with the boy was that he and the girl would not concern themselves with me as long as I didn't get involved with them. In other words, the boy had been telling me to find some subject other than Morino if I wanted to take my pictures.

That night, I didn't go back to my apartment. I drove to a shopping district, started talking to a bored girl in the lobby of a bowling alley, and invited her out. We played a claw crane game, I treated her to a juice from the vending machine, and I got her into my car. The photo shoot was finished that night. The fact that this girl had black hair was not unrelated to my meeting Morino.

A week went by, and the police still hadn't forced their way into my apartment. For my part, I had also not attempted to look into the identities of Morino or the boy. I turned the power off on the cell phone and kept it, together with the bandage.

Moreover, when I photographed the other girl, I came full circle to being glad I hadn't been able to make Morino my subject that day. If I had photographed her face in death, my oeuvre would have, at that moment, been complete, and I would have spent the rest of my life simply admiring those photos. I chose to be more positive, taking the attitude that this sense of loss, my dissatisfaction no matter how many photos I took, could be transformed into my passion.

That said, I did wonder if Morino had made it home safely that day. When I had free time, I would remember her as I looked through my album of dead faces.

When you run, go in the direction of the setting sun.
I checked a map. There should be houses that way.

That's what the boy's email said, but the sun was already starting to set then, wasn't it? The temperature had also dropped significantly. But it would have been on the news if she had gotten lost and frozen to death in the mountains. The fact that it hadn't meant that she'd managed to get out safely.

Although even if she had managed to make it to the nearby houses without incident, she could have been mistaken for a ghost because of the rumor the boy had started; she might have had a fair bit of trouble getting help. Had she tried to hail a passing car, the driver might have screamed and driven right past her. I suddenly saw her clucking her tongue at ending up in such an absurd situation.

She knew nothing.

Not that she might have died that day.

Not that the person walking with her on that path in the woods was a murderer.

ABOUT THE AUTHOR

Born in 1978 in Fukuoka, Otsuichi won the Sixth Jump Short Fiction/Nonfiction Prize when he was seventeen with his debut story "Summer, Fireworks, and My Corpse." Now recognized as one of the most talented young fantasy/horror writers in Japan, his other English-language works include the short story collections *Summer, Fireworks, and My Corpse/Black Fairy Tale* and *ZOO* (Haikasoru). *GOTH* won the Honkaku Mystery Award and was adapted into a feature film starring Rin Takanashi. The English-language edition of *ZOO* was nominated for the Shirley Jackson Award.

HAIKASORU
THE FUTURE IS JAPANESE

THE OTSUICHI LIBRARY

ZOO

A man receives a photo of his girlfriend every day in the mail…so that he can keep track of her decomposition. A deathtrap that takes a week to kill its victims. Haunted parks and airplanes held in the sky by the power of belief. These are just a few of the stories by Otsuichi, Japan's master of dark fantasy.

SUMMER, FIREWORKS, AND MY CORPSE

Two short novels, including the title story and *Black Fairy Tale,* plus a bonus short story. *Summer* is a simple story of a nine-year-old girl who dies while on summer vacation. While her youthful killers try to hide her body, she tells us the story—from the point of view of her dead body—of the children's attempt to get away with murder.

Black Fairy Tale is classic J-horror: a young girl loses an eye in an accident, but receives a transplant. Now she can see again, but what she sees out of her new left eye is the experiences and memories of its previous owner. Its previous *deceased* owner.

ALSO CREEPY:

APPARITIONS—MIYUKI MIYABE

In old Edo, the past was never forgotten. It lived alongside the present in dark corners and in the shadows. In these tales, award-winning author Miyuki Miyabe explores the ghosts of early modern Japan and the spaces of the living world—workplaces, families, and the human soul—that they inhabit. Written with a journalistic eye and a fantasist's heart, *Apparitions* brings the restless dead, and those who encounter them, to life.